KNIGHT

IN THE

MUSEUM

KNIGHT IN THE MUSEUM

A JORJA KNIGHT MYSTERY

ALICE BIENIA

Issued in print and electronic formats.

ISBN 978-1-990193-11-8 (Paperback)

ISBN 978-1-990193-12-5 (EPUP)

Editing by: T. Morgan Editing Services

Cover Design by: Damonza.com

Published by: Cairn Press | Calgary, Alberta, Canada

ALSO BY ALICE BIENIA

Jorja Knight Mystery Series
Knight Blind
Knight Trials
Knight Shift (prequel)
Three Dog Knight
Knight Vision
Knight In The Museum

Anthologies
Last Shot
Crime Wave
The Dame Was Trouble

on, and nothing we could do would change it. I shook off a twinge of melancholy and crossed the lane to where my car was parked.

Resting my coffee momentarily on the car roof, I noticed the barista had spelled my name Georgia not Jorja. I had equal luck with the correct spelling of my last name, Knight. I unlocked the door and slid in. Resettling my coffee in the cup holder, I pulled down the sun visor, applied lip gloss, and tucked a strand of my newly cut, dark-brown hair behind my ear.

A noise startled me. I turned as the passenger door opened. The man I'd noticed in front of the Starbucks jumped into the seat next to me.

"Drive! Drive!" His blue-grey eyes bulged as they darted from side to side. His head whipped around to the rear window and back to me.

My hands tightened on the steering wheel, my nails digging into my palms. Blood pounded in my ears. He was beyond twitchy now. I could smell his frenzied panic.

"Go, dammit. Go."

He glanced over his shoulder and swore. He turned to me, his eyes jumping wildly, his forehead beaded with sweat.

The noise of the outdoor mall faded. Everything around me slowed, each second stretched to ten.

His face was thin and pockmarked. One of his front teeth was angled to the rest. His thin lips moved. He was shouting again, but the words didn't register. A speck of spittle left his lips and arched toward me. My eyes locked with his, my breath caught in my throat. A drop of sweat rolled down his face and dangled at his jawline.

This can't be happening.

A burst of adrenaline shot through me.

ONE

I NOTICED HIM RIGHT away. The guy was twitchy, like he'd just done something stupid or was about to. You didn't have to be a cop or a private investigator to figure out he was up to something, although being the latter made me predisposed to noticing such things. I pulled my sunglasses down over my eyes, shook back my shoulder-length bob, and stepped out of the Starbucks into the sunshine.

Keeping a firm hand on my pocketbook, I strode past several patrons lingering on the sidewalk in front of the coffee shop. The man with the shifting feet and buggy eyes stepped closer to the cluster of people, trying to make it look like he was one of them, and doing a poor job of it. His eyes never focused on any one thing; his head swivelled from side to side as he scanned for who knows what. I gave him a wide berth and gazed across the parking lot. The sun gleamed off the rows of cars. Everyone moved at a leisurely pace.

The maples and ash trees were ablaze in autumn colours, their red and golden leaves a sharp contrast against the pale-blue sky. Soon they'd be carpeting the ground. It would happen quite suddenly; a gust of wind would strip the branches, sending down a cascade of leaves from their lofty heights. Nature's reminder that life marched

For Sean and Katherine, with love.

I turned. My hands clawed at the door handle; my shoulder rammed the door. My foot shot out onto the pavement. I felt the car shift.

I scrambled out, wasting a precious second to glance back.

The passenger door stood open. The man was gone. My knees already rubbery from the adrenaline spike.

Leaning one hand on the car roof, my eyes swept the parking lot. Customers sauntered down the aisles, the sun glistened off the cars around me. All the familiar noises of the outdoor mall returned.

Someone shouted.

I turned in time to see my unwanted passenger push a man aside, leap over a black lab that was tied to a lamppost and disappear around the corner of the Starbucks. Several people stared after him.

I blew out the breath I'd been holding. The world was churning out more and more crazies. The stress was going to kill us all.

I shook my head and slid back into the car.

My hand trembled as I pushed up my sunglasses and stared into the visor mirror. Hazel eyes speckled with yellow flecks looked re markably unperturbed despite the loops and gyrations my organs performed inside. I slid my glasses back down, picked up my coffee and took a sip. Cradling the hot cup against my chest, I tried to process what just happened while the rest of me caught up. An attempted carjacking? Should I report it? More than likely just a poor soul suffering from a psychotic episode. I scanned the parking lot, but all was calm, everything back to normal.

I turned the key, still dangling from the ignition, and the engine sputtered to life. A light on the dashboard told me one of the doors was still open. I glanced at the passenger door. It had swung closed but wasn't quite shut. I set my coffee down, leaned over the passenger seat, tugged the door handle, and it clicked shut. That's when I noticed it.

A small white triangle poked up from between the door and the passenger seat, barely visible. Sprawling across the seat, my fingers teased the white triangle upward until I could get a grip. I pulled out a business envelope, folded over in half. It wasn't mine. My heart rate shot up.

I unfolded the envelope. There was nothing written on either side. I lifted the flap and peered inside. Puzzled, I pulled out two pieces of newsprint, each folded over several times. A headline came into view as I unfolded the first newspaper clipping. "Massive Winnipeg drug bust collapses. Defence claims police accessed lawyers' communications."

I scanned the article. Apparently, the largest drug bust in the region's history collapsed before it reached trial. The prosecution's case crumbled after defence lawyers attacked police conduct in the investigation, claiming they violated solicitor-client communication privileges. Charges were stayed.

I folded the article, and the headline of the second clipping caught my eye. "Ancient curse drives businessman to take his own life." My right eyebrow rose.

I spread open the second article and skimmed the story. Guy Palermo, a well-known businessman in the energy service sector, had thrown himself off a forty-two-storey high-rise, here in Calgary. An avid collector of Mesoamerican and pre-Columbian artifacts, Palermo had blamed a string of bad luck, including a house fire, the death of his wife, and failure to win an expensive lawsuit, on an ancient jade statue he had recently acquired. The article went on to talk about the power of myths and referenced several ancient artifacts said to be imbued with supernatural powers to heal the sick, curse wrongdoers, or bring people back from the dead.

I checked the dates of the newspaper clippings. The first one was three years old, the one about Palermo had been published last month. I slipped the clippings back into the envelope and threw it onto the passenger seat. I didn't know much about ancient civilizations, but I did know that since the earliest of times, humans have attributed events, both good and bad, to creatures, gods, entities not of this world. It's much easier to believe that the universe is ordered, that the chaos around us isn't random, that someone or something is in charge.

The man's face came back to mind as I exited the parking lot, my hands still shaky from our brief encounter. It brought back memories of my assailant, Jason Marr, the man who became the impetus for my decision to leave my job as a forensic lab analyst to become a private investigator, but I had never seen anyone's eyes look as terrified as the stranger who tried to hijack my car. If anyone feared for his life, it was him.

TWO

I LOOPED THE BURGUNDY strips of silk into a loose bow, admiring the well-defined muscles in my arms. My last few cases had required more of me physically than I ever imagined, so I started lifting weights and joined a kickboxing class. Who knew six months could make such a difference? I debated going as is, then reminded myself the men at the event would likely be wearing suits. I pulled a black jacket from the closet and slipped it on over my sleeveless blouse.

As I walked back into the living room, something on the TV caught my eye. I reached for the remote and turned up the volume.

"Police have identified yesterday's hit-and-run victim as Jeff Nickleson. Nickleson was found on 14th Street SW, just south of 90th Avenue, at around 4 p.m. He was declared dead at the scene. A light-grey or silver, newer-model Toyota GT86 was seen speeding away from the area. Police would like to speak to the driver of that car or with anyone who saw the incident or has information about what happened."

I stared at the photo that popped up on the screen. It was the man who had jumped into my car. I thought back to how he had shifted from group to group on the sidewalk in front of Starbucks, how his eyes had searched the parking lot, how his face twitched as he tried to blend in. And his obvious fear and panic in my car. Poor guy. He must have run into traffic.

I turned off the TV, grabbed my purse, and locked up. Yesterday's incident replayed in my head as the elevator whisked me down to the underground parking garage. Should I let the police know I saw Jeff Nickleson shortly before he was killed? I wouldn't be able to tell them much, other than he appeared frightened and panicked. Had someone been chasing him? And what about the newspaper articles he left behind. Could they have any significance? Of course, his state of mind could have just as easily been drug induced. Either way, the poor man had run into traffic and lost his life.

Downstairs, I thumped the hood of my 2004 Ford Taurus wagon, and a black cat shot out from underneath. I climbed in and immediately rolled down the window. A faint fishy odour materialized whenever the vehicle was parked for any length of time. I was certain a fish monger had previously leased the vehicle, and not just because of the odor. In the right light, I could make out the outline of a fished-shaped logo that had once graced the driver's door.

The Taurus was leased from JumpIn Jalopies, where I leased all my vehicles. They offered older-model vehicles for a great price. The lower price compensated for some slight issue the vehicle came with, usually trivial but too expensive to warrant fixing, given the vehicle's age. The leasing agent had assured me the Taurus was mechanically sound and this model rated high on crash-test scores, a feature I didn't necessarily appreciate him pointing out. I did, however, appreciate the power of its V6 engine, and the missing back seats didn't bother me a bit.

I pulled out of the parking garage and turned right. I loved the location of my condo. It was located a short twenty-minute ride to

Calgary's downtown, yet close enough to Glenmore Reservoir to let me commune with nature.

I knew something was up when it took three lights to make my left turn onto 14th Street. Traffic was backed up behind and in front of me as far as I could see. I glanced at my watch. I hated being late almost as much as Luis hated me being late.

Detective Inspector Luis Azagora headed up the Special Crimes Unit in Calgary Police Services. We had been seeing each other on and off for over a year—perhaps more off than on. Neither of us wanted a relationship that followed the traditional steps of dating, cohabitating, engagement, and marriage, but we both enjoyed each other's company—and the sex. We had formed this casual yet committed relationship, with an unspoken understanding that work would likely take priority over personal wants and needs. So far it was working out. Then again, we hadn't spent enough time together to really get on each other's nerves.

Stuck at a red light near the Rocky View Hospital, I sent Luis a text, telling him a massive traffic jam on 14th Street was hindering my progress. I didn't have many route options as I was heading to the university, to a charity fundraiser being held in MacEwan Centre. I suddenly noticed the three-car gap in front of me and moved forward before someone honked.

Finally on the ramp to Glenmore Trail, I could see what caused the snarl. Several emergency vehicles stood on the right side of the freeway. The fire department rescue boat slid quietly across the water to the northern shore of the reservoir. Looked like there might be a covered body in the boat. Lights flashed behind me, and traffic shifted over as far as possible to let a police vehicle and a car with the Medical Examiner logo on the door squeeze past. Being stuck in traffic now seemed less inconvenient somehow.

·‧•●‧●•‧‧·

I paused just inside the door to the reception area on the second floor of MacEwan Centre. Azagora stood talking with a high-powered group of men and women. The man to Azagora's right was the current Chief of Police. Next to him, a city councillor. I recognized the tall man with silver hair as Franklin Dirks. He was a real-estate developer and had recently announced his plans for an entertainment park just north of the city. Next to him stood a blonde woman, thin as a rail, with perfectly coiffed hair that didn't move when she did.

Another man I didn't recognize stood with them, and a woman from the Chief Prosecutor's Office stood on Luis' other side. She touched Luis' arm, and I watched as he bent his closely shaved head toward her, presumably to hear what she was saying. He threw back his head and laughed. I gritted my teeth and headed to the bar.

I had noticed little miss prosecutor on several other occasions. Even though Luis and I were spending time together, he often chose to go to public events, like this one, on his own. I got the distinct impression he didn't want to raise speculation that we might be a couple. Azagora had his eye on deputy chief or chief of police, but it wasn't his ultimate goal. The man had political aspirations and his squeaky-clean reputation made him a good future candidate, although some days I wondered if that was no longer needed as a qualifier for public office.

He had no problem being photographed with *her* though. Of course, Luis and I weren't exactly a couple. That word had implications, at least in my mind, which weren't being fulfilled. I pushed away the little green dragon flicking its fiery tongue in my head, as the rest of the group surrounding Luis joined in the laughter.

We had both received an invite to tonight's fundraiser, an annual event hosted by Inner Light, a street ministry raising funds to tackle drug addiction and homelessness in the city. Once we discovered we were both attending, we decided to meet here and planned to grab a late-evening bite once the event ended.

I took the glass of red wine the bartender poured for me and headed for the tables displaying the items in tonight's silent auction.

A voice called out, "Jorja."

I turned and smiled. "Adan. Long time no see. Your events are getting bigger and better attended each year. Congratulations!" I held up my wine glass. "Here's to a wildly successful night."

Adan leaned forward and brushed his lips against my cheek. "I'm so glad you could make it tonight. Nick's here, too." He looked around. "He's working as one of my volunteer servers tonight, but he's also agreed to speak later on."

I met Adan—a street minister who offered up messy church to his growing flock and ran a halfway house for recovering addicts—when I found myself looking for a client's long-lost relative, rumoured to be living rough. Nick was one of the street people who helped me find my way through the streets and alleys where the homeless lived, and in the process managed to find himself.

"I'll have to find him later. Glad to hear he's doing well." I noticed Luis staring in our direction. "And you, too." I laughed and touched Adan's arm, hoping it would spark the same feeling of jealousy in

Luis that had run through me a moment earlier. Feeling just a tad mortified at my blatant tit-for-tat move, I dropped my hand. "I'm glad your work is getting the support and recognition it deserves. I see the Chief of Police is here. And Franklin Dirks, and oh, there's the mayor."

"Speaking of which, I guess I should go mingle, although I'd much rather stay here." His warm grey eyes crinkled as he smiled. "Stick around after, if you can, and we can get properly caught up once this is over."

I nodded. "I'll try. Now go and remind all these well-heeled people why they're here."

I watched Adan walk away. The man was beautiful, and not just on the inside. I had once made a play for Adan, but it turned out being God's servant was a full-time job. I looked over at Luis. Maybe being a cop was, too.

I walked over to the silent auction tables and picked out two items to bid on. A watercolour painting of a meadow filled with bright-yellow flowers immediately caught my eye. It reminded me of the flowers I used to pick as a child that grew wild behind my parents' house in Timmins, Ontario. We called the flowers buffalo beans because each green stalk contained a cluster of yellow bean-shaped flowers. Which didn't explain the buffalo reference. Then again, we were just kids.

I was upping the bid on the second item I had chosen, a pair of tickets to a scotch-tasting event that included dinner and an overnight stay at the Banff Springs Hotel, when I noticed Luis making his way over. God, that man was hot. Six foot two, with dark-brown eyes and skin no glancing touch of the sun could produce. He exuded confidence and his slight swagger—just enough to soften his mostly serious demeanour—made him seem more human, more approachable. I knew what lay underneath that well-cut brown suit and felt a familiar flutter stir in my stomach.

He looked down at the bid I just made and winked at me. "You'll need to do better than that." He took the pen from me and upped my bid by a hundred dollars.

"Maybe we should pool our resources on this one." I took the pen back and immediately upped his bid by another fifty. Last winter, Luis and I managed an incredibly sexy getaway weekend at Emerald Lake. We holed up in a cabin for two whole days, the fireplace crackling day and night, the snow drifting down steadily, erasing all signs of human presence. Perhaps this year's getaway could be at the Banff Springs.

"I saw you talking to Adan. He's really done an amazing job with his annual charity event. Remember the first fundraiser he had, in the basement of Inner Light?"

I laughed. "Yeah, with a potluck supper to boot."

Azagora's eyes darkened. "I still remember what you were wearing—that green silk thing with no back."

I remembered the night, too—it was the first time Luis sent me any indication he was even slightly interested in me, although I had spent months fantasizing about him.

Luis stepped away and pulled his phone from his inside jacket pocket. I hadn't heard it ring, but he probably had the ringer turned off. He rubbed a hand over his short-shorn hair, nodded his head several times, then said something I couldn't make out. He put the phone away and stepped back. "Mierda," he muttered.

"What's up?" I asked but needn't have bothered.

"Sorry, babe. I have to bail tonight. Can I call you tomorrow?"

"Of course. Be careful."

I wanted to lean in, kiss him goodbye, but he was all business now, already heading for the door. I watched as miss prosecutor set her glass on a passing waiter's tray and rushed off to catch up with Luis.

They wouldn't have...would they?

THREE

THE LIGHTS IN MY office flickered and went out. I got up from my beat-up wooden desk and made my way to the grime-encrusted window. The building across the alley still had power. I sighed and returned to my desk.

I hadn't stayed long at the charity gala on Friday night. Adan and I only managed to snatch a few minutes before other gala guests, eager to talk to him, descended upon us, so I left.

I looked around the office. A faint stale-cigarette odour clung to the walls and remained permanently ground into the carpet. It would probably continue to ooze out of the furnishings until the building was refurbished or knocked down and replaced with something new. It was rather depressing. More so now that my best friend, Gab Rizzo, the prime lessor of the space, was in Paris, enrolled in a nine-month cooking program at the Cordon Bleu. Her personal catering company sign, Thyme to Dine, no longer graced our door, leaving me the sole occupant. Her most recent emails and texts were full of talk about wanting to take a year off to travel after her program ended—a gap year, like the one neither of us had after finishing school.

I'd have to decide if I wanted to stay here if Gab didn't return.

My phone vibrated against the top of the wooden desk, startling me. Mike Saunders' name and number popped up on the screen.

"Hey, Mike. How are you doing?"

"I'm okay. Is this a bad time?"

"No, not at all. Just finished up the paperwork on the Lane case when the lights went out in the office. I was getting ready to pack up for the day. Why, what's happening?"

Gab Rizzo might be my best friend, but Mike was a close second. I met him at my former place of employment. I had just taken a job at Global Analytix when Mike, recently retired from the Toronto Police force and bored with his newfound freedom, signed a contract with them to help set up training and procedures for their field analysts.

This week, Mike was in Vancouver, then heading east. He was part of a national task force set up to develop an empathy-informed procedural framework for decentralized 911 calls. Calls that could, in certain instances, be assigned to social workers, drug councillors, or psychologists, and not police.

"Glad I caught you. What's your schedule like? Any chance you have a few spare days?"

"I'm doing some background checks for one of my insurance company clients but we're talking hours of work here, not days. Do you need me to do something for you?"

"Yes, if you don't mind."

Maybe he needed me to check in on his two Persian cats. His neighbour, a spiteful little Polish woman, usually looked after them when Mike was out of town, but on occasion he had needed me to fill in for her when she went to look after an ailing sister somewhere. Probably Transylvania.

"Sure. What do you need?"

"You know the body they recovered from the reservoir last week?"

"No. Oh, wait. I did notice some emergency vehicles down there when I was driving by on Friday night. I wondered if someone drowned. There's been nothing about it on the news, or if there was, I missed it." Not that I paid attention to every death in the city—like some ambulance chasers I knew.

"Yeah. Well, they recovered the body of a cop I knew. A former mentor of mine. He retired when I was still on the force."

"Sorry to hear that, Mike. What happened?"

"His daughter said the ME ruled it an accidental death. She's adamant it's not. She thinks he was murdered."

"That's tough. The ME usually gets it right. What do you think? Could it have been an accident, or maybe suicide?"

"I guess it's possible. He was diagnosed with lung cancer last year. He wasn't the kind of guy who would've taken to dying slowly in a hospice—then again, he wasn't the kind of guy who would kill himself. Can you give Donna, his daughter, a call, talk to her?"

"Sure. She lives in Calgary?"

"Yeah. I'll send you her contact info. Her father's name was Howard Bergman. After Howie retired, he became a private investigator. He moved out west last year—wanting to reconnect with his daughter. He didn't see much of her while she was growing up since his ex-wife moved to Calgary after they split up."

"Oh, that's too bad. She was probably just starting to get to know him."

"She's had a big shock and she's upset. Maybe all she needs is to talk this through. Or maybe she knows something. When she called, I told her I was tied up here, but that I'd contact a good friend of mine who might be able to hear her out—look into what happened."

"Okay. Send me her name and number and I'll give her a call."

I didn't believe for a moment that Mike believed Donna just wanted to talk. After thirty-some years in policing, Mike had a sense for when things didn't sound right.

FOUR

Donna lived in a modest 1950s bungalow just off Elbow Drive, near Henry Wise Wood High School. I parked and made my way up a crumbling sidewalk to the front door and pressed the doorbell. The door opened to reveal a woman in her mid-forties. She was a few inches shorter than my five feet and eight inches, and her wavy, light-brown hair was cut close to her head.

"Hi. I'm Jorja Knight. Mike Saunders' friend."

Her green eyes lit up. She smiled and held out a hand to me.

"Nice to meet you, Jorja. Come in, come in."

I stepped into a bright, well-lit interior. Someone had renovated the place, if not recently then certainly in the last decade or so. Several interior walls had been removed and I could see past the living area to my left all the way back to the kitchen, which looked out onto a sunny, treed backyard.

"Would you like a coffee? I just made some."

"A coffee sounds great. Your place is lovely. Did you do the renos?"

She laughed. "No. I moved here about eight years ago. The former owner had just reno'ed the place. That's why it appealed to me."

I followed her back to the kitchen and after she poured two coffees we sat at a small table next to a set of patio doors which opened to a large backyard.

"Love the backyard. With all the trees, it's like you have your own little park."

"I do love all the trees, but now that my daughter is off at university, I'm going to have to rake up all those leaves myself."

"Oh—yes, there is that. Where's your daughter studying?"

"Lethbridge. She's enrolled in the Criminal Justice Policing Program." Her voice caught. "My father was pretty darn proud of her."

"I'm sure he had good reason to be. I'm so sorry for your loss."

She nodded. "A police officer came to the house on Saturday. He wanted me to provide confirmation that the man they found in Glenmore Reservoir was my father." She picked up her coffee, cradling it in both hands, and stared out at the sun-dappled yard. She turned back to me. "I drove down to Lethbridge on Sunday to tell Amanda in person. She took it pretty hard. She wanted to come back home with me, but I told her to stay, focus on her studies. I'm organizing a memorial service for him. She'll come home for that."

"I'm so sorry. This must be so hard for you."

"Thank you. The suddenness of his death makes it worse. I never got a chance to say goodbye."

I knew exactly how that felt. My own mother had been killed while I was away at university. For years, I wondered if I could have somehow changed the outcome if I had been there.

"I was just getting to know him. My parents split up when I was five. I don't have many memories of my dad from my childhood. He wasn't around all that much—which is why they split up in the first place. Work always came first to my father, and it didn't mesh with what my mom wanted from a marriage."

My mind immediately flashed to Mike and then to Azagora. Both of Mike's marriages had ended for the same reason. He once told me that even when he was home, he really wasn't emotionally available. His work and the cases that haunted him were like a constant third person in their relationship. Azagora had never married, didn't want to.

"Yeah, unfortunately, the divorce rates for police officers are some of the highest in the country."

Donna nodded. "After my parents divorced, we moved to Calgary. My grandmother, my mom's mother, lived here. She helped raise me and looked after me while my mother went to work."

"Your father didn't visit?"

"He came out here maybe three or four times while I was growing up. It was hard to stay in touch—we didn't have the technology we have now. Thank goodness we do now. Amanda and I text every day and we FaceTime two or three times a week. Of course, Lethbridge isn't that far away, and I'm sure she'll be home for weekends whenever she can get away."

"Mike said your dad retired about fifteen years ago, but he only moved out here last year."

"That's right. A lot of his cop friends back in Ontario were already retired, but as people get older, they move on, either to follow their children and grandchildren to wherever they've settled or to move somewhere warmer."

"I guess it was the former reason for your father. He sure didn't pick Calgary for its short, balmy winters."

Donna laughed. "If Amanda ever got a job on the west coast, I'd be heading out right after her. But you're right. One day, right out of the blue, he called me. I hadn't seen him in over ten years. He said he was in Calgary. I thought he'd come for a visit, but he said no, he'd relocated here."

"That's nice. Did you see him often after that?"

"Comparatively speaking, yes. It was awkward at first. We didn't have much to talk about. After five or six visits, things got easier. I had him over for supper every couple of weeks. Amanda would join us if she was home."

"I understand he was still working as a private investigator. I gather he worked for himself?"

"That's right. He loved his work. Or maybe that was just the nature of the man—and he loved to work. It gave him purpose. That's one of the reasons I know he didn't kill himself."

Sadly, I knew people who were gainfully employed, seemingly doing okay on the outside, who suffered tremendously and silently on the inside until they lost their grip on life. I glanced up. Donna was still talking, her voice quicker now.

"The trip back from Lethbridge gave me time to think. Before that, I was in shock—working on autopilot. A few days later I managed to contact the ME. She told me her first thoughts were that he died by suicide but after further examination decided it was an accident. She seems to think he slipped and fell, hit his head on a rock on his way down the slope, and drowned once he went into the water. But it couldn't have happened that way. So, I called Mike."

"Mike told me you think your father was killed—murdered. What makes you think so?"

"Dad was working on a new case the last few weeks. He was onto something big. He seemed happier and more excited than I've ever seen him. He said after this case he might properly retire. That he always wanted to move somewhere warm and live on a beach. Costa Rica really appealed to him. He said he knew he hadn't been a good father, but he meant to make it up to me...and Amanda. That I deserved to have a better life than the one I had growing up. That he was going to make sure I never wanted for anything, anymore."

"Do you know what he was talking about? Or what he was working on?"

"No. He was excited, but secretive. The last time I saw him was Tuesday...three days before they found his body. Something had changed. He told me to be careful, to take care of myself. He said if anything happened to him to call his friend Mike. He often talked about Mike, and I met him this spring when I ran into him and Dad having a craft beer on a patio at the farmers' market."

"That's interesting. He didn't elaborate on what he meant or why he thought something might happen to him?"

"No. I laughed it off and told him nothing was going to happen to him. But it did." She wiped at a lone tear that spilled from her tear-filled eyes.

I took a deep breath, hoping I wasn't about to reveal something she hadn't already known. "Mike said your father told him he had lung cancer. Could he have maybe gotten a more devastating diagnosis? Maybe he was talking about insurance money being left to you."

Donna shook her head. "He went through chemo last year. The tumour in his lung shrank considerably. They had him on an experimental drug, but one they have found to be promising at keeping the tumour from growing. He knew his life expectancy would be shorter than most, but there's no way he killed himself. As far as insurance money goes, he only had a small policy, just big enough to cover his burial costs, he used to joke. His police pension died with him. Besides, why would he have told me to contact Mike if anything happened to him?"

"And he made that comment, what? Three days before he died. I can see why you'd think his death might be suspicious."

She looked at me, her eyes serious. "So, what do we do now?"

When Mike first told me Donna might just want to talk things over with someone, I didn't believe him. And now that I had met Donna, I was positive she hadn't just contacted him for sympathy. It wasn't just the comments her father made to her in the weeks before his death. Donna said something had changed when she last saw him. And now that I had met Donna, I could see she was a rational woman, one who would be prone to think about things before offering up her opinion. In that regard, she reminded me a bit of myself.

"Did your father keep an office, or did he work out of his home?"

"He worked from home. A studio apartment. He has this massive desk where he kept his files and computer. Took up almost a third of his living space."

"Well, it may turn out he did fall, hit his head, and drown. But from what you've told me, I have a sense that there was something else going on that might have contributed to his death. It warrants a look."

"Thank you so much, Jorja. I didn't know what to do. If someone killed my dad..." Her voice trailed off as her eyes welled up again. "My dad deserves to have someone pay attention to his death."

I left Donna's with the address and the keys to her father's apartment in my pocket. If nothing else, I would love to get Donna the closure she needed. Closure I never got with my own parents' deaths.

FIVE

I PAUSED IN FRONT of the three-storey walk-up. This was the place. The once-cream-coloured stucco was chipped and streaked with dirt, the windows dark with grime. Several faint numbers were etched into the wall above the front door. 1912. Not the address, but the year the building was built. The front glass door had a crack running through it. I pulled it open and stepped inside.

A set of mailboxes lined the wall to my left. Each was labelled with its apartment number, made by one of those handheld Dymo printers. I counted eighteen units. Howard's apartment was 302, which I assumed would be on the third floor.

I climbed the once-navy-blue carpeted stairs, now black with decades of dirt and grease. The cheap, metal stair railing wobbled under my hand, and the sticky feel of its chipped plastic top was enough for me to move to the right and avoid touching it at all.

The apartment building was just a long, rectangular box. A hallway on each floor ran from the front staircase straight through to a second set of stairs at the back of the building, with four units on the left, four on the right. I reached the third floor, which was darker than the previous two levels as the light from the front door didn't reach this far. Apartment 302 was the first unit on the right.

I pulled out the set of keys Donna had given me. Four keys on a plain metal ring. Two of the keys had a Chevrolet symbol on them. Donna had told me he drove an old blue Chevy Malibu but wasn't sure where it was now. I selected one of the other keys and reached for the doorknob, the tarnished gold of the metal mostly worn off.

The doorknob wobbled loosely in my hand. The security in this building was nonexistent. I reached to fit the key into the lock, and the slight pressure I applied opened the door before I even had the key fully inserted.

I pushed the door open further. The jamb was nicked and battered. I stared at a ten or twelve-inch crack in the wood frame. My heart hammered against my chest.

Taking one last look down the long, dim hallway, I stepped inside. The place was dark. My fingers ran over the rough plaster, searching for a light switch. Finding none, I reached into the back pocket of my jeans, pulled out my cell phone, and tapped the flashlight icon.

I was in an entryway, six or seven feet in length. I spotted the light switch several steps in from the door. *Handy.*

I flicked the switch, hoping the power hadn't been turned off for some reason. A blue-grey light flickered ahead, and the familiar buzz of a florescent light broke the stillness.

"Hello?" I called out tentatively, getting ready to beat a hasty retreat. No one answered.

I slid forward, keeping my back to the wall. I was breathing fast, like I'd just finished a 10K run, which I never do.

The hallway opened into a living area and a small kitchenette on my left. The fluorescent light buzzed, flickered, and finally emitted a garish bluish-white light. I gasped.

Tan couch cushions lay strewn at odd angles on and around the couch, the stuffing visible through deep slashes in the fabric. An old wooden desk stood against heavy, dark drapes that covered the front window. The desk drawers had been pulled out; papers scattered everywhere. A small bookshelf lay tipped on its side, books strewn across the floor.

I stepped further into the living area and shone my cell phone light around the room. The hairs on the back of my neck prickled.

I whipped around. No one there.

I rushed out of the apartment and into the hallway. My fingers shook as I keyed in Donna's phone number on my cell. She answered on the third ring.

"Hi, Jorja. What's up?"

"I just got to your father's apartment. I think you should come down here. Someone's broken into the place and trashed it."

"Oh my god. Okay. I'm on my way."

"In the meantime, I'll give the cops a call. They might want to see this."

· · • • · • • • · ·

Donna arrived before the police did. We were careful not to touch anything as we tiptoed through the apartment. A bed was wedged into an alcove partially tucked in behind the kitchenette, the mattress pushed to one side. Clothes from the one small closet in the room lay on the floor. We stepped back out into the hallway.

"Someone was looking for something," Donna said, her eyes growing wide.

"No doubt about that. I know it's hard to tell, but do you notice anything missing?"

She bit her lip, then glanced back through the door. "The computer monitor is lying on the floor, but I didn't notice the computer."

"He didn't have a laptop?"

"No. I mean, maybe he also had a laptop, but he definitely had a desktop computer with a good-sized monitor. His eyes weren't as good as they used to be."

We both turned as footsteps came up the stairs. Two uniformed police officers arrived at the top of the stairs, both young, both blond.

"You call in the break-in?" the male officer asked.

"Yes. My name is Jorja Knight. This is Donna Hart. This was her father's apartment."

"Was?" He turned to Donna. "He doesn't live here anymore?"

"My father died last week. I've been busy organizing his memorial service. I asked Jorja to come here and check in on the place." Donna looked over at me, her eyes pleading for help.

"I got here about an hour ago," I said. "As soon as I put the key into the doorknob, the door opened. I noticed the frame is splintered."

"Did you go inside?"

"Yes. I touched the wall on the right—looking for a light switch, and then the switch, of course. As soon as the light came on it became obvious that someone ransacked the place. I called Donna to tell her what I found and then called you. We both went in and just surveyed the place from the edge of the living area."

We spent the next hour answering questions. They wanted more details about Howard's death, then seemed to lose interest when they heard it was officially labelled an accident.

Donna did a walkthrough with the officer and confirmed his computer was gone as well as his old trusty Nikon camera. She said his cell phone also seemed to be missing and hadn't been among the personal items that had been returned to her at the morgue. Beyond that, it was hard to tell if anything else was gone.

While Donna was talking to the police, I went down the back stairs and found the parking stall for Unit 302. Howard's Chevy Malibu wasn't there. I headed back upstairs to share my findings with Donna and the police. Either someone had taken it, or it was still parked somewhere near where Howard's body was found.

The building manager had been located and was talking to the police. He looked to be about eighty and was shaking so badly, I worried he might need medical assistance.

An hour later, Donna and I were on our own.

"Constable Abbot told me he sees this sort of thing all the time. People post an obituary for their loved ones in the paper and the next thing you know there's a break-in at their residence."

"Did you post an obituary?"

"No. Dad didn't know many people out here and he doesn't...didn't have many friends. I just phoned the few people he knew and told them we're having a private memorial service for him on Monday at the Grayson funeral home. I suppose I should post something in the paper. His former work colleagues might want to know that he's...gone." Her voice broke.

"I think the police have this one wrong."

"I'm so glad you're here, Jorja. I can't imagine having to deal with this on my own."

"Glad to give you a hand." I stared at the papers scattered on the floor, a mixture of newspaper articles, printed pages from his files, invoices, and handwritten notes. God knows what was taken. It was going to be a challenge to sort and put the contents back together into some meaningful order. Maybe his files would hold some clue as to what he'd been working on.

"If you don't mind, I'll stay awhile and start straightening up the place. I'll come back in the morning to pack up his files and take them back to my office. Hopefully, there's something in there that will be of use to us. I can drop off his house keys when I'm done, so you can sort through his personal belongings."

"Thanks, Jorja. I guess I should clear out Dad's stuff sooner rather than later. The building manager was grumbling about having to secure the door—I suppose he'll be changing the locks."

I nodded, but I was quite sure the door locks hadn't been changed in years.

After Donna left, I walked over to the Safeway just down the street from the apartment, picked up a sandwich and a coffee, and headed back. Newly built apartment buildings defined the neighbourhood, with only the odd, old single-family home left wedged-in between. Howard's apartment building, and the three-storey walk-up next to it, were relics from another era. Whatever once stood behind them had been torn down and the reinforced concrete walls rising from the ground told me another gleaming muti-story tower would soon stand there.

Reluctant to leave the sunshine and fresh air behind, I climbed the dingy stairs back to Howard's apartment. It was going to be a long day.

SIX

THIS MORNING I ARRIVED prepared. Coffee in one hand and a few packing boxes tucked under my arm, I climbed the stairs to Howard's apartment. It appeared the building manager had tightened the door handle, but my key still worked in the lock.

Yesterday I had searched every crevice of the couch, examined each cushion thoroughly, and set them neatly back on the couch. I didn't know what I was looking for but hoped that whatever someone had been searching for hadn't been found.

I set my coffee down, crossed the room, and pulled apart the heavy damask drapes covering the front window. A cloud of dust floated out into the room. Each fold in the material was faded from the sunlight, leaving a light-coloured stripe running through the botanical pattern. Thistle flowers, red pomegranates, and green vines wove in and around each other on an indigo backdrop. The fabric felt brittle in my hands.

The building manager had made it clear last night that the furniture, drapes, and the kitchenware had come with the place and were not to be removed. As far as I was concerned, he was welcome to it. The only items that belonged to Howard were the heavy wooden desk, a microwave, his clothes, books, computer, and a few personal mementos.

I had a quick look through the kitchen cupboard and the medicine cabinet in the bathroom last night. The fridge hadn't held much—two containers of leftovers from a takeout dinner, some wilting vegetables, and half-empty jars and condiments, some already past their best-before date. I found nothing hidden in the coffee beans or box of cereal.

Nothing in the medicine cabinet gave me pause, just the usual stuff—toothpaste, deodorant, antacids, Aspirin, and Benazepril, a medication for high blood pressure. I made note of the prescribing doctor's name, although I'm sure privacy laws would prevent him from sharing any useful information about Howard's health.

This morning I tackled the books and papers. I picked up each book, held it upside down, and riffled the pages. Assured there was nothing hidden between the pages, I placed each book in one of the boxes I brought. Most of the books were thrillers—Michael Connelly, Ludlum, Harlan Coben, and a few true crimes. Then I started on the papers. They were going to present a bigger challenge, as many of the pages, once held in individual file folders, were now intermixed, and scattered everywhere.

I packed the papers into a separate box to take to the office with me. I would sort them later and hopefully be able to figure out what he had been working on. I checked each desk drawer, inside and out, before sliding the drawers back into place. I checked the back of the desk and the underside.

By noon, the place was almost back to normal, other than for the obvious damage. Everything on the floor in the living room had been picked up, allowing me to move around unencumbered. I stacked the boxes of books and papers that I was taking with me in the hall. A bag of garbage stood ready to take out to the dumpster—full of stuffing from the torn cushions, along with the kitchen contents that had been dumped onto the floor.

As the chaos and clutter diminished, a sense of melancholy had grown. Howard's death was another reminder of how short our time on earth was, how it could all end in a blink of the eye, usually unexpectedly. His few earthly possessions, regardless how inexpensive or worn, possessed an energy of their own. They were no longer inanimate objects, they had Howard's emotions, thoughts, and feelings attached to them. I wondered if Donna would keep them or give them away. Sometimes mementos from departed loved ones became a source of constant sadness instead of comfort. That's why I rarely wore my mother's watch, the one and only keepsake I had of her. I was glad I wasn't the one who would have to decide what to do with them.

Suddenly feeling the need for a quick break, I grabbed the bag of garbage and made my way down the hall to the back stairs. After depositing the bag in the garbage bin behind the building, I continued down the street to a coffee shop and sat there for a while to clear my head. Before leaving, I called Donna and gave her an update. I let her know I'd be returning Howard's keys later this evening.

Once back, I made my way into the alcove off the living room that served as the bedroom. All that was left to straighten was the nightstand, which lay tipped over on the floor, and to pick up the clothes where they lay after being pushed off the few shelves or torn from their hangers. I checked the underside of the mattress, the bedframe, and pushed the mattress back into place.

An obviously well-used coffee mug labelled Best Dad remained on a closet shelf. I picked up and folded the small pile of clothes that had been torn from the hangers and placed them on the bed. Under the pile, I found a black photo frame holding a picture of Donna and Amanda, the glass now shattered. I shook the shards of glass into a garbage bin and laid the photo next to the pile of clothes.

I righted the nightstand and crouched to pick up the drawer, which lay on the floor, taking a minute to shift through the contents, some of which had spilled onto the floor as well. A few pens, a small flashlight, a couple of screwdrivers, a small sewing kit, a tube of gorilla glue, and some change. I put the items into the drawer and lifted it to slide it back into the nightstand. It wouldn't go.

I stuck my hand into the opening and felt something on the underside. Grabbing my cell phone, I tipped the nightstand onto its side and shone the light into the space for the drawer. Something was taped to the underside of the nightstand top.

Excitement replaced my earlier melancholy. I picked at the corner of the tape holding the item in place until it gave way enough for me to pull out a small, thin notebook. My fingers shook as I opened the faux-leather cover.

Each page was divided into three sections, each section a separate day of the year. I flipped through it. This was Howard's appointment book. Many of the pages were blank, but some had notes, initials, dates, and times jotted in them.

I sat back on my heels. Why would Howard have needed to hide his appointment book?

SEVEN

THE LITTLE COGS IN my head had been whirling all day, but now I was done. I rubbed the back of my neck and looked at the mounds of paper around me. Six piles on my desk, five more on the small round table that was crammed into the corner of the office between two file cabinets and the window. It had taken me six hours to sort and shift through Howard's papers and group them into related stacks. A thankless job but needed.

Several piles were from cases he had worked on in 2020. The files were pretty typical—cases involving cheating husbands, a divorce dispute where the soon-to-be ex-wife was claiming her husband was hiding assets from her, and a woman who hired Howard to track down her kids, missing since her ex-husband refused to return them after a court-approved parental visit.

Another pile held notes and invoices for some work he had done for a law firm. I found a scanned copy of an insurance policy, which I added to the pile. The relevant names, dates, and many of the details had been blacked out, leaving me not much to read. Looked like he may have been investigating an insurance fraud.

A separate yet unsorted pile contained a hodgepodge of material, everything from receipts for gas, food and office supplies to newspaper articles, computer printouts and pages torn from magazines. This pile also contained his tax filings, banking statements, and various invoices related to his phone, internet, cable services, and car insurance. I wasn't ready to go through them, as I really didn't know how they could help me at this point, but they might offer up useful information once I figured out what Howard was working on.

I also had a three-inch-high stack of pages I hadn't been able to assign to one of the other eleven piles I had already made. It was also possible one or more pages might now be sitting in the wrong pile but, as a first cut, they made sense where they were.

My cell phone rang, providing a welcomed distraction.

"Hi, Donna."

"Hi, Jorja. I just wanted to let you know I got a call from the police this morning. They found Dad's car in the Heritage Park parking lot. The driver's window was smashed out and someone used a crowbar to pop the trunk. The glove box was empty. I've found an autobody shop that will fix the trunk and window on the car using used parts so it will keep the costs down. They're going to go pick it up."

"Hmm, the police don't think it odd that someone broke into his car *and* his apartment after he was found dead?"

"I asked the same thing, but they said they see this kind of thing all the time. The car was in a paid parking lot that gets locked overnight. The culprits see these left-behind cars and know that no one will be coming for them until morning."

My previous job as a forensic lab analyst had honed my inclination to consider risk and probability when examining evidence. I quickly considered the probability of would-be thieves randomly breaking into a car that was owned by someone who had died under somewhat unknown circumstances, then had their apartment ransacked. A red flag popped up.

I refocused. Donna was still talking.

"There's another reason I'm calling. The building manager from Dad's apartment called me just now. He wants the whole place cleaned out by the end of the day tomorrow. He says he's got a renter lined up and if I don't get the place cleaned by then, he's going to hire cleaners to shampoo the rugs, clean the oven and all that, and send me the bill."

"Whoa. You can tell the old vulture to cool his jets. I've been going through your father's files, and I found his rental agreement in the mix. He's paid up until the end of the month—so that means you don't have to give the apartment back for two and half more weeks."

"Oh, thank goodness."

"Let me scan and send it to you. He put a five-hundred-dollar damage deposit on the place, which you won't get back unless he took out insurance on the contents of his place, which is probably unlikely. If the building owner didn't have his own insurance on the furniture, then too bad for him. I suspect most of it was left behind over the years, by previous renters. Unless you want to remove and keep your father's desk and the microwave—which belonged to him, not the apartment—you don't have to do anything."

"Well, what the...the manager must know this."

"Of course, he does. My guess is he wants to get a tenant in there right away so he can pocket two weeks of rent before the new lease at the beginning of next month is made known to the building owner."

"I can't believe it. He knows that the apartment wasn't only broken into but that my father recently died."

"Believe it. I was once hired to find out who was stealing this woman's jewellery and turns out her dear old mom was taking her things and selling them on eBay. When I caught her and provided proof, she told her daughter her mind must be going because she didn't remember doing it. Except she was stealing from a whole network of friends and acquaintances."

"Wow. The dementia card. Who would have imagined?"

I laughed. "Something to file away in case I end up homeless and the government cheques aren't enough."

"Oh, and there's one more thing. The funeral home phoned to see if I could bring some clothes down...for Dad. I guess it was just old habit, but I checked all the pockets of the clothes I picked out. I found a key in the jacket pocket."

"Can you tell what it's from?"

"No. I used to have one that looked similar, from a safety deposit box. I don't have it anymore."

"That's interesting. Do you know what bank he used?"

"I have no idea."

"Okay. I have a big stack of personal papers, including tax filings from previous years, his CPP payments, that sort of thing. I'll have a look, see if there is anything that will tell us where he banked."

"Thanks. And Jorja?"

"Yes?"

"I know this isn't what you usually do. It's not what I expected, either. Please keep track of your time; I'll pay you for all this extra time you're spending to help me."

"Don't give it another thought, Donna. Your father was a good friend of Mike's, and any friend of Mike's is a friend of mine."

I hadn't intended to look through Howard's financial information until much later, but a possible safety deposit box key changed all that.

I pulled over a three-inch-high stack of papers I had labelled *personal finances*. Donna needed to know where he banked if she were to have half a chance of finding the location of his box. Assuming the key fit a bank safety deposit box.

I was halfway through the pile when it occurred to me: wouldn't Howard's wallet have been returned to Donna? He would have had credit cards that told her where he banked.

I finished shifting through the pile and called Donna.

"Hi, Donna. I found credit card statements from RBC and one of those credit card term agreements from American Express. I'll scan and send them over to you. You could call the RBC and see if he also had an account with them. A credit card with the Royal Bank of Canada doesn't necessarily mean he banked there, or had a safety deposit box with them, but it's a good place to start."

"If the key I found belongs to one of their safety deposits boxes, will they even give me access to it?"

"You'll need to get a copy of his death certificate and provide proof that you're his next of kin. I'd do it for you if I could, but they're going to want your information, your signature, and proof of ID on the request forms anyway."

"Okay. Thanks, Jorja. I don't know what I'd do without you. It's like my brain's turned off."

"Don't worry. It's been a big shock, and it's hard to know what to do unless you've been through it yourself once or twice before. Donna, while I have you on the phone, quick question. Wasn't your father's wallet among his personal effects?"

"No…now that you mention it…oh my gosh, it wasn't. Just clothes, his watch, keys, and his old army tag he always wore on a chain around his neck."

"I just thought of it myself as I was going through his financial papers. I wonder if that's how whoever broke in knew where he lived."

"So, it would mean someone was there. Someone killed my father."

"It's a stretch in logic, but possible."

After I hung up, it continued to nig at me. I suppose Howard's wallet could be lying on the bottom of the reservoir. Or perhaps his wallet and cell phone had been in the car and someone lifted them there.

I finished sorting the last few papers and another troubling thought occurred: why had the police been okay with finding a man wearing street clothes in the reservoir, with no phone or wallet, and not investigated further?

EIGHT

I SLID OPEN MY balcony door and stepped outside. The traffic noise wafting up from below acted more like white noise by the time it reached my condo eight floors up. I set my glass of wine on a small metal table between the two white composite deck chairs I kept on the balcony. The plexiglass railing sheltered the space from the wind and offered up unencumbered views of treelined streets below and a glimpse of the reservoir itself. I took in a deep breath then shuddered, suddenly realizing Howard's dead body had been floating in our drinking water. Good thing I had wine.

After spending six hours at the office, I had returned home with Howard's appointment book. No use wasting the entire day inside a dingy office when I could study it outside, with a glass of wine to boot.

The brown faux-leather cover was well worn. I flipped it open. An appointment book, like the ones you could buy each new year at any office supply store, was anchored inside. I checked the front and back openings in the leather wraparound to make sure nothing was in between it and the appointment book covers tucked into it.

I flipped to the front page. There was a space for the owner's name and contact information, but Howard hadn't bothered with either.

My first pass through the appointment book was a quick one. Looked like Howard used it to jot odd notes, mileage on his car—expenses, appointments, and meetings, many apparently at restaurants.

The second time I went through the book I placed a sticky post-it tab on the pages of interest. He had met or called someone named Milt on August 24. A phone number was jotted down under the name, and near the bottom of the page a number, 204. A different pen had been used than the one to note the name and phone number. Maybe he had driven somewhere to meet this Milt and the number was his mileage for the day.

I drew a circle on my mental map of the area surrounding Calgary. Assuming the mileage was for a round trip, he could have driven to Banff, Olds, High River, Beiseker, or any number of smaller towns near Calgary.

A second trip—or at least that's what I interpreted the numbers to represent—occurred a week later, this time with the number 272 behind the notation. There was no other information on the page.

There were also three meetings over the last month with someone only identified by the letters JN. Usually at or near the noon hour. Of course, I was assuming these were meetings with someone, but the initials could be a place. Could be anything. One of the pages contained the word *Bale*, which was circled several times, as if it were important.

The rest of the notebook contained doctor appointments, notes to take his car in for an oil change, haircuts, that sort of thing. Donna was right. He didn't have a full social calendar, or if he did, it wasn't reflected in his notebook.

I kept flipping pages. One of the pages had a list of numbers written on it.

05, 07, 18

12, 11, 19

06, 03, 20

24, 02, 21

17, 10, 21 bsag

No idea what *bsag* meant. The numbers could be dates. Or his picks for a lottery ticket. It didn't give me a whole lot to work with.

I continued page by page. The last entry Howard had made was on a Monday, four days before his body was pulled from the reservoir. Just two words, *call Donna.*

I pulled out my cell phone and typed the phone number below Milt's name into the 411 reverse-call website. A message came back that it didn't have enough information on the caller. I went inside, retrieved my burner phone. I didn't want my own phone number showing up in the call log, especially as I had no idea who this Milt was.

The call went directly to voice mail. A raspy voice announced, "I'm not in. You know what to do next." I didn't bother leaving a message.

Returning to the balcony, I sat, took a sip of wine, and contemplated my next move.

All I had were a few first names, an initial or two, and a phone number. The other useful piece of data I had, if I could call it that, was a copy of a heavily redacted insurance policy from Carson Milford. A five-million-dollar insurance policy isn't that common. At least in the circles I travelled in. But I didn't see any mention of Carson Milford in Howard's appointment book. For all I knew, it had nothing to do with whatever Howard had been working on recently.

I picked up my phone and googled Carson Milford Insurance. They had branch offices in major Canadian cities, seven in all. I had to assume the policy had been issued in the Calgary office, but it was an assumption predicated on nothing.

The big question of course, was what was Howard doing at Glenmore Reservoir? My guess was that he was meeting someone there. Odd place for a meeting—unless you didn't want to be seen. A fifteen-kilometre trail ringed the reservoir with several smaller offshoots. Some sections of the trail were well travelled by cyclists, runners, and hikers but other sections, particularly those that wound through the marsh and wooded areas, were less popular.

Trying to reconstruct Howard's movements in the weeks and days before his death was going to be a challenge. Unless the key Donna found in her father's jacket pocket led to something related to whatever Howard was working on, we might be done. Of course, the box it opened might simply hold important papers like his will, or information on his personal assets or finances. But based on what I had seen to date of Howard's record keeping, I doubted it.

I picked up my now empty wine glass. Time to call it a day. But instead of putting thoughts of Howard away, I found myself pouring through his appointment book a third time. There was something in here that made Howard hide it in his nightstand. Donna said he had been excited to be working on a case but then something changed. He had told Donna to contact Mike if something happened to him, just days before he died.

The more I thought about what I knew of Howard's death, the more convinced I became that whatever Howard had been working on had gotten him killed. I just had to find what that was.

NINE

It was one of those days that made you forget winter was even a possibility. The trees were brilliant yellow under the palest of blue skies, the air still and warm.

The funeral home Donna had chosen was a few blocks east of Macleod Trail, in a mostly commercial area. A small, family-run funeral home, it appealed to people with limited funds and no need for a large gathering.

I slid out of the Taurus, smoothed down my black pencil skirt, and walked the half-block back to the funeral home. A woman in a black suit stood at the doorway. She smiled as she handed me a memorial card and pointed out the way to the Trinity Chapel. I was glad I had gone with a simple cream-coloured silk blouse and dispensed with the black jacket that came with the skirt, otherwise I could have been mistaken for her.

The room was small. Three rows of chairs had been set up to face a tablecloth draped round table at the front of the room. A spray of white roses lay on the table next to a gleaming burl walnut urn and behind it, an 8-by-10 photo of Howard Bergman in police uniform.

"Hi, Jorja." Donna came forward to greet me. "Come—I want to introduce some people to you." There were ten people in the room, including Donna and myself. Donna started with her daughter Amanda, who was the spitting image of a younger Donna. Next, she introduced me to her sister and brother in-law, a nephew who looked to be about Amanda's age, and her mother, a tiny woman sitting in a wheelchair.

She led me over to three people standing off to one side. I recognized one of them—a man named Lennie, whom Mike had introduced me to a couple of years earlier. Lennie had worked with Mike in the Toronto Police Service and must have also known Howard. The other two people standing with Lennie were Howard's cousin, Barry, and his wife, Elsa.

The officiant arrived, and we settled into the chairs arranged at the front of the room. Just as the officiant was introducing herself, a woman arrived and slid into a chair in the last row. She looked to be in her sixties and wore a flowy peasant dress with a loose mauve scarf wrapped around her neck.

The officiant talked about death, losing a loved one, the grieving process, and reminded us we were all here to celebrate the dedicated, hardworking, and kind spirit Howard had been.

Amanda got up next and, as she made her way to the front of the room, I noticed a man had slipped in and was standing by the back door. Amanda read a lovely poem she wrote about her grandfather.

The officiant then read out several messages that had been left on the memorial page the funeral home had set up for Howard on their website, and a telegram from Mike. Mike's telegram expressed his sympathy and went on to say how great a mentor Howard had been to him and how stellar a police officer he'd been—always allowing other people's grief, pain, and need for justice to overshadow his own personal needs.

I watched Donna wipe away a tear as her daughter leaned in to give her a hug.

Once the formal part of the service ended, the funeral home caterers brought in sandwiches, salads, as well as desserts, coffee, and tea, and set them up on two tables at the back of the room.

I chatted a bit with Howard's cousin and wife before joining the woman who had come in late.

"Lovely service, wasn't it? I'm Jorja," I said, stretching out my hand.

She wiped her hand along her dress and took mine in a loose grip. "Hi. I'm Marie."

"I know Donna through my friend Mike, who worked with Howard when he was with Toronto Police Services. How do you know Howard or the family?"

"I'm his neighbour. Or I guess, I was his neighbour."

"Oh. From the apartment on Fifth Street? Or from one of his former residences?"

"No, Fifth Street. I live in Unit 301, right across from Howard's apartment. I couldn't believe it when I heard he was dead. I had just been talking to him a few days before."

"I'm sure it came as a shock. Did you know Howard well then?"

"I was starting to." She gave me a small smile. "He kept pretty much to himself, but he was a nice, kind man. If he saw me carrying in groceries, he'd always give me hand. Fixed the tap in my kitchen once, too. The constant dripping was driving me crazy, and the building manager is useless. When I saw the cop, the first thing I thought was that old Larry had croaked in his sleep. Then I saw him going into Howard's place."

"Oh, you mean the police officers that came on Thursday?"

"No. On Saturday. Not this past Saturday—the Saturday before that."

Howard's body was found on a Friday night, and the police had contacted Donna the following day. Maybe they had gone to his apartment before contacting Donna, in case Howard had a wife, or someone else he was living with. Odd, though.

"Are you sure? I mean, that you saw the police at Howard's apartment on Saturday."

"Yes. Well, one cop. I was looking out my front window when I saw him pull up, get out of his car, and come up the sidewalk to our building. Like I said, I thought maybe our building manager had died. I'm surprised he hasn't."

"Was he driving a police vehicle?"

"I guess so. It had a light on the roof but was one of them unmarked cars. That's what really got my attention."

"And you saw him go into Howard's place."

"Yes." She nodded her head firmly. "I didn't see Howard let him in, but he went in. Of course, I didn't hear about Howard until the other cops came on Thursday. You were there."

"Right. Did you see the cop leave? The one who was there on Saturday?"

"No. My daughter called right then, and we had a good chat on the phone. After we hung up, I looked out the front window, but the police car was gone."

"Did you know Howard's place was broken into?"

"Yeah. I cornered Larry in the laundry room after the cops left. He said the place was trashed. He was whining about the couch being a write-off. Ask me, the couch was a write-off about two decades ago."

"Howard's daughter told me the two officers who came to the apartment on Thursday thought someone knew that Howard had died and then robbed the place."

She pressed her hand to her cheek. "Do you think the man I saw did it? The one who came by the place on Saturday. But I was sure he was a cop."

I shrugged. "Maybe he wanted people to think he was a cop. What did he look like?"

Marie's eyes grew fearful. "He was big. He had these big shoulders." She stretched her hands six inches out from her shoulders.

"Was he wearing a uniform?"

Marie frowned. "No...now that I think about it, I don't believe he was."

"Could you tell how tall he was? Colour of his hair?"

"Don't know about his hair colour. Light coloured, maybe. It was short and he wore a ball cap. He was at least six feet tall. Six-two or six-three if I had to guess. A big guy. Of course, you know how those peepholes distort everything. You think I should tell someone?"

"Yes. The officer who came to investigate the break-in is Constable Abbot. He works at District C. You might want to call there and talk to him. I'll bet he would want to hear about what you saw."

Marie set her plate down on the edge of the table. "You got a pen? I want to write that down."

After jotting down Constable Abbot's name and District number on the back of one of my business cards for her, I looked around for the man I'd seen standing by the back door during the service, but he was nowhere to be seen. I made my way over to Lennie, who had just finished saying his goodbyes to Donna and was heading to the door.

"Lennie. Long time no see." I held out my hand. "Jorja Knight. I'm a friend of Mike Saunders."

"Jorja. Right. I recognized you. I once secured an apartment for one of your clients."

"That's right. I suppose you knew Howard from your TPS days?"

"He was my captain for about ten years. When I heard he moved out west, I looked him up."

"Did you see much of him?"

"We had lunch a couple times this summer. Why? Don't tell me Howard was another client of yours?"

I lowered my voice. "No. Howard's daughter called Mike after Howard died. She doesn't buy into the whole accidental-death story she's been given. Mike's tied up on a special project, but he asked me to poke around a bit, see what I could find. I'm starting to think Donna might be right."

Lennie rolled his shoulders as if he'd been standing too long and nodded. "I wondered myself. Then again, he wasn't in the best of health, so a slip and fall is possible." He rubbed his chin for a second, pulled a business card out of his jacket pocket, then jerked a thumb toward the door. "Sorry, I gotta run, I have someone coming by the office at 4 p.m." He handed me his card. "Give me a call. We should chat."

I glanced down at the card. *Lennie Popovic, On-Call Security*. By the time I looked up, Lennie was gone.

TEN

THE SUN DIPPED BELOW the spruce trees, but the air was still warm. Luis reached across the table and put his hand over mine. He flashed me a boyish grin. "Sorry about the other night. I was disappointed to have to cancel our plans for the evening."

I stared into his warm brown eyes. "Me, too." I knew better than to ask him what the emergency was. My eyes shifted to the surrounding hills, blanketed in spruce and pine, the odd larch adding splashes of brilliant yellow. "This more than makes up for it. It's beautiful out here."

"The view *is* stunning." I turned back; his eyes were focused on me.

I laughed. "Flattery will get you everywhere."

A server approached with our appetizer, a charcuterie board with chicken liver pâté finished with a cherry glaze, duck ham, coriander beef salami, and a variety of cheeses. Luis gave my hand a squeeze before letting it go.

"Got anything exciting happening?" he asked as he dipped his knife into a triple-ale onion spread, smoothed it over a thin sourdough crostini, and added a slice of salami and Colston Bassett Stilton blue cheese.

"No...not really. I've been doing some work for a woman whose father died. Someone broke into his apartment a few days later and trashed it. His car, too. I spent the last few days helping her deal with it. His memorial service was yesterday afternoon." It was mostly the truth. Besides, if he couldn't share the minutest details about his work, did he really expect me to be an open book about mine? "I'm so glad we could get away tonight. Just coming out to Bragg Creek for dinner feels like a mini vacation."

"It's been a while since we spent any real time together. We should go back to Emerald Lake this winter."

My heart fluttered and my face grew warm. I picked up a seed cracker, added cheese, and looked at him from under my eyelashes—which were ridiculously long, but I wasn't about to complain about the gift nature bestowed on me. "Maybe this time we can actually leave our cabin, get to see the place."

Luis cocked his head to one side and winked. "We could check out one of the rooms in the main lodge...or the heated pool." He reached under the table and squeezed my knee. "I bet the place is spectacular in the fall."

I felt my heart jump. My eyes travelled down his chest, his pecs visible under the black Henley crew-neck shirt molded to his body, down his strong muscular arms and to his long fingers. I took a sip of wine. Then another. This was the Luis I was interested in getting to know better.

Dinner conversation turned to where we would like to travel next, assuming money and time were no object. "Venice, Rome, Tuscany, the Amalfi coast, Alberobello. The weather, the scenery, the history, the food, the people. I want to see and experience it all. What about you?"

"Italy."

My eyes widened. "You're just saying that." I laughed.

"No. I'm dead serious."

"Okay. Tell me why Italy is your first choice, too."

"I like their policing model. Italy has one of the best police forces in the world."

I did an internal eye roll. Of course. If you're going to take a vacation from work, why not go somewhere that exhibits best-in-class work practices.

Luis leaned forward. "They've got over three-hundred-thousand police officers, split into five national and five local police forces. The Italian National Police has the highest-trained officers in the world. They've established an Italian Anti-Mafia division, which has already taken down two of the most violent and dangerous Mafia Bosses."

"You don't say." I speared an olive and popped it into my mouth. "I can see how turned on you are. Maybe we should talk about the Mafia more often."

"You think I'm kidding? They were even gifted a couple of specially designed Lamborghinis for their excellent work. Those cars can reach speeds of up to three hundred and fifty kilometres an hour. The officers who drive them have to have special training before they're allowed behind the wheel."

We didn't linger after the plates from our main course had been cleared away. We didn't quite make it home, either. The sexual tension between us grew so strong that we pulled over onto a forestry road halfway to Calgary. If we hadn't been so busy, I might have noticed a black SUV take the same turn behind us.

·•••••••••··

My phone woke me in the morning. I rolled over and picked up my cell. Ten after seven. Luis was already gone. I vaguely remember hearing him head out around five this morning. I sat up and brushed the hair back off my face.

"Hey, Mike. You're up early."

"Hope I didn't wake you. I'm just heading to the airport; we're flying out to Halifax today."

"Things must have gone well if you're heading east."

"We wrapped up our working draft yesterday. Now the fun begins."

Mike's cohort was now going to cross the country east to west—getting feedback, holding workshops and seminars, using the input to fine-tune a national framework, or rework huge sections of it, if need be.

"I just wanted to touch base as I'll be hard to reach for the rest of the day. How's it going?"

I gave Mike a quick update about the break-in at Howard's place, the missing Nikon camera, cell phone, and computer, as well as the hidden appointment book. I ended with: "It's possible someone just broke in and took the few things of any value, but the way the place was trashed...I don't think so."

"I agree. Usually when these punks rob and trash a place, it ends up with spray paint on the walls, ketchup on the carpet, or the sink stopper in place with the taps left running. Make anything of Howard's appointment book?"

"Not really. There's a phone number I'm running down. I'm also going to see if I can find out anything about a copy of a five-million-dollar insurance policy I found in Howard's apartment, issued by Carson Milford Insurance. Heavily redacted, of course, including who it was issued to. It may have nothing to do with whatever Howard was working on, but he did hint to Donna that he might be coming into some money…so it makes me wonder if there's a connection somehow. Oh, and I ran into Lennie Popovic at Howard's memorial service. It sounds like he might have something for me."

"Okay. Let me know if you need anything, although I know I'm of limited use to you right now."

"Just having an ear to bounce things off from time to time will be a big help. I'll let you know what I find."

I hung up. There had to be something in Howard's appointment book or files to point me in the right direction. Maybe Donna would find his safety deposit box with something revealing inside. A thumb drive with all his computer files would be a good start.

I put on the coffee, had a quick shower, did some yoga, and ate a bowl of cheerios. At nine o'clock, I retrieved my burner phone and called the number written below Milt's name in Howard's appointment book. If it went to voice mail again, I'd leave the number of my burner phone and a message saying it was urgent. But I didn't have to. This time the gravelly-sounding voice answered.

"Landen."

"Oh hi. Is this Milt? Milt Landen?"

"Who's asking?"

"I'm a private investigator. I'm calling about a phone call or meeting you had with Howard Bergman. On August 24 of this year."

"I don't know anyone named Howard Bergman."

"I found your name and this phone number in his appointment book. Can you tell me if this is a private number or your business number?"

"Look, lady, I said I don't know any Howard Bergman." He hung up.

I stared at my phone. "You knew him, you little creep."

ELEVEN

The Trolley didn't take reservations, but I arrived at eleven-thirty, hoping to beat the noon-hour crowd. I managed to get the last table in the joint. The open window next to my table overlooked a small patio, and the slight breeze made my spot inside perfect. My mind drifted back to my evening with Luis, which left me feeling happy, content, and somewhat lazy. I stared mindlessly out the window and promised myself I would find more time to enjoy life. A promise I had made at least a hundred times.

Lennie arrived twenty minutes later and slid into the wooden chair across from me. "Glad you could get here early. This place serves an insanely good short-rib sandwich and some of the best locally brewed beer you'll find in the city."

"Judging by how busy the place is, word's gotten out."

A server arrived and we both ordered the short-rib sandwich and a pale ale for him, a white wine for me. After getting him caught up on Mike's newest assignment and his current whereabouts, the conversation turned to Howard.

"You mentioned you'd seen Howard a few times over the summer. Any idea what he was working on?"

"No. But he was hyped up about whatever it was."

"His daughter said the same thing. Donna said he was working on something big, something he was excited about. He didn't drop you any clues?"

Lennie picked up the fork lying on the placemat in front of him and shifted it over an inch. The knife followed. He reached up, rubbed his chin, then crossed his arms, resting them on the table.

"Howard and I would get together every couple weeks—you know, grab a beer or a bite after work and get caught up. A lot of times we just rehashed old cases, a few of which still aren't solved. The last few times we met, he talked about going to Belize or Costa Rica, said he might retire, start enjoying life."

"He was upbeat, then."

"Oh yeah. I hadn't seen him that excited in a while. Then in September, I had him over to my place. I wanted to show him the renos I've been doing. Besides, university had started, and the bars were filled with students. I knew something was up as soon as I saw him. I showed him the renos, and we ordered pizza and sat on the deck with a beer. Hard to put my finger on it, but he seemed different that night, distracted. He was there physically, but his mind was somewhere else."

I nodded. "Did he say anything, about what was going on with him?"

"Not that night."

I knew Lennie was about to drop something, the way he was now leaning forward, his head nodding ever so slightly as he recalled the day.

"Two days later, he calls me. Says it's important. Can I meet him downtown, at Starbucks? Sure, I tell him. Howard hated going downtown, but I figured he might already have a meeting down there."

"That's interesting. Sounds like it was somewhat urgent, as well as important."

"I thought so too, but when I got there, he didn't seem interested in telling me why he wanted to meet. We spent the first half hour just chatting, how the Stampeders were shaping up, his granddaughter had gotten accepted into Lethbridge University, his place was stinking hot with the weather we'd been having. He laughed about that, said maybe moving somewhere hot wasn't such a good idea since he couldn't take the heat."

Our server arrived with our mains. Lennie sat back as the server placed his food in front of him. The warm, spicy aroma filled my nostrils, and I could feel my forehead getting warm even before taking the first mouthful. Lennie ordered another beer. I asked for a glass of water. We each dug in. The meat was so tender it melted in my mouth, the sauce buttery smooth, then as I swallowed the heat kicked in. After a few bites I put down my sandwich, wiped my hands on my napkin and took several swallows of water.

"Wow. That's the best rib sandwich I've ever tasted. I don't suppose they bottle and sell that sauce?"

Lennie laughed. "You and I wish," he said around a mouthful.

Finally, having taken the edge off our hunger, I asked, "So did Howard ever get around to telling you what the important thing was that he wanted to see you about?"

Lennie swallowed and put his sandwich down, now pretty much just two bites left. "Not in so many words, but he wanted to know how the new security systems could be circumvented." Lennie laughed. "I asked him if he was planning a heist."

"Did he say what kind of security? I assume he was talking about something complex, not like a home security system for his place."

"I told him security systems have come a long way since we used to investigate break-ins back in the day. Today's systems provide twenty-four-seven surveillance, monitor motion, smoke, sound, provide continuous audio and video feed to an offsite server. None of this video-loop feed that gets overwritten after a few days. Although there are still a lot of those around."

"I see. Nothing specific though, right? He just wanted the general lowdown on how these systems work?"

"Mostly. He wanted to know if they could be hacked. I told him there are lots of ways to get around them—even with all of today's safeguards. Unlike what most people think—security systems don't prevent someone who is determined to get in from getting in, they just make it more difficult."

"He never said why he was suddenly interested in security systems?"

"No. He wanted to know if the data could be altered, how easily someone could hack such a system, and how this whole cloud thing worked. The conversation went all over the place."

"But something about the meeting stuck with you."

"Yeah. He got into a rant about dirty cops. If there was one thing that could set Howard off, it was the idea of a dirty cop. We had a case once, back when I was still on the force. A guy who took money to not sign in a critical piece of evidence from a crime scene. Of course, things are much tighter these days."

"What got him started? He wasn't just reminiscing, was he?"

"I got the distinct impression all these questions about security systems were secondary. That maybe he knew something about a cop who had managed to circumvent a system or alter the data."

"But he didn't say?"

"No. Just a gut feeling I had. I wish there was something more specific I could tell you. I didn't really give it much more thought until I found out Howard was dead. I've started to think the two might be connected."

Lennie had an appointment right after lunch, so I told him to go, I was getting the bill. I lingered after he left, taking time to finish the coffee I had ordered. I hope Lennie's joke about Howard planning a heist was just that—a joke. More than likely, he had been looking into a robbery. A robbery which may have been aided by a cop.

I settled my bill and left the restaurant feeling somewhat unsettled. A fleeting thought about a robbery passed through my mind but dissipated as quickly as it appeared.

My mind churned as I drove home. Howard had a copy of a heavily redacted insurance policy for something that could be worth up to five million dollars. He had been interested in security systems, died under possibly questionable circumstances, hid his appointment logbook. Someone broke into his place, trashed it, and made off with his camera, computer, and god knows what else.

My brain was telling me Howard was working on a robbery. But what robbery? And who was he working for? Himself? Or did he have a client? And what about that beefy guy his neighbour had seen letting himself into Howard's apartment?

TWELVE

I parked the Taurus in the underground parking stall, took the stairs to the lobby, collected my mail, and took the elevator up the eighth floor. My neighbour was prowling the hallway. I stepped back, intending to escape into the elevator, but she'd already spotted me.

"Good afternoon, Mrs. Wilson." I tried to slip past her. Mrs. Wilson had the demeanour of a hardened prison warden, self-assigned to keep order on the floor.

"You see my cat?" she barked at me.

"Did you lose one of them?" Mrs. Wilson had three cats, or by now it could be nine for all I knew.

"No, I'm playing twenty questions, what-do-ya think?"

"Sorry, no."

"Some detective," she muttered as I slid past her.

What a troll. I opened the door to my condo and hurried in.

I paused at my vision board, hung on the short wall between the entrance and the living area. It was filled with pictures of exotic locales, stunning homes with spectacular views. Several pictures of tropical patios and a sleek yacht were pinned on top of the previous layers of photos. A confident and fit woman, with a rakish shoulder-length bob, was pinned to one side, a fluffy grey kitten underneath.

I shook my head. It was time to create a more ordered, more realistic vision board. I mean, why had I pinned a yacht? I didn't particularly like being out on the water, and I didn't know enough people to host a dinner, let alone a weekend yacht party. Of course, if I owned a yacht, I might have more friends.

Now, as I stared at it, another observation hit me. I hadn't pinned any pictures of houses with white picket fences, children playing on swings, or anything that smacked of domesticity. Maybe Luis Azagora and I were better suited for each other than I thought.

Still feeling the effects of a large and spicy lunch, I poured myself a glass of Pellegrino, squeezed in a shot of lemon juice from one of those fake plastic lemons, and plunked myself down on the couch. I set down my drink and picked up my laptop from the coffee table.

I opened the file I had created for Howard and jotted some notes from my meeting with Lennie. I scrolled back and reread the notes I had made in the last few days. The answer to what I was looking for had to be in Howard's appointment book. But what useful information did it provide?

At least now I had a name to go with the phone number I had found in Howard's book. Someone named Landon or Landen had answered the phone when I called this morning. Since the number didn't provoke long-distance charges, I assumed it was within the same area code I was in, which really wasn't of much help. Area code 403 covered a large swath of southern Alberta.

Landen sounded ancient, although I suppose a medical condition could be responsible for his raspy voice. I hoped he wasn't one of those fellows who had let the whole technology trend pass him by.

I pulled over my laptop and typed in Milt Landen, Milton Landen, and Milt Landon. My browser page filled up with hits. The majority of the articles were about a family of well-known, historical archeologists, named Landen. One of the Landen's, a Milton Landen, was still alive and rumoured to be living in Alberta. *Lordy, lordy.* Could this be the Milt Landen whose telephone number was in Howard's logbook?

I skimmed the articles. Some were interviews, some were articles about the early archeological expeditions carried out by members of the Landen family. I found several interviews with Milton Landen, along with dozens of articles in which he was quoted or referenced. He even had a Wikipedia page. I turned to that.

Milton Landen was born in 1942, the only child of Albert Landen, a well-known archaeologist, as was his father before him. Grandad Horatio Landen was part of a National Geographic-funded team sent to South America at the tail end of World War I, to map the many undocumented ancient cities rumoured to exist there. His next expedition took him to Honduras, where he was part of a team searching for the Lost City of the Monkey God, which was eventually found but not in his time, and was expected to yield hundreds of artifacts from a mysterious pre-Columbian civilization that worshipped a monkey-god deity.

Milton deviated slightly from his father and grandfather's paths but remained connected to the ancient world. He studied art history in university and then acquired a law degree from Columbia. He articled at a law firm in Montreal and in 1973 joined Kaufman and Kaufman, a firm run by two brothers who were expanding their preeminent niche practice in art and cultural property law. The Kaufmans developed their interest in art theft after assisting law firms in The Hauge to recover and rightfully restore art works stolen during the Holocaust.

Morty Kaufman was quoted as saying "Justice is slow to come in art theft cases, as most involve the upper crust of society, money, sophisticated global smuggling networks, and galleries and museums as beneficiaries of the stolen art."

Landen left the Kaufmans in 2002 under a cloud of controversy. By 2004 he had set up his own business. This may have been predicated by a large windfall left to him upon his father's death in 2002. As his father's sole living heir, he inherited the Landen family's substantial private collection of artifacts, rumoured to be worth several million dollars.

Four hours later, I had several pages of notes and had built a rough timeline of Milton's escapades. As best as I could tell, Milton's new business provided authentication services, and he also bought and sold rare antiquities for a private and moneyed clientele. His work and travels took him around the world.

As time went on, Milton's business ventures and his personal interests and behaviour became more varied and outlandish. In 2009, he bankrolled and produced a short film on the White City, a mystical, Eden-like paradise rumoured to have existed in what is now Honduras, but which has never been confirmed.

In 2010, he bought a 120-acre strip of land adjacent to Skinwalker Ranch in Utah, a site well-known for its documented UFO sightings and other paranormal activity. He gave an interview on 60 Minutes claiming aliens have lived among us for thousands of years and even attributed evidence of ancient mysterious civilizations to aliens.

Then, in 2015, he bought an old gallery and museum near Drumheller and disappeared from the public eye. That cinched it for me. Drumheller was well within a round trip of 272 kilometres from Calgary, assuming the number I found in Howard's hidden notebook was indeed a mileage.

I read the last interview Milton gave. He seemed to have not only left his public life behind but also parted with reality. He alluded to the Illuminati and hinted that he had been helping their members acquire ancient artifacts known to hold great power. Although he wouldn't say where, he was building an eco-compound around a location he had found in Alberta that channelled energy from several energy vortices, similar to those found in Sedona, Arizona.

WTF. I sat back and rubbed my temples. The guy sounded certifiable. Then again, given his age, he might just be an old rich guy who was slowly losing his grip on reality or giving in to his personal theories and whims, and with no family of his own, no one really cared.

Now I just had to figure out how Howard had managed to get his phone number and why.

THIRTEEN

My eyes snapped open. I peered through the darkness. The space along the sides of the blinds told me it was still dark outside. I listened for what woke me, but all was quiet. Too quiet.

What had I been dreaming about? Something important. This sort of thing had happened to me before when working on a case. My body might eventually fall asleep, but my brain worked overtime. I lay still, closed my eyes, and breathed in deeply...slowly.

A fragment of the dream came back, then disappeared. *Relax. Breathe.*

I'm running from someone. Running up the stairs. Fragments of the dream drifted in and out of my consciousness. I was in a stairwell. I see a door and a number—twenty-nine.

Keep going. Two more turns, there's floor thirty-one.

He's closing in. I can hear him. I grip the handrail, pulling myself along, my legs burning with effort. He's right there, right behind me. I don't dare turn. I don't dare stop.

Level thirty-seven. I grab the door handle. It's locked. I continue up the stairs...how many more flights? Where am I running to?

Forty-two. I throw the door open. The air feels cold on my face. I'm outside. I'm on the top of a building. I run to the edge; the

Calgary skyline spreads out around me. I look down. My hands are empty. Where is it? I can't fly without it. I turn. He's in the doorway now. I can see his eyes, bright red. I must fly...

I bolted upright. I was drenched in sweat yet shivering. My heart pounded against my chest.

Forty-two floors. A cursed object...suicide.

I ran into the living room and flicked on the light. "Where the hell did I put it?" I muttered as I riffled through the stack of papers I had brought home from Howard's place. No. The paper I was looking for hadn't come from Howard.

My mind flashed back to the day that man had jumped into my car. That man. *Mackerin? No, that's not right.* Had I been wearing a coat that day? I rushed to the closet. There was nothing in my coat pockets. *I hadn't been wearing a coat.* I ran my hand along the top shelf. My fingers closed in on the envelope.

Taking it with me, I hurried over to the couch, my fingers already pulling at the article inside. *Ancient curse drives businessman to take his own life.* The article was written by someone named Barbara Oates.

I sat down and reread the article, focusing on the bits I had skimmed over the first time I read it.

"Guy Palermo, a well-known businessman in the energy service sector, was found dead Thursday night, after falling to his death from the top of the forty-two storey Ventura Tower in the downtown core. His death has been ruled a suicide."

It was well known that Palermo's company, RioTec, was facing bankruptcy. RioTec's fortunes turned after a 2018 terrorist attack in Yemen destroyed a warehouse, killing three employees and injuring seven more. Palermo, an avid collector of Mesoamerican and pre-Columbian artifacts, blamed a string of bad luck on an ancient statue, including a house fire, the death of his crew in a plane crash, his own failing health, and the death of his wife.

During an interview earlier this year, Palermo claimed his luck had changed after he acquired a jade statue while in Colombia. He purchased the object at a street market. It was shortly after he acquired the statue that his luck turned.

Palermo leaves behind one daughter, from a previous marriage. Speaking to news media after her father's death, Kelly Montgomery said her father was never the same after twelve of his crew members were killed when their plane went down in the jungles of Colombia. Ms. Montgomery has hired an auction house to divest the seven hundred ancient artifacts in her father's collection. The proceeds of the sale will go to the families of the Yemen and Colombian plane disasters."

The article went on to talk about several such ancient artifacts that were supposedly cursed. In 2004, a German man visiting Egypt acquired a tablet displaying hieroglyphic text. Soon after, the carving was returned by the man's stepson. His stepfather had suffered unexplained paralysis and fevers after acquiring the tablet, then fell ill with cancer and died, all within eight months. I continued reading.

"Perhaps there is something to these myths—and Palermo paid the ultimate price for the jade statue. After his death, I contacted his daughter. The statue was not among his effects. Perhaps he was successful in divesting it himself, or perhaps he simply buried it, where it will remain for several more thousands of years. In any event, there is no sign of the statue—perhaps just as well."

I opened the second newspaper article, about a drug bust in Winnipeg that never made it to trial. Six individuals had been charged but all six had their charges stayed. The lawyers for the accused claimed the Crown's case was premised purely on suspicion and unsubstantiated allegations.

A spokesperson for the Winnipeg police said while they were not in a position to comment on the decision to not proceed with the prosecution, they worked collaboratively with the Crown from the onset of the investigation and remain proud of the members of their team who worked so tirelessly throughout the entire investigation.

I was certain that reading about Milton Landen's fascination with the Illuminati and their belief in powerful ancient artifacts, combined with the spicy food at dinner and the lingering memory of Jeff Nickleson—the poor hit-and-run victim who dropped these articles as he fled from my car—had created the bizarre dream.

Then again, Nickleson was dead, Howard was dead, and Palermo was dead, all within weeks of each other. And Howard did have Milton's phone number squirrelled away in a hidden appointment book. I just had no idea how or if any of this fit together.

Fully awake now, I shivered, got up, schlepped to the kitchen, and put on a pot of coffee. While it finished dripping, I went into the bedroom and pulled on some clothes. The clock on my nightstand read four twenty-two. Mike would already be up having breakfast on the east coast, Gab finishing lunch in Paris. My body wanted to crawl back in under the warm covers, but my mind jumped like a Russell Terrier chasing a butterfly.

Could the articles and Nickleson's death have any connection to Howard or his suspicions about a dirty cop? Could that cop have been involved in the Winnipeg drug bust mentioned in the one article? How would a suicide and a missing cursed statue fit in?

Giving free rein to my imagination, I came up with all sorts of implausible stories about how or why Howard ended up dead. Had

Howard been running from someone when he slipped and fell? But after giving it additional consideration, I figured I was letting the hit-and-run victim and the articles he left behind in my car colour my thinking based on absolutely nothing.

I grabbed a coffee, settled back on the couch, and googled Guy Palermo. He started his career in the oil patch as a reservoir engineer. In the eighties, he formed his own company, RioTec. Palermo's company revolutionized the science around preventing well blowouts. His company grew rapidly, and he quickly earned a reputation as an innovator when he developed an electrically powered blowout preventer, which could be combined with the intelligent drill pipe technology that was coming onstream. He took his company public, and the company's stock price soared. Then, disaster in Yemen. RioTec's offices were attacked by a terrorist group and fewer than half of the personnel working at the facility escaped. Three of his crew died that day and seven others were injured. I entered more search terms into my browser. A faint pale-orange streak appeared in the eastern sky.

Everything had been going swimmingly for Palermo until 2018. By then, his company had operations in three countries. Besides headquarters in Canada, RioTec had field offices in Yemen and Colombia.

The year after the attack, RioTec pulled out of Yemen. The following year, his crew of twelve and three airplane personnel on board died when their plane lost an engine and plummeted into the jungles of Colombia.

That same year, Palermo returned home from a trip to shutter his office in Yemen to find the house he had been building—meant to be his retirement home in California—was destroyed by wildfire. His wife died this March from brain cancer.

By the time the sun was up, my head was spinning, and not from the four cups of coffee I had consumed. I could see why Palermo would have wanted to lay the blame for this horrible end to a stellar career and a fully lived life, on a cursed object. Why else would so much bad luck have befallen him?

Why had Jeff Nickleson been carrying around a newspaper article about Guy Palermo's death? Had he known Palermo? Could his and Palermo's deaths be somehow connected? Nickleson died in an apparent hit-and-run on September 14. Howard's body had been pulled from the reservoir the next day. Could they have both been running from the same thing?

FOURTEEN

When Mike first asked me to call Donna and talk to her about her father's death, I had fully expected my role would be to help convince her the ME's report was the only logical conclusion that could be drawn. Now I had so many tangents to follow up on that I didn't know what direction to take next. I solved the issue by changing into running gear and heading over to the pathway ringing Glenmore Reservoir, hoping a run would reinvigorate me after a mostly sleepless night and reveal the direction I should take.

I was approaching the western edge of the Reservoir when I noticed it. A black SUV on 90th Avenue seemed to be creeping along at the same speed I was. I checked over my shoulder. No one here but me.

I had only seen two other joggers on this stretch of the pathway in the last half hour. The path was slowly veering northward and would skirt the western edge of the reservoir. Soon I'd lose sight of the car on 90th Avenue and the reservoir. Here the trail was ringed by trees and would be until I hit the Weaselhead Flats at the most western end of the reservoir.

My breathing sounded ragged and loud in the morning silence. I took a sharp breath and glanced behind me. I peered to my right, then my left. Someone could be waiting for me, hidden in the trees, just a few quick steps off the path.

A branch snapped to my right, and I jerked my head in that direction, then stopped. My chest rose and fell rapidly as I tried to quiet my breathing. Probably just a porcupine. Or maybe one of the dozens of homeless people who set up makeshift camps in the trees along the reservoir each year. I moved on, trying to keep a nice steady pace, but every fibre in my body told me to run.

I hated that I couldn't feel safe having an early morning run by myself, but the little voice in my head told me it was better to be cautious than stupid. I turned around and headed back in the direction I'd come from.

A figure now appeared ahead. The sun blinded me, leaving details hidden. I balled my hands into fists and my breath quickened. *Be prepared, mentally and physically.* I slid my keys out of my pocket and slipped them into my hand, leaving one key protruding from between my fingers.

The threat turned out to be an older man out for a jog. He lifted a hand in greeting as he passed.

The sun was already high on the horizon by the time I reached my condo building. Traffic on 90th Avenue was building as the first tranche of commuters headed off to work. Soon it would swell even more with students, and parents driving their youngsters to school.

Once upstairs, I made a fresh pot of coffee and hit the shower. After yet another cup of coffee, which I swore would be my last for the day, I opened my laptop and pulled up the list of names, times, initials, mileages, and so forth, that I had compiled from Howard's appointment book.

I bolted upright. *OMG*. I don't know why I hadn't made the connection before. The initials JN had been listed three times in Howard's appointment book. JN...Jeff Nickleson. It had to be.

I had Nickleson's obituary up in a flash. He left behind two teenage boys and a wife. His wife's name was Edith Stark. She must have kept her maiden name. The rest of the obituary talked about his love of the outdoors. He was an avid fisherman and had a black belt in karate. His life revolved around family.

I pulled up the white pages and searched for Edith Stark. Nothing. I typed in Jeff Nickleson. *Bingo.*

I checked my watch, pulled out my phone, and dialled the number.

The phone on the other end rang ten times, then went to voice mail. A woman's voice repeated back the number I'd called and instructed me to leave my name, number, and a short message.

"Good morning. I'm trying to reach Jeff Nickleson's wife, Edith Stark. I heard he was killed in an accident. A hit-and-run. I...I might have some information regarding his death." I read off the number of my burner phone and disconnected. Now I'd wait.

I hadn't expected a female voice, but on the other hand, if this was Nickleson's landline, his wife might not have had a chance to change the name on the account. Or maybe the voice on the recording wasn't Edith Stark, but his mother, or another woman.

I opened my laptop and sent Mike a text asking him if he could find out Howard's actual time and date of death. I added a short note to say I was making progress, although nothing was adding up yet that would allow me to theorize what happened. Then I went back to googling Jeff Nickleson.

The first few articles that came up were about the hit-and-run incident that ended his life. It didn't say much about his personal life, other than he was originally from The Pas, Manitoba, and was a retired former police officer.

I pulled over Howard's appointment book and flipped through it for the umpteenth time. I sat up, my heart beating faster, my senses tingling. I slid the appointment book out of the faux-leather cover. Why had I not done this before? I had checked inside the cover flap but hadn't slid the whole book out.

I turned the appointment book over. Two business cards were taped to the back cover. The first card was from the Black Stilt Art Gallery, located on 13th Avenue, here in Calgary. The card stated: Private Fine Art Dealer: Acquisition, Sale & Appraisals.

The second card was one of these generic business advert cards, from 4SiteSecurity. A line below the company name read, "Located in Calgary and serving southern Alberta." I peeled the card off the back cover, as it was stuck somewhat, and turned it over. My heart skipped a beat. Jeff Nickleson's phone number was handwritten on the back.

FIFTEEN

It was evening by the time Mike had a chance to call me back. They had finished up their sessions in Halifax and were heading to New Brunswick in the morning. I gave Mike a recap—the lone cop seen entering Howard's place three days before the break-in was discovered, the hidden appointment book with the name and number of an antiquities dealer in it, as well as the initials JN, the same initials of a man who had recently been killed in a hit-and-run the same time Howard had died. Both near Glenmore Reservoir.

"I'm not sure if I told you, but I saw Nickleson right before he died." I told Mike about the newspaper articles he had dropped in my car and about Lennie's last few conversations with Howard.

"Interesting. You think this Nickleson character was meeting Howard at the reservoir—and that somehow whoever caused Howard's accident also ran him down?"

"I don't know what to think, Mike. I mean, I can accept that me running into Nickleson that day was a coincidence, but not that Howard and Nickleson were killed only a few kilometres from each other and on the same day. Especially as Howard had the letters JN listed in his appointment book on three different days in the weeks before he died. I know there are a lot of threads to follow, and I'm not sure if all of them are related to Howard's death and the case he was working on, but I can't help thinking there's a connection between Nickleson and Howard that will help us find out what Howard was looking into, something that resulted in his death, accidental or otherwise."

"You figure the hit-and-run victim might know something about this collector, the one who committed suicide?"

"Palermo? Maybe. The article mentioned he owned an ancient statue that's supposedly cursed, but it's not among the other artifacts in the collection he left behind."

"Cursed, eh? The newspapers love that sort of thing. Makes for a more sensational story than if the guy had a string of bad luck and was depressed as hell."

"I'm not inclined to believe it, either, but I must admit, finding out Howard had a business card with Jeff Nickleson's phone number on the back and had a phone number in his appointment book that apparently belongs to Milt Landen tells me there is definitely something here. Landen owns a museum and collects, buys, and sells ancient artifacts. Makes me believe I might be on the right track."

"Donna did say Howard had been alluding to money coming his way. What is this supposed cursed object Palermo owned worth?"

"I don't know; the article didn't say. Maybe Howard reached out to Landen to learn more about the object, find out its worth."

"There might be something there. And now this statue is missing?"

"The article doesn't say much about it or what happened to it when Palermo died. Maybe his daughter knows. I'll try and track her down. Maybe it's the link to Landen, or the Black Stilt Art Gallery—Howard had a business card from there in his appointment book. According to Wikipedia, Landen's a big believer in the Illuminati and has an interest in unique artifacts, especially those that are believed to have provided their owners with great other-worldly power."

Mike grunted. "If this so-called cursed object is missing, maybe Howie was going after it, hoping for a reward. Or someone hired him to find it."

"Now you see why all of this has me believing these things may be related. Although certain things don't stack up. Like why Howard would have been on a tear about a dirty cop and why a cop was supposedly seen going into Howard's place the day after Howard's body was found. They're not in the habit of entering a deceased person's premises, are they?"

"They can if they suspect something illegal is going on. Not in an accidental drowning, though. Is the neighbour sure it was a police officer?"

"She says yes, or did at first, but she observed him through the peephole in her door. Not very likely she'd have seen the details needed to really confirm he was a cop. You wouldn't have any way of finding out if he was legit, would you?"

"That's a tough one. Even if I had a reason to ask around, theo-retically, there isn't anyone investigating Howie's death."

"Right." I shook my head.

"By the way—I talked to the coroner. Her preliminary assessment for Howard's death indicated suicide or accidental death. The au-topsy revealed several bruises, but they were consistent with what one might expect to find if someone fell down a rocky embankment. Given that most male suicide victims hang or shoot themselves, and as the cliff he fell down wasn't of sufficient height to guarantee death on impact, she didn't see that as a likely scenario."

"But he could have been pushed."

"I suppose that's possible."

"Do you know his time of death?"

"It appears he'd been in the water for about twenty-four hours. The pathologist estimated his time of death as sometime between noon and six o'clock the previous day."

I sucked in a breath. "That means he died within hours of Nickleson, our hit-and-run victim. Maybe they were working together on something."

"You know what they say."

"I know, I know. It's easy to jump to conclusions; it's harder to find the truth. But I'm finding the whole thing kind of creepy. To think I was there too and that I saw Nickleson that afternoon. He must have seen me leaving and followed me to my car. At first, I thought it was an attempted carjacking, but he was more terrified than I was. I'm convinced he was trying to get away from something or someone. Oh. I gotta go, Mike, I have a call coming in on my burner phone. Might be Nickleson's wife."

"Okay. Keep me posted."

I picked up my burner phone and hit accept.

"Hello?"

A woman's voice came on the line. "Who am I talking to, please."

"Who's asking?"

A pause. "Are you the person who called this number earlier today?" She rattled off Jeff Nickleson's number.

"Yes, that would be me."

"I'm not talking to any reporters."

"I'm not a reporter."

"You said you had some information. About Jeff."

"Yes. Are you Edith Stark, Jeff's wife?"

"Why don't you tell me what you know."

I had to hand it to her. She was being as cagey as a politician at an election rally. Of course, it was entirely possible that this was Jeff's wife, and she had caught him cheating on her and now thought I was his mistress.

"My name is Jorja Knight. I'm a private investigator. A friend of mine, also a private investigator, died under suspicious circumstances the same day Jeff Nickleson did, and in the same vicinity. His death has been ruled accidental, but there are some unanswered questions that led me to believe it wasn't an accident."

I paused. The silence on the other end was deafening. Finally, she spoke. "Are you saying they knew each other?"

"I found the initials JN and a business card with a phone number in his appointment book. The phone number I called to contact you. I don't know if he met with Jeff Nickleson that day or talked to him, but I can't help thinking that he might have had information related to what my friend was investigating. Information that maybe got both of them killed."

"What did you say your name is?"

"It's Jorja Knight. My friend's name was Howard Bergman. That mean anything to you?"

She didn't reply right away. I could almost hear her thinking.

"We should talk—can you meet me at the Pizza Shack in an hour?"

SIXTEEN

Edith Stark was waiting for me inside the Pizza Shack. I assumed the petite, dark-haired woman was her, because the place was empty. I walked over to the booth where she was sitting.

"Hi. Are you Edith Stark?"

She nodded. I slid into the bench across from her.

"Are you really a private investigator?"

"Yes."

I opened my pocketbook, took out a business card and my driver's licence and slid both across the table. She picked up my business card with both hands, the way Japanese businessmen do, and stared at it. I was certain she was reading each word printed there. She did the same with my driver's licence.

While she read, I gazed around the place. I could see a guy through the pass-through window making pizzas in the back. The six tables in front were all empty except for ours. It was more of a takeout joint than an eat-in kind of place.

Finally, she tugged at her shirt collar, slid back my licence, and tucked the card into her purse.

"Your turn. Are you Jeff Nickleson's wife?" My eyes dropped to her hand resting on the table. Her other hand flew to the missing wedding band on her ring finger. "Jeff," she swallowed hard, "Jeff...was my ex-husband. We divorced last year." She tucked a strand of dark hair behind her ear and turned away.

"I'm so sorry for your loss."

"Thank you." She pulled a tissue out of her coat pocket, dabbed at her nose, and turned back. "It's been so hard on our children."

The man working in the kitchen yelled out through the pass-through window, sparing me from having to reply. "Can I get you anything," he called in our direction.

"You want anything?" I asked.

She shook her head in reply.

I got up, went to the counter, and ordered wings and a Pepsi. I looked back at Edith, who was twisting a strand of her hair. "Maybe add another Pepsi to my order." I paid, he handed me two soft drinks from his soda fountain and said he'd bring out the wings when they were ready.

I carried the drinks back, set one in front of Edith, and sat down with mine.

She looked up and nodded. "Thank you."

For one brief second, I considered the possibility that I was being set up somehow. I mean, all I had was her word that she was Edith Stark, Jeff's ex-wife. But her slumping posture and wet, dull eyes convinced me otherwise. I decided to tell her most of what I knew, hoping she'd reciprocate.

"The police found my friend's body in the Glenmore Reservoir. They say he likely lost his footing, fell—hit his head, rolled into the water, and drowned. I have a hard time believing it for several reasons, I won't go through all of them now. More than likely, he was working on something that got him killed.

Edith sat up a little straighter.

"The days after he was found dead, someone broke into his place and trashed it. They took his camera and computer, and maybe some of his files, hard to tell. There were books and papers scattered everywhere. I found your husband's initials in his appointment book—looks like they might have met on several occasions. I also found a 4SiteSecurity business card with a handwritten phone number on the back of it. I called that number and you called back."

Edith shook her head. "Are you saying Jeff had something to do with your friend's death? Because that's ridiculous. Who hired you?"

I looked her in the eye and held her gaze. "I'm not blaming Jeff in any way. My friend's daughter hired me. She doesn't buy into the Medical Examiner's ruling that it was an accidental death. I'm starting to think maybe your husband knew something related to whatever Howard was working on, and it got both of them killed. Or maybe they were working on something together."

The man from the kitchen walked out with my order of wings and set it down on the table between us, along with two side plates. "Refills on the soft drinks are free. Just let me know if you want a second." We waited until he was back in the kitchen.

"Listen, Edith, as bizarre as this sounds, I saw Jeff the day he was killed by a hit-and-run driver. I don't mean to upset you, but when I saw Jeff, he looked terrified. Like someone was after him. Do you know what was going on?"

Her eyes widened. She pulled at the collar of her white shirt, layered underneath a black sweater, as if it were too tight, choking her.

"Did you see...the accident?"

"No. I saw Jeff at Glenmore Landing just before he was killed. He dropped an envelope, which I picked up. Inside was an article about a businessman who died by suicide, by throwing himself off a 42-storey building downtown. A second newspaper article was about some drug trial in Winnipeg that got dismissed, apparently because the police accessed the defence lawyer's communications illegally."

Her eyes grew wide and now her shoulders curved forward as she crossed her arms in a hug but remained silent.

I took a side plate and added three wings. "Please, help yourself." I picked up a wing and bit in. I was done talking. I wanted to hear something from her.

"Jeff was a good man. He was a good father. We...we just weren't a good match for each other."

"I'm sorry."

She nodded. "We stayed in touch, of course. We have two boys. Jeff Sr. is in high school, and Ethan is in grade eight."

"Sorry. It's rough losing a parent at that age." I took a sip of my Pepsi and picked up another chicken wing. I noticed she had side-stepped my earlier question. "Did your husband work for 4SiteSecurity?"

"No. He worked for a company called First Digital Surveillance. Jeff used to be a cop. Twenty-six years on the force. He retired two years ago, but he wasn't ready to just sit in a rocking chair and watch the world go by. So, he took a job with First Digital."

"What police force?"

"First Winnipeg and the last three with Calgary Police Services."

The hairs on my arm stood up. "He wasn't involved in that drug case in Winnipeg, was he? The case that got dismissed due to some questionable police procedures?"

"No, of course not." She shook her head, frown lines forming between her eyebrows.

"What unit was he with at CPS?"

"Drugs and Gangs." Edith's lips tightened at the mention.

"Jeff ever mention a Howard Bergman to you?"

"No. But then we didn't talk about much other than the kids, since the divorce. When they needed to be picked up, what they were up to, that sort of thing."

"The newspaper articles I mentioned earlier, the ones that Jeff dropped the day I saw him? One was about a man named Guy Palermo, who killed himself at one of the downtown buildings, the Ventura Tower. Could he have known Guy Palermo?" I set a chicken bone down on my plate and wiped my fingers with a napkin while watching her face.

"I don't know." She started to fiddle with a set of thin, stacked rings she wore on the middle finger of her right hand.

"Do you know where your ex-husband was providing security?"

"One of the office buildings downtown. I never knew exactly which one."

"Could it have been the Ventura Tower?"

"Possibly. I couldn't say for sure. He moved around a fair bit—it's the nature of the job." Her fingers spun the rings around faster and faster.

"I heard about the hit-and-run the day I saw Jeff at Glenmore Landing, but I didn't know it was the man I'd seen until the following day, when they put his picture up on the news. I haven't told the police anything yet—not that I have much to go on. Do you have any idea why Jeff would be interested in Guy Palermo's suicide, or be carrying around an article about it or the failed drug case in Winnipeg?"

"No."

"Edith, was anything troubling your ex-husband? Or was everything fine and he was just the unfortunate victim of a hit-and-run driver?"

She twirled the rings on her right hand faster, her eyes wide, staring somewhere past me.

"He liked his job well enough until a couple months ago—then he got all nervous."

"Nervous how?"

She leaned forward. "He started calling me at night to make sure I had turned on my security system, and that the windows and doors were all locked."

"Whoa."

She looked around the small eatery. Her eyes darkened with worry. "I don't believe he was an innocent victim of a hit-and-run. Witnesses say they saw a car, travelling at high speed, veer into the turn lane where Jeff was crossing, hit him, and then continue straight through. Sounds deliberate to me."

"So, you think he was targeted. Have the police located the car that hit him?"

"Of course not."

"What about his cell phone—you still have it? Is it the number I called?"

"Yes."

"Can you look through his phone log? I want to know if my friend, Howard Bergman, called him." I rattled off Howard's number, which I had taken off one of his Telus invoices.

I watched her pull a phone from her purse. I repeated the number I had given her.

"Oh my gosh." She lifted her hand to her throat. "Yes, it's here. He called twice on September 26th. Two days before Jeff died." She kept scrolling. "Here it is again, September 24th and September 19th."

I almost yelped in my growing excitement. Finally, a solid connection. On a wild hunch, I pulled up my phone log and read off the number I had for Milt Landen.

Edith scrolled for a minute. "No, nothing like that."

"Okay, thanks." I sat back and rubbed the back of my neck, then leaned forward again. "Would you be willing to share the other numbers in his phone log?"

She put the phone away and pulled back from the table. "I'd rather not."

"I understand your reluctance—you told me Jeff seemed worried about you and your sons' safety and I understand your need for caution. Look, you have my card. You saw my driver's licence. Google me if you want—I have a website. If you change your mind—think of something or want me to look into his death, give me a call." Now, I did feel like an ambulance chaser.

She nodded, but I could see something still troubled her.

"Is there anyone else I could talk to who might know more? A friend of Jeff's, a co-worker?"

She bit the inside of her lip.

She picked up Jeff's phone and scrolled. "He kept in touch with a good friend from his policing days. His name is Eli. Eli Yardley." She read out a phone number from Jeff's phone, then slipped it into her purse. "Please don't tell the police that I think Jeff was targeted by the hit-and-run driver."

I looked up, startled. It was the first definitive thing she had said this whole time and wasn't something I expected. "No? Why is that?"

She got up to leave. "Promise. Just talk to Eli."

SEVENTEEN

I stepped back and stared at the flip-chart paper covering my office walls. After my late-evening conversation with Jeff Nickleson's ex-wife last night, I had been eager to get to the office to map out what I now knew, hoping it would help me find the next thread to pull. Of course, Eli Yardley, Jeff's cop friend, was on the top of my list. I had left him a message as soon as I got to the office, but he hadn't yet called back.

My handwriting was scrawled on dozens of post-it notes, some of which were stuck to the sheets papering the walls. Howard's name was on the top sheet, and below that I had taped up three additional sheets of paper, one each for Guy Palermo, Jeff Nickleson, and Milt Landen. I had arranged several sticky post-it notes around these names, sometimes adding one then removing it and sticking it somewhere else.

At the bottom of this masterpiece were approximately twenty sticky notes labelled with dates, events, and locations that might be relevant or not. I had five solid lines on the wall chart.

I had drawn a solid line from Jeff Nickleson to a box labelled *First Digital Surveillance* and another linking his name to Howard's. I had a dashed line from Jeff Nickleson to the Ventura Tower and a solid line from it to Guy Palermo. Palermo had plummeted from that tower, and I needed to find out if Jeff Nickleson could have worked security there.

I still didn't know why Nickleson's phone number was written on the back of a business card for a security company he *didn't* work for—4SiteSecurity—which had been in Howard's appointment book. Howard had clearly been in contact with Nickleson, and likely Milt Landen too. How Landen fit, I didn't yet know, but both he and Palermo had some connection to antiquities. And Nickleson also had the article about Palermo's death and that cursed jade statue in his possession before he, too, died. Was it a stretch to think that Howard might have been looking into Palermo's death, or the missing statue?

I paused. Voices in the hall. The laughter and voices grew muffled. Sounded like students at the English As A Second Language school across the hall. I felt better knowing there were people around.

This morning was the second time I saw the black SUV. This time it tailed me from Glenmore Landing to a small strip mall on 21st Avenue. I had left my Taurus there since parking was cheaper compared to the downtown core. I couldn't make out the driver's features, other than he was a solid build, and he vaped. If I'd been unsure before that I'd stumbled into something sinister relating to Howard's death, the fact that I was being tailed by someone left me certain there was more to all of this. If only I knew what.

I checked my watch and called a number I had tracked down for Kelly Montgomery, Guy Palermo's daughter. Or at least, I hoped this Kelly Montgomery was.

A woman answered after five rings.

"Good morning. I'm looking for Kelly Montgomery, the daughter of Guy Palermo."

"Yes, this is she."

I explained who I was and that I was looking into the death of a friend, whom I believed might have been looking into her father's death.

"Was he with the police?"

"No. He was a police officer at one time, but he was retired and working as a private investigator."

"And he knew my father?"

"I don't know if he knew your father personally or not. But he was in communication with someone who did know him, someone who worked at the office tower where your father...worked."

Jeff's wife hadn't known where Jeff worked, but I had since confirmed that the company he worked for, First Digital Surveillance, did provide security services at Ventura Tower.

"I think maybe one or the other of them were looking into your father's death."

"I don't understand. Why would they be? The police said my father committed suicide."

"Unfortunately, the man who worked at your father's office tower is also dead. An unfortunate hit-and-run accident. Then my friend died...the same day as the hit-and-run. Supposedly, another unfortunate accident."

She didn't answer. It was a lot to take in. I was suddenly aware how wrong it was of me to mess with her feelings. Insinuating that her father might not have taken his own life, that something more sinister was going on, would certainly stir up emotions.

"Did you ever hear your father mention a Jeff Nickleson or Howard Bergman?"

"No. Those names mean nothing to me."

"What about someone named Milt Landen?"

"Why are you asking all these questions? Who are you again? Are you a reporter?"

"Sorry. I know this is a lot to take in. No. I'm a private investigator. I was hired by Howard Bergman's daughter to look into his death. She doesn't believe it was an accident. I'm trying to find out what he was working on. I think maybe whatever he was investigating got him killed."

"Yes, but what does that have to do with my father?"

"One of the articles I read about your father's death said he had recently suffered several severe losses, personally and professionally. The article went on to say that he attributed the disastrous misfortunes that befell him to some ancient artifact he picked up on one of his travels."

She gave a bitter laugh. "That damn reporter. Ever since she wrote that article, I've been fielding phone calls about that stupid statue. Is that why you're calling?"

"No...well, maybe. I don't know anything about the statue that was mentioned, or how it fits. All I know is my friend is dead and another man he was in contact with, who worked in the same building as your father, is also dead. I don't have anything more than that. It's not much of a stretch to think something they knew or were looking into got them both killed. I thought, maybe if the statue mentioned in the article was valuable or something, it might be related to his death."

"You said your name is Jorja. Knight?"

"Yes. Jorja with a J and Knight with a K. I'm a private investigator and I'm located in Calgary."

"Okay. Let me call you back."

I knew what she was doing. Smart woman.

My office landline rang a few minutes later. I answered. "Knight Investigations."

"Okay, so you are who you say you are, or you've gone to a lot a trouble to set this up."

"I appreciate your concerns. If I can provide you any further proof of who I am, I'd be happy to do it. I can scan my PI licence and email it to you. It has my photo on it. Then I can set up a zoom meeting for us to chat."

She didn't speak for a moment. "That's fine. That you offered to do so is good enough. It's just that ever since my father died, I've been inundated with calls about that stupid statue."

"Do you know anything about this statue? Where it is or what it's worth?" The statue mentioned in the newspaper article Jeff Nickleson dropped in my car was either a critical clue to what happened to him and Howard or I was following a red herring. I was determined to find out which.

"I don't have the statue. Its worth? I don't know. I do know that one way or another, that stupid statue cost my father his life."

EIGHTEEN

KELLY HAD HIRED AN auction house to divest her father's collection of art and ancient antiquities, as she had no interest in such things. The auction house had just finished cataloguing some seven hundred items, but the statue in question was not listed in the inventory.

"Did you ever see the statue that was mentioned in the newspaper article, or know which statue your father was referring to?"

"I only saw it once, shortly after my father bought it. It's six or seven inches high and not very pretty."

"What is it a statue of?"

"A jaguar. My father said it was pre-Columbian. Which means it's crude looking. Hideous is more like it. The statue was of this...thing, lying on all fours, with its front paws tucked in underneath. It had an oversized head and round eyes and its mouth pulled back in this awful grin. I didn't think it resembled a jaguar at all. My father said the statue was of a female jaguar, although how he could tell is beyond me. Like I said, I only saw it once. My father was over the moon with it...at least at first."

"Any special reason?"

"Yes. It was made of jade, rather than stone which was more commonly used during the pre-Columbian era. Apparently, using a semi-precious material like jade meant it would have belonged to someone important."

"So, the statue's importance is more of a cultural thing rather than what it is made of."

"Yes, but it's mind-blowing what some of this stuff goes for. Especially the really old items."

"Could your father have sold it?"

"Possibly. He had debts to pay. But if he sold the statue, it didn't make a dent in his debt or add much to his bank account. I'm planning to use most of the proceeds from the auction to start a trust fund in his name, for the families of his former employees, some of whom were killed in an accident."

"Do you know when or how your father acquired this statue?"

"He bought it on one of his business trips from some old lady in a market in San Augustin, Colombia. I think in 2018...or maybe 2019."

"Did he collect artifacts from anywhere in particular?"

"He had items from all over the world—the stranger the better. He had so many amazing stories from his travels working around the globe. He'd risk life and limb going to some godforsaken place because he heard someone had found an amulet worn by King Tut or Cleopatra's tooth or some such thing." She gave a sad laugh. "He was an explorer at heart, and when he found himself working in some remote or exotic place, it gave him the opportunity to explore the local history and culture. And"—her voice broke—"I suppose it helped him ward off the loneliness."

I felt a lump growing in my throat. There was always another side to our personal stories. "So," I cleared my throat, "he just picked this particular statue up at a market?"

"Yes. Well, not a market like we know. I gather there was an old woman selling things at the side of the road. My father stopped to have a look. She had a few broken pieces of pottery laid out on a blanket on the ground and some bits of siltstone embedded with fossilized ferns. He admired her moxie but felt sad for her at the same time. It wasn't the first time he had come across people like her, eking out a living anyway they can."

The scene Kelly described was vivid in my head. I had a feeling I would remember it for quite some time.

"Even though he could see right away that she had little of value to sell, he feigned interest in a few pieces, as he was intent on buying something from this poor lady."

"Your father was a kind man."

"He was. He had a big heart and would do anything to help you if he could. I'm going to miss him so much." Kelly's voice caught.

There was little I could say. I waited.

"Then this woman motioned for him to wait. She went back into this little makeshift tent she had behind her, just a ratty blanket spread over some propped-up twigs, and came back with a cloth bundle. When she handed it to him, she crossed herself several times and wouldn't meet his eyes. Dad said that should have been his first clue that the thing was cursed."

"Interesting."

"When my father unwrapped the bundle, he had a tough time seeing what he was looking at. The statue was caked with centuries of mud and dirt. He asked how much. She told him ten thousand pesos, which is like three dollars, but probably more than she earned in a month. My dad picked out a few fossils, some bits of pottery, and the statue, and gave her fifty-thousand pesos for the whole lot."

"Aww. What a nice man. But later he came to believe it was cursed?"

"When my father showed me the statue, he didn't say anything about a curse. But after all these bad things started happening, he said that the damn thing must be cursed. That's when he told me this woman crossed herself when she gave him the object."

"Did you get the sense that your father really believed the statue was cursed?"

"Not when he first mentioned it—he said it more like a joke. That changed later." She laughed bitterly. "With the string of bad luck my father had, it's hard to believe that one man could attract that much grief into his life on his own."

"Everything I know about your father is from the few articles I read on the internet. It seems like he got pummelled by one disaster after another."

"When I got a call from the Calgary police that my father had died, I was devastated. They wanted to know if he had been depressed or worried or anything. When I told them about his wife dying, the fire destroying the dream home they were building in California, the loss of his crew in Colombia...I guess it confirmed what they thought. That it was suicide. I should have reached out to him. I should have done something."

"It's hard not to feel guilty, but you can't put that on yourself. There really is nothing you could have done." I knew from experience what she was going through, the why's...the what-if's."

"Thank you for saying that. I'm sorry I can't be of more help."

"Believe me, you've been a big help. I'm sorry for dragging all of this up and raising all the emotions that come with it. I truly am sorry for your loss."

"Thank you."

"Earlier, you said the statue cost your father his life, one way or the other. What did you mean by that?"

"People are calling me, looking for it. It's not among my father's things. Maybe he got rid of it. Maybe it is cursed or maybe he just thought it was. All I know is his life took a rapid turn for the worse right after he bought the damn thing, and now he's dead."

After my call with Kelly, I sat back and rehashed the conversation. Kelly made it sound like the story about the object being cursed was just the sort of thing Palermo might have said to a reporter to try and explain the reason behind all the horrible things that had befallen him. The fact that it was missing wasn't all that disturbing either. Maybe he had simply tossed it in a bin.

A feeling of despondency settled over me. I didn't believe in curses and such either, but I had been hoping the statue was worth something...worth enough to warrant three lives. On the other hand, Guy Palermo had disaster after disaster hit him. It would take an exceptional person to survive all of it unscathed.

The police weren't looking into Palermo's death. No one was running around looking for conspirators that caused his crew's plane to crash, or for an arsonist to blame for the fire that burned down the retirement home he was building. Kelly seemed satisfied with the answers she had been given about her father's death. She didn't seem overly concerned that the statue he referenced in his newspaper interview with a reporter, was missing.

As far as Jeff Nickleson went, even though he had been frightened before he ran into traffic, it didn't make it an intentional murder. The hit-and-run driver could be hiding away somewhere, traumatized by what happened…unable to stop in time when Jeff appeared out of nowhere.

Donna might have to accept that Howard slipped, fell, hit his head, and drowned. And despite my desire to find her a more altruistic reason for his death, something that reflected the fact that Howard had dedicated his life to serving others, I might have too as well.

I rubbed my forehead, willing the knot of pain forming there to go away. But what about the break-in at Howard's apartment. Or the black SUV I had noticed on several occasions. Was I making connections where there weren't any? I stared at the post-it notes littering the wall. Maybe I'd reached a dead end.

I was packing up to leave when the email arrived. The email that would complicate things even further and make me realize I had only scratched the surface of what was really going on.

NINETEEN

The bar was tucked away at the end of a dead-end street under the elevated C-Train tracks on the western edge of the downtown core. One of these honky-tonk bars with barnwood siding, live music, and waitresses dressed in short cowgirl skirts. Not that any self-respecting, authentic cowgirl would ever wear something like that.

I paused at the door, waiting for my eyes to adjust to the dim light. Not many people here, but maybe it filled up later in the evening. A man sitting near a small, raised bandstand at the front of the room raised his hand. I walked over.

"Hi. Eli?"

He stood up, shook my hand, then pulled a chair out for me. "Have a seat."

I slid into the chair as he somehow caught the waitress' attention. "What would you like to drink?" he asked as she sidled up to the table.

I looked at the bottle of beer standing on the table in front of him. "I'll have one of those." I nodded at his beer. No use ostracizing myself by asking for a fine wine.

Eli was a good-looking man. Solid. Six one or two, with a dark buzz haircut and green eyes. A shadow outlined a strong jaw and accentuated a slight cleft in his chin. The muscles in his neck were tense.

"Thanks for meeting with me. Please accept my condolences on the loss of your friend."

He nodded, sniffed, but didn't look at me.

"Jeff's ex-wife tells me you and Jeff go way back. That you were in the police force together."

He brought his bottle up to his lips and took a pull. "We did our training together in Regina. We hit it off right away. He was ex-military, like me."

"Oh. Where were you stationed?"

"I did two tours in Iraq. Jeff did a couple of stints in Golan Heights."

"Thank you for your service. Living in our safe little country, it's sometimes hard to remember what members of our military face day after day to keep the peace elsewhere."

He nodded, but he still wouldn't meet my gaze. The waitress returned with my beer and a glass.

"So, you and Jeff must have started your careers in the RCMP."

"Yup."

I took a sip of my beer. I was annoying him with all my questions. I gazed around the room. A woman sat alone at the bar, nursing a cocktail. Two guys played pool in the back. When I thought I couldn't stand the silence one second longer, he broke it.

"What about you? You have a policing background?"

"Afraid not, although a lot of private investigators I know do." My thoughts drifted to Howard. "No, I was a forensic analyst before I became a PI."

He raised an eyebrow.

"Yup, a lab rat. After a while it just became too routine. Most days I couldn't tell you what month it was let alone what day. Life's too short, you know?"

"I get it. There're days it's hell being a cop, but I can't imagine doing anything else. I think I'm addicted to the adrenaline."

We sat in silence for a few more minutes. I wanted to scream out—*why did you agree to see me if you didn't want to talk?* I told myself to be patient.

His wedding band glinted in the dim light. "Were you married while you were in the military?"

He looked down at the ring and nodded. " Yup. Just celebrated our 30th anniversary. Married my high school sweetheart. We had our first kid a year later. Then two more, one right after the other. It's one of the reasons I left the military and went into policing. Not that it's that much easier on the family than being in the army, but at least I get to come home most nights."

I nodded. "Well kudos to you and your wife for sticking it out."

I lifted my bottle in a cheer and he lifted his bottle in return and tapped mine.

"Where did you and Jeff go after training?"

"We mostly worked the northern communities. The Pas, La Ronge, Frobisher Bay, 100 Mile House."

"Together?"

"No. But Jeff and I kept in touch. I was best man at his and Edith's wedding. After a few years, I got accepted by CPS and moved here. Jeff joined the Winnipeg Police Service."

I thought about my best friend, Gab Rizzo, whom I had met at university. We told each other everything. "Edith said you were still best of friends even after all these years."

"Yeah...well." He cleared his throat and took another swig of beer. Now, I realized his reluctance to talk might be driven by his inability to talk without giving in to his emotions. I knew someone like that. I was dating him.

"Edith told me he eventually wound up in CPS. Did you get a chance to work together in Calgary?"

"No. I was in homicide at the time, and he was with gangs and drugs. Although they are now part of the Special Crimes Division."

I could feel myself tense. I calculated the timeline in my head. Luis headed up Special Crimes—well, until a month ago. In all probability, he knew Eli. Maybe even knew Jeff.

"That must have been around 2016." It slipped out before I could stop myself. I hoped he wouldn't ask why I knew so much about Calgary's Special Crimes Division.

He tilted his head back for a few seconds. "Yeah, that's about right."

"Are you still with CPS?"

"Yeah. Strategic Enforcement Unit."

"Edith said Jeff retired in 2019."

"Sounds about right."

"He didn't stay retired though."

"Well…his kids are still young. He and Edith split. What was he going to do with himself? He figured it best to make a little money, leave the pension intact for later."

"I can't imagine he was thrilled about working security."

"You know, he really didn't mind. A lot of cops and ex-military types end up in security—especially armed security services. Jeff did some of that, but a lot of routine security, too."

"Oh. I didn't realize First Digital provided armed security services." I took a sip of my beer. Edith told me to talk to Eli. She must have thought he knew something about how or why Nickleson died. She said he'd become nervous, started checking in on her and the boys. But nothing Eli said was raising any red flags. I decided to bluff.

"Edith thought Jeff was working on something—maybe something from one of his old cases. She said Jeff was a career cop. His job always came first. It's one of the reasons they split up. Jeff was running from something or someone when he was killed. Edith said if anyone would have known what was going on with him, it would be you."

Eli took a long swallow of his beer, set the bottle down and stared at it. I waited while he sat, rotating the bottle with his fingers. Finally, he looked at me. His eyes met mine.

"Look, I'm still a cop. Jeff was a good buddy of mine—but there's only so much I'm willing to tell you."

I nodded. "I get it." But I really wasn't prepared for what I heard next.

TWENTY

"We were having a few beers one night, this was after Jeff joined CPS, and I asked him to tell me the real reason he transferred to Calgary."

I nodded but kept quiet as Eli spoke.

"He was settled in Winnipeg. The kids had friends there. I jokingly reminded him Alberta didn't exactly have a ton of lakes. He and Edith had a lakefront cabin at Sandy Hook, just a stone's throw north of Winnipeg. My wife and I used to pack up our kids and drive out there in the summer to hang out with Jeff and his family at the lake. He loved it there; he wouldn't have given it up lightly."

"What did he say?"

Eli shrugged. "He said he needed a change."

"You believe him?"

"No. He finally told me there were things happening in his old department he didn't want to have anything to do with."

I set my beer down, all ears. "Did he say what?"

"Not specifically. But the department was run by some ass-wipe who was power-tripping at the expense of those around him. Let's just say his attitude permeated through the unit. You know how it goes. The underlings, in turn, took their power-tripping out into the community. Cultural sensitivity was a word meant to be sneered at."

"Wow."

"Yeah. Well, things are taken a little more seriously now, but back then you kept your nose clean, your head up, and your mouth shut. Reporting a fellow cop for some wrongdoing was almost unheard of, and reporting someone for bad behaviour made you an active target."

"Is that what Jeff did? Report someone for bad behaviour?"

"Not just someone. He reported his partner. Jeff said this guy used to say there're two ways to get rich: become a drug lord or steal from one. They were working drugs. Cocaine was coming into the city, and no one knew from where. And a lot of it. His unit had guys undercover, working a network of snitches, making deals with the low-end dealers for information."

I nodded. Mike had shared similar stories with me from his time with OPP and the Toronto Police Service.

"Jeff said he'd noticed a few things about his partner that didn't seem right."

"Did he elaborate?"

"One time he blatantly denied being at a warehouse the night before a big raid. They had just gotten a tip that drugs were coming in the next morning. The day of the bust, the warehouse was empty. Another time, he noticed a report they filed had been altered. He also had a habit of pushing people for information, using Gestapo-like interrogation tactics. So, Jeff went to his boss."

"What happened?"

"His partner denied everything, of course. Jeff's boss chose to believe his partner. He even berated Jeff for being a snitch. Word got out. Everyone closed ranks. No one wanted to work with him."

"Shit."

"Right. Jeff knew he had to leave. It was only going to be a matter of time before someone did something in retaliation, set up him, made him the fall guy for something."

"Sounds like they forced him out."

Eli's jaw tightened. "That's about right."

"Good thing he got out of there."

"Sure, but it cost him. Moving his family, uprooting his kids."

"It probably didn't help his relationship with his wife. Is that when he and Edith split up?"

"It didn't help. They split up a year later."

"And he worked drugs and gangs here, too?"

"He liked drugs and gangs. In homicide, yeah, you can put away a killer. Sometimes a serial killer, who has hurt a lot of people. But drugs...Jeff believed it wasn't just about putting away these scumbags, he felt he was protecting the kids, the young and old people out there who fell victim to these sleazeballs."

"He like it here?"

"He seemed happy, despite things not being terrific at home. He was assigned a partner—the guy had been working drugs for years. He knew all the junkies, snitches, dealers, and where they hung out." He laughed. "They were like Starsky and Hutch. You ever watch that show? Two guys on a mission and nothing was going to get in their way."

"What happened?"

"His partner got caught in the crossfire between some punk gangs having an all-out war in broad daylight in Chinatown."

"Aw shit."

"Things changed for Jeff after that. At first, I thought it was grief over losing his partner."

"It wasn't?"

Eli shook his head, drained his beer, and asked me if I wanted another. When I declined, he motioned to the waitress and held up one finger.

"Maybe he had PTSD."

He looked over his shoulder, first to the right and then the left. "He might have had PTSD, but it was more than that. I think Jeff saw or knew something about the night his partner was killed. Something he didn't want to admit seeing or knowing. When I pressed him on it one night, he said he wasn't going to make the same mistake twice—that he learned his lesson in Winnipeg." Jeff paused as the waitress returned with his beer.

This was serious. I wasn't sure I wanted to hear any more. Before I could stop myself, I blurted out, "He couldn't have ignored something as serious as that!"

"He didn't. Anyone who knew him would have known that. He knew that if he was going to lob an accusation, he needed absolute proof of wrongdoing. He started his own side investigation. He got real obsessive about it. It ate up his evenings, weekends, any time off he had."

I knew how easily one could get sucked into something like that. I was a bit like that with my cases—once I ran into unanswered questions, illogical connections, or something that smacked of ongoing injustices, it became like a drug, one I couldn't let go of.

"So did he ever get the evidence he was looking for?"

"Not while he was working on the force. Then Jeff decided to retire."

"Why retire? Why right then?"

Eli shrugged. "He'd put the years in, so why not. I was glad to see him retire. Frankly, he was burned out. Maybe suffering from PTSD, like you suggested. His divorce took its toll and his partner's death really hit him hard. I actually worried he might do something stupid."

I stared at Eli. "So he dropped his investigation into whatever wrongdoing he noticed?"

"Oh, he didn't retire from that investigation."

"Is the cop he was suspicious of still on the force?"

"You know I'm not going to answer that."

I took a sip of my beer and thought about what I had just heard.

"You think his death might be tied to his continued private investigation into what happened the night his partner was killed?"

"It's best I keep my opinion on that to myself."

"Do you know which building Jeff was working at when he died?"

He turned; his eyebrows furrowed. "The new one, the split one—business on the bottom, condos on top."

"The Ventura Tower?"

"That would be it. Why are you asking?"

"A man by the name of Guy Palermo allegedly died by suicide at the Ventura Tower a week or two before Jeff died. He owned an ancient statue which may or may not be worth something. It's missing. I saw Jeff the day he died. A chance run in with him at Glenmore Landing. He was running from something or someone."

Eli took another swig of beer, but I could tell I had his attention.

"A friend of mine was also killed the same day Jeff was. He was a private investigator—another ex-cop. Jeff's initials were in his appointment book, listed on three separate days in the three weeks before their deaths. I told Edith this when I met with her. She confirmed that my friend's name appeared multiple times in Jeff's telephone log."

Eli emptied his beer. I saw a flicker of something in his eyes.

"Three men with connections, however loose, all dead within a few weeks of each other? It can't be a coincidence."

Eli rotated the now empty bottle sitting on the table in front of him. A muscle jumped in his cheek.

I continued. "Look, Edith doesn't believe Jeff's death was an accident. My friend's daughter doesn't believe her father's death was an accident. Did Jeff know something about Palermo? Could he have seen something the night Palermo died? I mean, Palermo was heavily in debt. An airplane accident killed one of his crew—fifteen people in total. There were other unfortunate accidents and deaths. Maybe someone blamed Palermo, helped him off the 42nd floor of the Ventura Tower. Now you tell me Jeff may or may not have been looking into the activities of a dirty cop. Why isn't anyone looking into this?"

"Looks like someone is looking into it now."

"I don't know, Eli. If I don't find something concrete tying any of this together, I might be at a dead end."

Eli sat for a long time, not saying anything. I let him sit.

After a while, he pushed aside his empty bottle of beer and stood up. He pulled out his wallet and threw two twenties on the table. He turned to me; his eyes dark with...what? Anger? Fear?

I waited, hardly wanting to breathe lest I break the moment.

"I told Edith I would meet with you. For old times' sake. I can't tell you anything more."

"Can't or won't?"

I watched him swallow, the muscles in his neck tense. He leaned in toward me. "Palermo's death wasn't a suicide."

TWENTY-ONE

I barely had enough time to drive home after my meeting with Eli and change into something date-worthy before Luis came to pick me up. Eli's bombshell had left shrapnel-like fragments of our conversation embedded in my brain. It was painful to leave them there, but my desire to stay home and rehash details of our conversation was interrupted by the buzzing of my intercom.

"On my way down," I said into the speaker. On the other hand, giving my mind a chance to back away from the day's findings might do me good. I grabbed my bag, slipped on some ballet flats, and headed out the door.

Mrs. Wilson was doing her loop around the floor. Technically, not a loop, since the floors in the building were arranged like a giant U around a central dead zone containing the elevators, trash disposal chute, and other utilities. She walked the halls at least twice a day, claiming she did it to keep her arthritis at bay. I was certain she listened in at doorways and kept the neighbours under surveillance. On occasion she ventured outside, but her claim of being a fair-weather walker had her prowling the halls more days than not.

I smiled at her as she approached. "Lovely day out there, Mrs. Wilson. Did you find your cat? I hope he made his way back home okay."

She harrumphed as her beady eyes took in my jeans and short tweed jacket with fringed edges overtop a lacy camisole.

"You're not going outside for a walk today?"

"Does it look like I'm going out for a walk?"

I found myself wondering if there was an interior door somewhere that led to the roof of our building.

The elevator doors slid open, and I stepped inside. "Have a nice evening, Mrs. Wilson."

"Ya, ya." She waved me away.

After being her neighbour for three years, she was growing on me. Like black fungus. I couldn't help smiling as the elevator made its way down to the lobby. Despite her total disregard for social norms, she was independent and feisty, qualities I admired in a person.

The doors opened and I stepped out into the lobby. Luis' face broke into a grin as I stepped out of the elevator. He walked toward me. There was no question the man was handsome, but it was the little things that made my knees grow weak; the way he ran his hand over his closely shorn hair when he was thinking or frustrated, the way his eyes darkened when he looked at me, how he radiated calm and strength.

"God, you look hot," he whispered against my ear as he bent his head and kissed me. This was progress. Luis hated public displays of affection.

I reached up and laid a hand on the back of his neck, then ran my hand down his back until that spot where it took a dip, curling toward his hips. "You're looking pretty hot yourself, Inspector."

He pulled me in tighter and I felt his hands slide down to my waist.

After a second, he stepped back, took my hand, and pulled me toward the door. "We'd better go."

"I hope I'm dressed appropriately." I pointed at my jacket and jeans.

"Perfect. Although right now, I wish you weren't wearing anything." Luis grabbed my hand and pulled me through the lobby and out the door.

His car was parked in front of the building in a bus pullout, a no-parking sign prevalently displayed. I felt a twinge of something I'd never felt before. What the hell was happening? A kiss in public—although the lobby of my condo building wasn't exactly public space—and he even risked a parking ticket for me.

He opened the car door for me, then ran around to his side and slid in. He had to hunch over ever so slightly to keep his head from touching the roof of the car. His arms were strong, and the muscle in his forearm flexed as he gripped the steering wheel.

"So, what are we doing tonight?" I asked as he put the car into gear, did a quick shoulder check, and gunned it.

"It's a surprise."

I don't like surprises—maybe because all the surprises in my life have been bad ones. "How about a hint?"

"I already gave you a hint."

He hadn't told me what we were going to be doing but his text had read, *Dress for speed and bring something warm.*

"Well give me another hint."

"Okay. How about speed, heat, and sweet?"

We laughed ourselves silly at my attempts to guess as to what the evening might hold. Leaving the city behind, Luis turned off onto Highway 566 and then turned onto a small single-lane road.

We passed a large billboard at the side of the road announcing the area was soon to become an international destination entertainment park. The developer's photo—a six-foot, photoshopped picture of Franklin Dirks—beamed down on us as we passed.

I turned to Luis. "I'm impressed Adan managed to get Dirks to his Inner Light charity gala."

"I know Dirks. He's a decent guy, down to earth, easy to talk to."

Now I remembered Luis had been standing talking to him when I arrived at the gala. Him and miss prosecutor.

"Actually, he's one of the reasons we're out here."

I looked around in the gathering dusk. I knew a raceway had been recently completed at the western end of the park, and a horseracing track was now going in on the east end.

Luis pulled up to the Saddle Ridge Raceway and grinned at me.

"Is it open already? Are we watching a car race?" I turned to Luis, my excitement obvious.

"Oh, we're not watching."

The two and a half mile, fifteen-turn circuit was designed to host both IndyCar and NASCAR, but between races would be offering race car enthusiasts the opportunity to try it out through open lapping or by signing up for various levels of racing.

Luis had heard they were in their testing phase and allowing enthusiasts to book a time to try out the track. I had to admit, there was something intoxicating and sensual about feeling the car's vibrations and hearing the engine rumble as I sped after Luis. Of course, he left me eating his dust, but I attributed him beating me to all those high-speed car chases he had practice with.

"Okay, that was sweet...fast and hot," I admitted afterwards.

"Are you always this bad with clues? The night's not over."

After leaving the raceway, we drove back to the city. Luis had reserved a firepit for us at Sandy Beach Park. I watched him arrange the already splintered wood in the firepit, light and coach it into a nice blaze. I think I went into shock when he pulled out a small cooler he had brought with him and took out a bottle of wine and the fixings for smores.

I inched closer to the fire, propped up against Luis, who sat behind me. His arms curled around me as we stared into the fire. I didn't often get to see this side of Luis. The soft, vulnerable side. Only once in the evening did I catch myself staring at Luis and wondering if he was paying me all this attention out of guilt.

Luis was married to policing. Would he lie or look the other way to protect the department's reputation or image? Despite our desire to believe that most human beings were honest and kind, we were all capable of lowering our moral standards if the stakes were high enough.

· · · ● · ● · · · ·

This morning I was still riding on last night's high. Luis and I were finally getting to know and trust each other. One of these days we might even have an actual conversation about what we expected of the relationship. Something worth broaching in the near future.

A few months ago, I had finally told Luis about my parents, that my father killed my mother and then himself. He didn't say a word when I told him, although I suspect he already knew. He just leaned over and kissed me.

Last night was only the second time Luis ever opened up to me. The first time was a few months after we started seeing each other. He came to my office looking for comfort after watching a man kill his own child and then himself.

I didn't know much about Luis, other than he was born in Puerto Rico and his mother was from Brazil while his father was American but never in the picture. His mother couldn't afford to look after him and his siblings and had sent Luis to live with an aunt in Chicago. I had assumed it was an act of love and sacrifice on her part, but last night I learned otherwise.

Luis told me he barely knew his two sisters who were already teenagers by the time he and his brother arrived, each from a different father. His brother was three years older than Luis but died when Luis was ten.

Luis said his mother was a drug addict. A steady stream of lowlife boyfriends passed though their lives. One of the lowlifes thought it was a good idea to send his brother out to score drugs for them. By the time his brother was thirteen, he was making drug runs for more than his mother and her boyfriend. He was found shot dead in a farmer's field.

The police told his mother that his brother had joined a gang and they were certain his death was gang related. They had no interest in pursing his killers. His mother and her deadbeat boyfriend decided to move to the Dominican Republic—and they didn't need a kid tagging along.

The night explained a lot about Luis. It also made any future conversation or questions about a potential dirty cop on his team just that much trickier.

TWENTY-TWO

I DIDN'T SPEND MUCH time flitting around the condo like some schoolgirl who had just been asked to the prom by her fantasy crush. Yesterday's conversation with Eli came back like a tsunami, obliterating thoughts of Luis.

Palermo's death wasn't a suicide. Eli's statement kept circulating in my brain. Eli was in a precarious position. I had no idea what he knew, but he wasn't likely to have made that statement without some idea of its truth. By telling me Palermo's death wasn't a suicide, he pretty much told me he wanted me to keep investigating.

Why wasn't Eli taking his belief that Palermo was murdered up through proper channels? Maybe it was simply a case of no evidence. Or maybe there was a dirty cop in the mix somewhere. But given his reluctance to offer up more last night, I also knew he wasn't going to offer up anything else.

I reminded myself I hadn't been hired to find out if Guy Palermo's death was a suicide or not. Likewise, I wasn't on a mission to find out if Jeff's accident was a hit-and-run or not. But Howard's death and each man's link to the other, however dubious, were all I had in my search for truth about what happened to Howard Bergman.

Palermo's daughter thought the statue was likely worth more from a cultural perspective than a financial one. So, what happened to it? If it was worth anything, she hadn't come across a sale record or noticed a bump in her father's financial records to indicate he had sold it.

Could someone have stolen Palermo's statue? Maybe it was worth more than Kelly thought. In which case, Palermo might have hired Howard to try to find it.

I reached for the phone and called Palermo's daughter. She answered on the third ring.

"Kelly. It's Jorja Knight. We talked the other day about your father, and a possible link to the case I'm investigating."

"Oh yes. Of course. You know, after your call, I contacted the auction house that's going to be selling my father's collections. They're certain this statue you were asking about isn't there."

I wasn't about to tell her what Eli said to me. But if I could find out who killed Palermo, or why he was killed, I might be able to figure out if Howard's involvement was even a possibility.

"I know you said the statue might not have a lot of monetary value, but I'd like to find out more about what happened to it. Maybe it went missing before your father died. It got me wondering if your father hired my friend to try to find it. I mean, he was a private investigator."

"Oh, well...I can't pay."

"No, no. Sorry. I'm not looking to be paid for this, Kelly. I already have a client and my one and only focus is finding out what happened to her father. He was a good man and a mentor to a close friend of mine. If the statue figures into it somehow and I discover what happened to it, I'd be more than happy to share that information with you. I just want to find out what Howard Bergman was working on. If he wasn't hired by your father to find the missing statue, at least it will shut that avenue of inquiry down and let me move on in another direction."

"Well...okay. If you want to look into it, go ahead."

"Kelly, you told me when your father first got the object it was encrusted in years of sediment and dirt. Did he do his own restorations, or did he have someone do that for him?"

"I don't know. I never thought to ask him."

"What about having the object authenticated? You said he collected a wide range of artifacts. Hard to be an expert in everything. Could he have taken the object to an expert, you know, to get their opinion on its age, its origin?"

"Possibly. I know my father had a good friend who is a professor of archeology. Just a minute, I saw his name in my father's contacts."

Kelly came back on the line a few minutes later. "Yes, here it is. Dr. Ian Garret. He's a professor at the University of Calgary." She rattled off his email address and phone number.

I felt my excitement growing. I was back to chasing this silly cursed statue. Did it really factor into what was going on, or was I just chasing a shiny object because it was easier than the real task at hand?

TWENTY-THREE

I had no trouble finding the Science Building, but parking was problematic. I arrived at Dr. Garret's office door a few minutes late. I knocked and waited. A small man with a thick head of grey hair came rushing down the hall. He wore a plaid, short-sleeve shirt, and a tie.

"My apologies," he called out. "Sorry to make you wait."

His glasses, hanging off a lanyard against his chest, swung toward me as he reached out to shake my hand.

"Quiz next week, and suddenly my students have all these questions. Please come in." He unlocked the door, swept a pile of papers off the lone chair parked in front of the desk, and motioned me to sit. "Can I get you anything, coffee, a soft drink?"

His head swivelled around the cramped room as if there should be a coffee machine or drinks somewhere in among the stacks of books and papers.

He looked relieved when I refused his offer.

"You said on the phone that you're an investigator?" He slid behind his desk and sat down.

"Yes, I'm a private investigator. I'm looking into the death of another private detective, a former police officer, by the name of

Howard Bergman. I've been trying to reconstruct the case he was working on at the time of his death and have learned that there may be a connection to your friend Guy Palermo. Guy Palermo's daughter, Kelly, kindly gave me your name."

He shook his head. "I can't believe he's gone. You know, Guy,"—he pronounced the name as *Gee*—"and I met at Simon Fraser. I was working on my Master of Arts. Guy was already working but taking additional courses in systems engineering. He was very creative. Always looking for ways to integrate disciplines like mechanical, electrical, and software engineering to find solutions to complex engineering problems." He smiled. His eyes had that faraway look. "Guy claimed he knew what he wanted to do since he was ten. He wanted to be an inventor. I had no bloody idea what I wanted to do when I was that age." He laughed. "I was interested in so many things—plants, the solar system, the monarchy. I found all of it fascinating. I don't know how useful becoming an archaeologist is, but I stumbled into it in my second year, and the rest, as they say, is history." He laughed at his own joke.

"It sounds fascinating."

"It some ways it is. Archaeology makes use of principles and information gathered from other disciplines, including anthropology, history, art history, religion, and geology. We used to have some great discussions around the rather myopic way our learning institutions have been organized."

"His death must have come as a huge shock."

He nodded. "Guy had this vigour about him, a classic type-A personality. He took everything in stride...good or bad. But the last few times I saw him, I could see something had changed. He was struggling. If only I had known how much..." His words trailed off.

"None of us can really know what is going on with someone, unless they want to tell us."

Dr. Garret remained wherever his memories had taken him, then shook his head, and sat up. "I saw him about two months before he died. He came here to the university—no heads-up, no indication he wanted to see me. He just showed up. Of course, I always had time for Guy. Although I admit, I was in the throes of final exams, and I may have been a bit distracted."

"You said he seemed changed?"

"He was subdued. When I asked him how he'd been, he said life was kicking the crap out of him. Those were pretty much his exact words. I knew his wife had died earlier that year, and I'm sure he was still suffering her loss."

"His daughter told me his wife died from brain cancer. And that a house they had been building in California was destroyed by fire. She said her father jokingly told her he thought the statue he'd recently acquired must be cursed. She said he had a great sense of humour."

"That he did. It's a lot, to see the life you've built crumbling around you. I knew he was having financial difficulty, too, and that terrible plane crash in Colombia. That really hit him hard." Dr. Garret sat for a minute, lost in thought. When he spoke again, it was with more vigour. "The Guy I knew would have never blamed someone or something else for his good or bad fortune. He used to say, we make our own luck. But that day, it seemed like he had given up."

"I know this must be hard for you, but did he ever show or tell you about a pre-Columbian artifact he picked up in Colombia a couple of years ago? Apparently, it's a statue of a jaguar."

"Yes, one of the Vanderburg Panthers. Or at least that's what I thought he might have in his possession. It looked to be made of jade—not commonly used in pre-Columbian sculptures. It had a shallow depression carved into its back, which would have held a ceremonial bowl used to burn seeds or certain plants, as offerings to their many and various deities. It was not a common, everyday object.

"You called it something...a Vandenburg Panther? You recognized it?"

"Vanderburg," he corrected. "Not exactly. My speciality is classical archaeology. I mainly study ancient Greek and Roman cultures, but I do have a smattering of knowledge around anthropological archaeology; that's the study of prehistoric societies, such as the pre-modern people of Asia and the Americas. I'm by no means an expert though." He lifted his glasses from where they hung against his chest, cleaned the lenses with a tissue, and positioned them on his nose.

"What's so special about these Vanderburg statues?"

"They were named after a famous archeologist, Friedrich Vanderburg, who discovered them in 1723 in Honduras. He had been following tomb and cave drawings that indicated a pair of jaguars—or panthers, as he called them—had been gifted to a king. The king was viewed as the supreme ruler who held semi-divine status, which meant he could act like a mediator between the mortal realm and that of the gods. The Vanderburg statues are said to be about six inches in height, eight inches long, and made of jade. They contained a depression said to have held a ceremonial bowl and were believed to be infused with the powers of unearthly deities."

"So not made by these deities but *infused* with their powers. Clever."

Dr. Garret chuckled. "Seems to be a long-standing tradition of those who reach power. I mean, who dares to question the authority provided them by an almighty yet invisible and usually vengeful being."

"And you thought the statue Guy had might be one of this pair found by Vanderburg?"

"Like I said, I'm not an expert in Mesoamerican art. But it was old and somewhat crude in design, befitting the form of statues made in that era."

"Guy's daughter described it as a hideous-looking thing."

"Such anthropomorphic figures, those merging animal and human features, were representative of the times. I have seen similar such forms in my own work. Many ancient Near East deities were personified as anthropomorphic figures. Such images evoked the belief that power could be obtained over the physical world by combining the superior physical attributes of various species."

"And you thought the statue Guy had was one of the pair of statues found by Friedrich Vanderburg?"

"Difficult to say. Tests would have to be run, and jade artifacts are very hard to date. But the figure he showed me could have been made around twelve-hundred to five-hundred B.C. There isn't much data on the Vanderburg Panthers, other than they were supposedly a male and female pair. There is a crude drawing of the statues made by Vanderburg in the archaeological archives, which is perhaps why they came to mind. But of course, testing back then was limited. Most of the data used to substantiate such a find would have come from ancient writings, and of course comparisons to other known artifacts from the area of discovery."

"What happened to the Vanderburg Panthers and how would one of them have ended up with an old lady near San Agustin, Colombia?"

Dr. Garret looked at his watch. "I have a tutorial I must attend in about twenty minutes. Unfortunately, it's across campus. If you're interested and have time to walk with me, I can tell you what I know."

Ancient kings and rare artifacts infused with otherworldly powers? It would take an army of unearthly deities to pry me away from Dr. Garret's side.

TWENTY-FOUR

I FOUND MYSELF ON the other side of the campus, with little idea of how I had gotten there. I'd been so engrossed in what Dr. Garret had been saying that I hadn't paid any attention to the circuitous route we had taken, some of which involved cutting across parking lots and through buildings.

"The Vanderburg Panthers were taken back to Germany by Friedrich Vanderburg. Handed down generation to generation. The statues were last seen in 1902."

"They weren't kept in a museum?"

"Oh no. It was quite common for the early archaeologists to claim and keep their finds as their own. Even today, many looted or stolen artifacts are finding their way into private hands."

I nodded. "What happened in 1902?"

"Those times, until the November Revolution in 1918, were tumultuous, especially as the Imperial State of Germany—or the German Reich, as it was more commonly known—was undergoing unification. Not to mention World War I. Whatever the reason, the statues left the Vanderburg family hands and disappeared. Perhaps the statues were stolen or perhaps they were sold.

"The next time the Vanderburg statues are mentioned comes to us anecdotally. The statues were now called jaguars to recognize the fact that the jaguar was only one of the four panther genera to be found in the Americas. It was rumoured the jaguars had fallen into Hitler's hands. Some even speculated his aggression and belief he was invincible may have been bolstered by his acquisition of the jaguars and other such ancient artifacts."

"Really? I never knew Hitler had a fascination with such things."

"Oh yes. When he was first sworn in as Chancellor of Germany and leader of the Nazi Party, he took control of all the state's institutions, museums, universities. It was all part of his plan to prove the Germanic people were descendants of the original master race."

"Why take over museums and universities?"

"He wanted to rewrite the curriculum of the educational institutions to align with his doctrines. He even sent teams of archaeologists around the world to excavate sites to prove the Aryan race lived there first and that they were entitled to take back what was rightfully theirs. Hitler ordered his teams of researchers to prove the existence of a mythical prehistoric population. The Nazis believed the German people were the descendants of this race. His party funded archaeological excavations all over the world."

"Really? And these jaguars were believed to hold special powers?"

"Yes. Certainly. In pre-Columbian times, the jaguar was seen as a symbol of strength and power. This belief carried over into later civilizations. The Aztec kings or rulers were victorious generals who conquered many towns and villages around them. They commanded the army. The jaguar was seen as a representation of the ruler as warrior. They even formed an elite warrior group known as the Jaguar Warriors."

"The man was truly mad. Were the rumours about the Vander-burg Jaguars falling into his hands ever substantiated?"

"No. But some of Hitler's loot and wartime spoils were relocated when it looked like the Nazis were going to lose the war. Some of his war spoils ended up in Bavaria, but some ended up as far away as South America."

"Wow. That's amazing. How would it have gotten into a simple countrywoman's hands?"

"Someone may have found and stolen it. Or maybe it was buried somewhere and never retrieved, only to be found years later by someone who did not know its value."

I nodded. "I see. These statues were associated with otherworld powers, but Guy believed them to be cursed."

"Yes. According to Vandenburg, a rumour or myth propagated by the local people of the area said that whoever possessed the jaguar pair would hold great power, but they would bring bad luck to anyone who only possessed one of the pair."

"Ah, I see. The implications being that something happened to weaken the king if one was able to make off with a statue, snatching it from under the nose of a great warrior or his elite army."

"Exactly."

"If the statue Guy had was one of the Vanderburg Panthers—or rather, the Vanderburg Jaguars as they were later called, how much could it be worth?"

"It's difficult to say. I told Guy the same thing. Authenticating it would be difficult."

"Why is that?"

"For an object like that—the authentication process can take years. It would likely be evaluated by dozens of top experts in the field. All sorts of tests would be run. There isn't much documentation on the Vanderburg Jaguars to support a solid authentication. How do you validate a piece which is described in ancient script or drawn in cuneiform on the walls of a cave? None of Vanderburg's ancestors, who may have seen it, are alive today. Nor is anyone in Hitler's inner circle."

"So how would it be validated?"

"One can look at where it was found, trace the source of jade that was used, examine the minutest of details in the actual carving and compare it with known artifacts from the era and region it came from. You need agreement among the experts. Even then, the so-called experts have gotten it wrong from time to time."

"If it were deemed to be authentic, what could something like that be worth?"

"The Guennol Lioness—an ancient Elamite figure from an area which today is known as Iran, believed to have been carved around twenty-eight hundred B.C.—sold for fifty-seven point two million."

"What? Did you say fifty-seven million? Dollars?"

"Yes, but it's an extremely rare object. Its historical significance as one of the oldest examples of Mesopotamian art found is what gave it that value." Dr. Garret's face lit up. "Imagine. It was carved at approximately the same time as the first known use of the wheel." He held his hands out in front of him. "I'd love to hold it in my hands. It's not just a work of art—it's a part of our human evolution. Priceless, if you ask me."

"Well, even if the jaguar was worth a tenth of that, it's a lot of money."

"True. On the other hand, the authenticators might conclude the object Guy had was not one of the Vanderburg Jaguars."

"What would its worth be, then?"

"Hard to say." He pursed his lips. "The right collector, someone who isn't purist about such things, might pay upwards of a million or two. Sometimes the story being sold with the object is worth more than the object itself, if you get my meaning."

"Guy's daughter told me the statue wasn't among her father's possessions."

He stopped mid-stride and turned toward me. "What are you saying? You think someone could have stolen it? Maybe, what...killed him for it?"

"I have nothing to suggest that, except pure speculation. But Guy Palermo is dead, the statue is missing, a security guard working at his office building was killed in an apparent hit-and-run. My friend was found dead the next day, his apartment and vehicle trashed. He had the security guard's name in his appointment book. I'm trying to find out if this statue could be worth enough to have set off this string of...deaths. Not from the perspective of the object being cursed, but its dollar worth. Do you know what Guy's plan for the statue was? If it was worth a few million, it would go a long way to getting him back on his feet."

Dr. Garret continued a few more feet, then stopped again, this time in front of a long, low building. He adjusted his glasses and rubbed a hand across his chin. "I had no idea it was missing. I assumed he found a buyer, or it was now in his daughter's possession."

I suddenly remembered the insurance policy I had found among Howard's papers.

"Do you know if he had it insured?"

"No. I suspect not. Most insurance companies need the item to be authenticated before they will issue insurance. And insurance is costly, depending on the value of the object, of course."

"Do you know what he ended up doing with it? Did you provide him with any advice?"

"I got the impression he wanted to get rid of it—the sooner, the better. I'm not sure if it was because he needed the money, or because he really believed the statue was cursed. Maybe both. I told him a private sale would be his best option if he wanted to sell it quickly."

"How would he go about finding a buyer?"

"I gave him the name of someone who could guide him on a private sale. He was once considered somewhat of an expert in Mesoamerican artifacts. These days, he's a purveyor of fine art and antiquities."

Something about the way he said *purveyor* made me believe Dr. Garret didn't think much of this so-called expert's service.

"Is he not reputable?"

"It's not my intent to question his reputation, but I do question his ethics. I was reluctant to give Guy his name, but he kept pressing me for help."

"Who is this so-called expert and purveyor of antiquities and fine art?"

"Milton Landen."

TWENTY-FIVE

My head was still spinning after my meeting with Dr. Garret. Now I was certain Milt Landen knew something that would be useful to me. Too bad he was somewhat of a recluse—at least, that's what Dr. Garret told me. Before he ran off to his class, he gave me the same number I had found in Howard's appointment book, the number I had called. My excitement grew. The fact that I found the same number in Howard's appointment book must mean I was on the right track.

Donna had told me Howard had been excited until just a week or so before his death. He was working on something big. Suddenly talking about retiring somewhere warm, making sure Donna and her daughter were well taken care of after he was gone. Sounded like he might be coming into some money. But how did this all fit together? Thoughts, ideas, and fragments swirled around in my head like dust devils before a tornado.

I pushed aside the joking heist comment Lennie had made to Howard when he came looking for information about a security system. More likely he was trying to figure out who breached Palermo's safe or security system. Is that how Jeff Nickleson fit in? He worked in the building where Palermo died. Maybe Howard questioned him, maybe Nickleson saw something the night Palermo died.

Milton Landen had already declared he had never heard of Howard. I supposed I could call again and ask him if Guy Palermo had ever contacted him about a possible priceless artifact. Somehow, I didn't think the direct approach would get me what I was looking for.

If Palermo had brought the statue to Landen, why hadn't he returned it to Palermo's estate after his death? If he sold it, why hadn't a deposit been made to Palermo's account? Maybe Palermo never got a chance to connect with Landen or the statue had turned out to be worthless in monetary terms. Or perhaps Landen did have the statue and was sitting tight hoping Palermo hadn't left a paper trail that brought police and lawyers to his door, demanding its return.

I parked the Taurus in an outdoor parking lot and hustled the six blocks to my office, using the time to formulate a plan. Once inside, I bypassed the ancient lone elevator, which only slowed one's progress, and ran up the stairs. By the time I was unlocking the door to the office, I knew what I needed to do.

As soon as I settled into my chair, I called Kelly, Palermo's daughter.

"Hi Kelly. I managed to get a hold of your father's friend, Dr. Garret. He told me your father did show him the statue—the jade jaguar. Apparently, your father was keen on selling it, maybe to a private collector. Dr. Garret gave your father the name of an art dealer—a purveyor of ancient antiquities, and someone who is knowledgeable about Mesoamerican artifacts. Milton Landen."

"Oh. Did my father take the statue to him?"

"It's a possibility. The man whose death I'm investigating also had Milton Landen's name and number noted in his appointment book. Not once, but three times. I called the number a few days ago, but Landen claims to have never heard of him."

"You don't believe him?"

"I'm not sure—at least not yet. What does interest me is that three individuals, all now deceased, who died within days of each other, either knew one another or had Milton Landen's name and number in their possession."

"Are you saying this Landen had something to do with my father's death?"

"No. I do think he might have some information that might be important in helping me to determine if Howard Bergman's death was an accident or not. There is also a question being raised by the ex-wife of the second man who died, a security guard who worked at your father's office building, as to whether his death was really an accident."

There was silence. "I see. I never even questioned my father's suicide."

"I don't mean to make you question whether it was suicide or not—or reopen that wound. It did make me curious though, if Milt Landen might know what happened to your father's jaguar."

"Oh. You think my father may have sold it to Landen?"

"Maybe. More likely, he asked him to broker the sale for him. Either way, the statue is missing. If it were authentic, Dr. Garret said it could be worth millions."

"What? That's incredible. Sorry...I'm having a hard time processing all of this."

"Well, keep in mind that the statue might just be, well, old, but not of any real significance, which isn't to say someone wouldn't want to pay a decent price for it. Maybe not millions though. But Dr. Garret did give Milt Landen's name to your father."

"Is there anything I can do? Should I be calling him? I mean if he has my father's statue..."

"You could call him. He might not tell you much, especially if he knows something that...well, let's say, isn't on the up and up."

"You mean he might have sold my father's statue and is keeping the money to himself, now that my father is dead? Should I be going to the police?"

This was the tricky part. An obvious and solid option. On the other hand, what were the police going to do? They would ask their questions and get answers, which may be truthful or not. If Landen had the statue or knew where it was—would he simply turn it over? If he had been predisposed to doing so, why hadn't he contacted Kelly after Palermo's death? Her name had been listed in the obituary as Palermo's only surviving daughter and she wasn't exactly hard to find.

There could be other explanations, of course. Maybe Palermo never got a chance to meet with Landen. Or maybe Landen had seen the statue and determined it wasn't one of the Vanderburg Jaguars, or anything of significance, and Palermo had just binned it since he felt it was cursed. However, none these options would explain why three men with links to each other, however tenuous, were dead.

"I'd like to find out more about what Landen knows about the jaguar statue, assuming your father did contact him, but if something nefarious is going on, he's not just going to offer up that information."

"Yes, of course. What do you suggest?"

"I've already called him, and I doubt that he'll be more receptive to me calling him a second time. He told me he didn't know Howard. He might be willing to talk to me if I tell him I'm looking into the missing statue on your behalf. That you have reason to believe your father showed him the statue."

"Yes...I see."

"Would you be willing to back up my statement if he should contact you for confirmation? It's entirely possible your father never got a chance to connect with Landen, but at least I'll be able to gauge his reaction to hearing someone is looking for the statue."

Luckily, Kelly agreed. It wasn't much of a plan, but at least it was a lead. Now all I had to do was find some way to roust out a recluse.

TWENTY-SIX

THE HEAT SHIMMERED OFF the asphalt as I turned off the QEII and headed east on Highway 566. The canola fields that previously flanked the highway with a blanket of yellow had been swathed and lay waiting to be harvested. The flat landscape now gave way to rolling hills. Further on, it would change again, into a dramatic patchwork of deep and winding gullies, known as the Drumheller Badlands.

Several hours of research had netted me little in the way of contact information for Milt Landen beyond the number I already had. I did find the name of his business—Traders of the Lost Art. The webpage didn't provide contact information, only a contact form. A little more digging had netted me a PO box number in Beiseker—not terribly useful.

I decided to focus on the museum he owned in Rosebud, a small town located about an hour's drive from Calgary and twenty minutes southwest of Drumheller and the world-renowned Tyrrell Museum. Rosebud has its own claim to fame. Home to The Rosebud Opera House and Theatre, it's a cultural mecca of sorts to those living in the rural heartland of Alberta.

I rounded the corner and began my descent into the river valley. I could see why two members of the Group of Seven had spent a summer in the 1940s painting in the area. The landscape changed and surprised at every corner. Finally, the tiny hamlet came into view. The tip of a tall turquoise structure turned out to be a grain elevator and stood out sharply against the brown-grey barren slopes of the surrounding terrain. It was pretty, in that '50s small-town kind of way.

The hamlet was intersected by two main roads, one running east-west, the other, north-south. I drove past a dozen or so shops and art galleries as well as the Rosebud Opera House and Theatre. The population of Rosebud was less than a hundred, but the hamlet swelled with visitors on weekends, coming to watch the live theatre performances, or to listen to the bands playing at the outdoor festival stage.

I slowed and turned into the parking lot of a white clapboard building. A sign prominently displayed across the top of the build-ing said it was the Hotel Rosebud. I opened Google Maps, looking for the Landen Museum.

Rosebud had a museum of its own, once the local Chinese laun-dry for the hundreds of miners who worked in the valley in the early 1900s, which now displayed artifacts and photographs of pioneer life. It wasn't the museum I was looking for. The Landen Museum was two kilometres outside of the hamlet, nestled into the hills overlooking the Rosebud River.

I reoriented myself, pulled out of the parking lot, and headed south. I almost missed the township road, little wider than a country lane. A few minutes later, I pulled into a gravel lot in front of a low building that looked like it was coming out of the surrounding hill.

The parking lot barely held room for ten or twelve cars but today two cars were parked there.

I parked, got out of my car, and stretched. The air was still, the hum of the electrical transformer on the overhead powerlines the only sound. The valley trapped the heat, and I immediately felt the moisture building on my neck.

A large swath of black rose from behind the museum and ran up the side of the hills behind. The scar from a fire looked to be recent, and by its close proximity to the museum, I gathered it wasn't the result of a controlled burn. High up on one of the hills, someone had spelled out the town's name with white rocks.

I followed a sign pointing me down a well-worn path. Several pathway markers explained what I would find inside—fossils, artifacts from indigenous peoples who occupied what was now known as Treaty 7 lands, and a collection of pre-Columbian artifacts, mostly from Latin America.

The path ended at a set of concrete stairs which led to double doors, both propped open to let in the afternoon warmth. I walked up the stairs and entered the building, dark after the glare of the sun outside.

A young woman sat at a table immediately inside the door. She closed the book she had been reading, shoved it under the table, and gave me a wide smile.

"Good afternoon. Welcome to the Landen Museum. Have you visited us before?"

"No. This is my first time." I pulled open my pocketbook and slid out a credit card, noting the ten-dollar entry fee.

"Well, you're in for a treat. We have some of the most unique artifacts ever found in North and South America. Our museum houses a sizable portion of the Landen Collection."

"Interesting."

"Dr. Horatio Landen was a famous archeologist who came to Alberta in the early 1920s. You know, he was one of the archaeologists hired by National Geographic in 1908 to map and find the Lost City of the Monkey God. That's a lost civilization in Mexico or maybe South America."

Cleary, she hadn't bothered to google it. "That's fascinating. Did he find it? The Lost City of the Monkey God?"

She giggled as she took my credit card and punched some numbers into her machine. "I think so."

"What brought him to Alberta?"

"He heard about the fossilized dinosaur bones being found around here and I guess he was fascinated by that. He travelled all over the world, to all the important digs and discoveries."

"The artifacts in this museum are from his collection, then?"

"I guess. Well, some of them, at least. His grandson inherited the collection. He's the one who opened up the museum."

"Is that Milton Landen?"

"Yes." She beamed as she handed my credit card back along with the receipt and a brochure about the museum. "You've heard of him?"

"I don't know anything about him. His name came up in conversation the other day, when I mentioned to a group of friends that I might be coming out here on a day trip—you know—staycation, see Alberta first. Does he spend time at the museum?"

She giggled. "I've never met him. I've only been working here a couple of weeks. My sister met him, though. She used to work here. I gather he's somewhat of a recluse. When he's not travelling places, like his granddad, he just wants to chill."

"I suppose." I put my credit card away. "I noticed the burn outside. Was that recent?"

"Oh my gosh, yes. It happened last month. Remember that super heat wave we had? Well, there was this grass fire. My sister was working here at the time. She said she could smell smoke but thought someone was just burning rubbish. Then one of the visitors noticed fire up on the ridge. Twenty minutes later, the firefighters came by and ordered everyone to leave. By then, the flames were already halfway down the hill. She said it was really scary."

"It must have been. Hope no one was hurt."

"No. They had it out by evening. They had to close the museum though, to get rid of the smoke smell inside. That's how I got this job, you know. My sister has a kid and can't afford to be off work. She didn't know how long the museum would be closed so she took another job, and I got this one." She gave me a whopping big grin.

"That's lucky." I held up my brochure. "I guess I should go have a look. Nice chatting with you."

"My pleasure." She flashed me a smile. "If you have any questions, let me know."

I pushed open the inner door and stepped inside. I could think of one question she might know the answer to...how do I find your sister?

TWENTY-SEVEN

The air was cooler inside the museum, a welcome reprieve from the heat outside, but it was darker, too. I startled, noticing for the first time a woman in uniform standing against the wall to my right. She wore navy pants, a light-blue, short-sleeved shirt with some sort of logo on the arm. Security. I nodded and stepped past her.

I found myself in the main room of the museum, which was devoted to America's early inhabitants, including the indigenous people of the northern plains and the Inuit people in the far north. I wandered past the glass cases, stopping here and there to read some tidbit about the shards of clay pottery, bone knives and needles, and various stone carvings.

After circling the North American exhibits, I exited into a smaller room dedicated to the Mayans.

Many of the Mayan artifacts were made of stone, semi-precious gems, and copper. Originally thought to be cliff dwellers, they left behind impressive temples and cities. Unlike the nomadic first peoples in more northern regions, they had access to food and water, the climate was mild, and the artifacts they left behind indicated a much richer and stabler lifestyle than their neighbours to the north.

I passed into yet another room leading off from the Mayan exhibit, housing pre-Columbian artifacts. Glass cases once again ringed the room, but here a large singular glass case on a square mahogany pedestal stood in the centre. The glass case was at eye height—for better viewing, I suppose. It was empty. I opened the brochure to see if there was any mention of what was meant to be inside. The brochure labelled it as the future exhibit of a rare jade statue believed to have been found in the Lost City of the Monkey God.

The brochure read, "Difficult to date, the statue is part of a collection of several artifacts brought back to Canada from Horatio Landen's expeditions to Honduras to search for the lost city. It is one of the earliest artifacts from the region, dating back to 1000 B.C. Although rumoured to be one of a pair of jaguars, the existence of the male version has never been officially documented."

My heart started to race. *What the hell*. Based on what I had read when researching Landen's family pedigree as world renown archeologists, the Lost City of the Monkey God hadn't been found until just recently, although many expeditions to Honduras had tried and failed to verify its existence.

A noise startled me. A tall swarthy man entered the room, hands behind his back, making his way around the room. The security guard had also shifted. I could see her through the open door into the Mayan gallery room. She had moved and was now standing directly in front of the connecting door.

I continued around the room, pausing here and there at a display case. My brain was still trying to process what I had just read about the exhibit that would supposedly be held in the large, now empty glass case in the other room. Was it meant for Palermo's statue? If so, why was he trying to portray it to be a statue found by his late grandfather? And from the Lost City of the Monkey God at that? I paused at a case and pretended to examine a copper amulet. Under the guise of referring to its reference in my brochure, I took a closer look around the room.

I noticed two security cameras mounted near the ceiling—one pointed toward the entrance to the room, while the other would provide a good cross view of the room and the doorway to the adjacent room that held artifacts from Honduras, El Salvador, and the Yucatán.

The man shifted closer. He had a beard, was four or five inches taller than my five feet eight inches, and smelled faintly of...what? Epoxy? Varnish? I completed my circuit of the room and entered the South and Central Americas exhibit.

This room was darker than the last despite the bank of windows near the ceiling of the room, which soared to a good fourteen or sixteen feet in height. Long, narrow windows ran parallel to the ceiling—the kind that provided ventilation, not views to the outside.

The wooden floorboards creaked as I hurried through the exhibit. As fascinating as the exhibits were, the place was giving me the heebie-jeebies. The bearded man entered the room as I exited back into the main gallery.

The remaining room in the museum housed a small shop which sold modern Inuit carvings, paintings, and handcrafted items. A door to the left of the shop's entrance was labelled as the emergency exit and advised visitors the door was alarmed.

The security guard avoided my gaze and shifted away from me as I turned in her direction. I entered the shop and made one round through the store, returning to a section that held books on Mesoamerican art, the history of indigenous peoples of Alberta, dinosaur discoveries, the Royal Tyrrell Museum in Drumheller, and various other local interest books.

I parked myself in front of the shelf, selected a book on coal mines in the area and pretended to read the description on the back. The bearded man had re-entered the main gallery. I watched him under the guise of reading as he milled around in the main gallery. Mostly I just wanted to get out of here and think about what I had discovered.

The woman sitting on a stool behind the cash register was reading a book. I took this as a sign the museum didn't get many visitors, or maybe it did during the summer months, prime tourist season, and when the Rosebud Opera House and Theatre was in full swing. After about ten minutes, the woman behind the counter looked up.

"Is there anything I can help you with?"

"Oh thanks. All of these are so fascinating, I'm having a hard time deciding which to buy."

That seemed to satisfy her. I flipped pages for another ten minutes to make sure the swarthy man was gone, then selected two books and made one last round of the shop. Seeing no sign of the bearded guy through the door to the main gallery, I made my way to the cash register and paid for my books.

"Great little museum. I feel kind of spoiled. I had the place almost to myself."

She smiled. "June through August are our busiest months. And of course, Saturday is usually our busiest day."

I nodded, took my books, and headed backed through the main gallery to the entrance. Odd place for a museum like this. Maybe Landen meant to piggyback off the tourists coming to Rosebud or on their way to Drumheller—which did have about half a million visitors each year. But why not set up in Calgary—or Edmonton, which had over five million tourists annually.

I did a quick mental calculation. Two visitors to the museum in two hours—twenty bucks. Even if I quadrupled it and Landen paid staff minimum wage, it would hardly be enough to pay their wages, let alone maintenance on the place. Maybe he didn't need the money and the museum was a labour of love.

I paused at the front desk on my way out. This time the girl didn't try hiding the fact that she was reading.

"Hope you enjoyed your visit." She beamed.

I noticed her name tag. Aubrey Knott. "I did. I'll have to tell friends; I never knew this place existed. I noticed one of the cases that is supposed to hold a jade artifact, apparently from the Lost City of the Monkey God, is empty. Do you know anything about that?"

She looked around, then leaned forward and lowered her voice. "I heard the museum was bringing in a special piece. But then the fire happened, and now I don't think it's coming."

I looked around and lowered my voice, too. "Why not?"

She leaned in even further. "It might be missing. I heard the museum wasn't left properly locked up during the evacuation. Something happened to the security system—maybe the heat made it wonky. The security company technicians were here for days afterwards."

"That's interesting. So, it was stolen?"

She nodded knowingly, leaned in closer and whispered loudly. "I think the security guard who used to work here knows something about what happened. He's gone, too."

"You mean they fired him?"

"I think so. Now we have her." She nodded in the direction of the gallery where I last saw the security guard.

"How do you know all this?"

"My sister Bonnie told me."

"Do you remember the security guard's name, the one who worked here before her?"

"Thanks!" She sat back and smiled brightly. "Don't forget to tell your friends to come out for a visit."

I glanced over my shoulder. The security guard stood at the entrance to the main gallery, her arms crossed, a frown creasing her forehead.

"And try the Last Chance Saloon on the way to Drum. My sister works there, and the food is really good."

"I will. Thanks again. Great little museum—I'll be sure to tell my friends." I waved my brochure at her in a goodbye and stepped outside.

I hurried down the path toward my car. As the parking lot came into view, I could see a fourth vehicle now parked there. I walked the remaining few feet to the Taurus. A black SUV stood in the far corner of the lot, its windows darkened, its motor running.

TWENTY-EIGHT

As I drove back through Rosebud and onto Highway 841, my mind kept going back to the empty museum display case and the rare jade jaguar supposedly from the Lost City of the Monkey God. Explorers and archeologists have been looking for the lost city for hundreds of years. If indeed the empty glass case in the museum was meant to hold an artifact from such a revered site, why would it be on display in a small obscure museum on the road to nowhere. If Landen's grandfather had found the jaguars at the Lost City of the Monkey God, as the museum brochure claimed, he would have heralded the news to the world, wouldn't he have? More likely the empty exhibit case had meant to hold the statue Guy Palermo once had in his possession. Hard to believe that there could be two such artifacts, both jaguars that supposedly wielded great power, echoing what Dr. Garret told me. Even more astounding, both were missing. I shook my head. I didn't buy it for a minute.

I stopped at the junction to Highway 9 and checked Google Maps. The turnoff to Wayne—billed as a ghost town—was a few short kilometres from here. The Last Chance Saloon seemed to be the biggest reason anyone went to Wayne, other than the thrill of driving over eleven bridges to get there.

I had been checking my rearview mirror for a black SUV every few minutes, and almost missed my turnoff. Since Wayne was a tourist attraction, I was expecting a much bigger sign pointing the way, and since I hadn't checked the distance, it came up on me rather suddenly.

I counted off the bridges as I passed. After the fifth bridge, the road narrowed. I still hadn't seen another vehicle and I felt a bit creeped out. Especially as some clouds had moved in and obliterated the sun. I had driven out to the museum in hopes of locating Landen. I wanted to follow up with him to see if Palermo ever managed to talk to him about the artifact he had brought back from Colombia. Now I needed a different plan.

After several more curves in the road and six more bridges, I found myself at the entrance to a parking lot in front of a pale-yellow, three-storey wooden building called the Rosedeer Hotel. The Last Chance Saloon jutted out to the right from the main hotel. The date—*Est. 1913*—was emblazoned over the front entrance of the single-storey structure. A makeshift fence made from old wagon wheels separated the sidewalk in front of the hotel from the parking lot.

The place didn't look all that busy, but then not many people were likely to book a night stay in a ghost town, assuming the hotel still functioned as a hotel.

I parked, crossed the parking lot, and headed toward the saloon. An open sign hung next to the door, and a larger wooden sign indicated the establishment provided family dining. I paused to read the handwritten message on a sheet of paper taped to the entry door.

"*At this time of year, many of our seasonal staff have returned to school. It may take us a while to get your order out to you. We're doing the best we can. Please don't give our remaining staff a reason to quit. Thank you."*

Blunt and to the point. I opened the door to a wall of noise. Several people stood waiting just inside the door. One of the women told me they had been waiting about fifteen minutes and that there was a group of six ahead of them and a foursome in front of that group. I did a quick count—eight tables. I hoped the restaurant wrapped into an L shape at the back. I sighed and queued up behind the two women in front of me.

The sound of dozens of conversations bounced off the low ceiling. The walls were covered with old black-and-white photos, steer horns, pickaxes, and other mining memorabilia. A chalkboard just inside the door, highlighted the day's specials—a toasted clubhouse sandwich, a veggie wrap, or tomato soup and a grilled cheese sandwich. Three of the six items listed there were crossed out. The clubhouse called my name and my mouth watered. I realized I hadn't eaten much in the last two days.

A young woman came out from the kitchen, a plate in each hand. She balanced two more plates on her left arm. I was too far away to see her name tag.

She set the plates down at a table with two adults and two kids, then hustled back.

I stood in my spot by the door, cleared old emails out of my phone log, and tried to stop my brain from churning through what I learned this morning for the hundredth time. Half an hour later, I was seated. The place was still busy, but now only a young couple who had come in after me stood waiting for a table.

A young boy of about fifteen or sixteen cleared and wiped tables and then motioned for the remaining couple to take their seat.

Ten minutes later, the young woman I'd seen earlier appeared at my table and handed me a menu. A minute later, she was back to take my order. A quick glance at her name tag told me her name was Bonnie.

"Sure is busy in here. I see you're short-staffed."

"Now that school is back, a lot of our summer help has departed for university. What can I get you?"

Thankfully, the clubhouse was still on the menu. I ordered it, coffee, and water.

"I stopped by the Landen Museum earlier—your sister told me you used to work there."

"That's right. Sorry, excuse me."

She dashed off before I could ask her anything and a few minutes later returned with my coffee and a glass of water.

"Any chance you get off soon? Your sister said you might be the best one to answer some questions I have about the grass fire, and a jade statue that was supposed to go on display there."

"Are you a reporter?"

"No, I'm a private investigator."

She raised her eyebrows. "Cool."

"I'm looking for a statue similar to the one that was supposed to be on display at the museum. A jade jaguar. I'd sure appreciate some of your time."

She pressed her lips together and looked around. The place was only just starting to get back to normal. Several tables still needed to be wiped down.

"No break for me today. I finish my shift at four…if you want to come back then."

"Thanks, that'll be great. I'll see you then."

She left for the kitchen. I glanced at my watch—it was one-forty.

I finished eating, drank my coffee, and left the diner half an hour later. No one was lined up at the door. I went next door and browsed a small shop. Then, with an hour and a half left until Bonnie was free, I decided to go for a walk to clear my head.

I headed back up the road. The air was still, noiseless. The Red Deer Creek flowed slow and muddy. I was approaching the third bridge and thinking of turning back when I saw it. A black SUV with tinted windows. It was parked about ten feet off the road, and partially hidden by a stand of willows.

TWENTY-NINE

IT BEGAN TO DRIZZLE on my way back. I kept glancing over my shoulder, half expecting the SUV to suddenly come up behind me. I couldn't be a hundred percent certain, but if I were a betting woman, I'd put all my chips on it being the same one I'd seen at the museum.

Relieved to finally see the hotel, I crossed the parking lot and with one last glance over my shoulder, entered the restaurant. The place was half full now; an older woman was serving customers. Bonnie came out a few minutes later.

We chose a table by a small window overlooking the parking lot. "We haven't properly met." I stuck my hand out. "My name is Jorja Knight. Thanks for meeting with me."

She shook my hand. "Do you mind if I order something—I haven't had a chance to eat all day."

I glanced over at the chalkboard—the lunch items were gone. The dinner specials included a beef taco salad, pan-fried trout, and meatloaf with mashed potatoes and gravy. There was homemade rhubarb and strawberry pie for dessert.

Bonnie ordered the meatloaf and I ordered coffee and the pie—telling myself the walk more than wore off lunch.

"You said you're a private investigator. Are you looking into the fire behind the museum?"

"Not exactly. It's a bit complicated. My client's father owned a pre-Columbian jade statue he was looking to sell. His friend, an archaeologist, suggested he contact Milton Landen. That he might be able to find a buyer for it. Unfortunately, he died recently, and the statue isn't among his possessions. His daughter asked me to follow up with Landen to see if maybe he sold it or knows where it went."

"I don't understand. How can I help you?"

"Do you know how I can find Milton Landen? All I've been able to find is a post office box in Beiseker for his purveyor business."

"Sorry." She shook her head. "I've only ever seen him twice. Once was last year when he delivered some things to the museum. There's a workspace underneath the museum where the artifacts are either prepared for display or stored. He occasionally rotates the collection to keep it fresh for the visitors."

"And the second time?"

"That was the day of the fire."

"What can you tell me about the fire?"

She shrugged. "The fire department said it was arson."

"The museum was evacuated that day?"

"Yeah. It was around ten-thirty in the morning. We had just opened up. There were two visitors in the building, besides me, Carolanne who runs the shop, and our security guard, Jason. When the firemen arrived to tell us to leave, Jason told me to go. He went to find the two ladies in the museum, get them out, and then lock up."

"Your sister said something about the museum not being locked up properly?"

Our food came. Bonnie picked up her fork and took a bite. I did the same. She chewed thoughtfully for a minute.

"I don't know if that really happened. My sister has a wild imagination, always reading those mystery books of hers. What I do know is that after the fire was out, Mr. Landen arrived, then a couple guys came out from 4SiteSecurity—that's the company that provides security at the museum. They all went inside. After about half an hour, one of the security guys came out and told Jason, Carolanne, and me that we should go home for the day. Later that night, I got an email saying the museum would be closed indefinitely, due to smoke damage."

"What about the glass case I saw in the pre-Columbian room? The brochure said it was coming soon. It's supposed to hold a jade jaguar from the Lost City of the Monkey God—a civilization Landen's grandfather had been searching for."

"There was no statue in the case before the fire. I haven't been back to the museum since it reopened. I got my email the night of the fire, that it would be closed indefinitely, so I gave my notice the next day and started working here."

"What about the security guard who was working that day? Does he still work for 4SiteSecurity?"

"Jason? I don't know. 4SiteSecurity works all over southern Alberta, so I guess he could be working at a different location. I'm pretty sure he's not around. Rumour is—he's left town."

"Do you know where he went?" I really needed to talk to this Jason character. Howard had a 4SiteSecurity business card hidden away in his appointment book. Now I knew that Howard had at least gotten this far in his investigation. I just needed to find out what happened next.

"No. He used to live in the Haywood Court apartments in Drum. The apartment manager is a friend of mine. Devlin was pissed because Jason was two months behind on his rent and then one day, he discovers Jason is gone. Just packed up his clothes and split."

"Interesting. Do you know Jason's last name?"

"Sure, it's Gray."

"Your sister said she heard several items in the museum went missing during the evacuation. Some of the cases that once contained objects are now empty."

"I don't know about that. Did she tell you Landen is selling the museum?"

"No. She didn't mention it."

"I'm sure he's opened it up to show potential buyers it's open for business. I hear he's selling everything, the building and a lot of the artifacts as well. Maybe he's taken out the items he wants to keep." A heaviness formed in my gut. *One step forward, one step back.*

"Do you know why he's selling it?" My first guess would be that it was losing money hand over fist.

"No idea."

I picked up our tab by way of thanks and climbed back into the Taurus. I googled 4SiteSecurity. Was this going to be a dead-end lead? Decision time. Do I head back to Calgary or go into Drumheller? I did a mental coin flip. *Drumheller it is.*

I pulled back onto the road and headed to the main highway. The black SUV that had been parked by the bridge earlier was gone, but I kept one eye on my rear-view mirror anyway.

Bonnie's sister heard that the museum hadn't been properly secured during the fire and items had been taken. If that were the case—surely it would have made the news. Especially if this rare jade statue was one of the items taken. That it and Palermo's jaguar were both missing was hard to believe. *What the hell is going on?*

THIRTY

I ROLLED INTO DRUMHELLER shortly before six. Most businesses were already closing for the day. It took me ten minutes to find 4SiteSecurity. They were housed in what used to be a private residence. I drove past the place and parked down the street. Bonnie said Jason had split, but he could still be on 4SiteSecurity's payroll. I pulled my burner phone out of the glove compartment and called the number on their website.

I told the woman who answered the phone that I was calling for a reference check on one of their former employees, Jason Gray. She transferred me to her boss.

"Hi, I'm with the Talent Seekers Agency. I'm phoning for a reference check on a former employee, Mr. Jason Gray. He's on my client's short list and I'm conducting candidate reference checks on their behalf."

I hoped like hell Jason wasn't this guy's nephew or still on their payroll, and merely working at one of their other locations. "Can you confirm that Mr. Gray was employed by your company?"

"Yes. Jason worked for us."

Past tense. I breathed a sigh of relief. "How long was he with your company?"

"Three years."

"How would you describe Mr. Gray's work?"

"He's a personable young man. The customers seemed to like him, for the most part."

"Was he reliable? Punctual? Was he willing to take shift work?"

A pause, never a good sign. "For the most part."

That was the second time he used that phrase. I could tell he was trying hard not to black ball the guy, but I wanted to know the nitty gritty.

"Our client provides security services to a variety of customers. Many of the larger companies have their own security requirements. We're looking for someone who works well with other team members, who follows protocols, who is punctual, dependable, and personable. Would you say that describes Mr. Gray?"

"For the most part."

I took a deep breath. That was the third time I heard him say *for the most part*. "Have there been instances where Mr. Gray did not follow protocol?"

Another pause, then he cleared his throat. "There was one instance I can think of, yeah. But there were extenuating circumstances."

"I see. Can you share that with me?"

"He was providing services at a facility that had to be evacuated immediately. During the process, one of the side doors was left unsecured. There was a lot of chaos, the building and people were in imminent danger. His main concern was to get everyone out safely. I don't think he should get a black mark for not wanting to risk his own life to go and double check that all the doors were locked. He did engage the main security system on his way out."

"Were there any consequences to the building being left unsecured during the evacuation?"

"I'm not in any position to say."

"Okay. Can you tell me when he left your employ?"

"A few weeks ago."

"And his reason for leaving?"

"I had to let him go."

"Oh. May I ask why?"

"With the economy tanking, I've lost a few clients. A few of our clients have downsized or sold their businesses entirely. I couldn't keep all my staff; I had to adjust my employee pool."

"I see."

"Look, miss—what was your name again?"

"Beddingfeld. Anne." I used the name whenever I had to provide a fake one, stolen from a character in one of Agatha Christie's murder mysteries.

"Look...ah...Ms. Beddingfeld. I'll be totally honest with you. I liked the kid. Like I said, he was very personable, upbeat. Always willing to jump in. Maybe he exhibited a little too much youthful exuberance from time to time. He's learning. I think partnered with the right people, he'd do an awesome job for your client. I'm a small firm, most of my clients are small to mid-size. I don't have a lot of spare staff. When I need my people out there, I need them out there. He missed more days of work than the other people on my payroll. I told him straight up when I let him go, but I also told him I wasn't going to black ball him. I hope letting him go has been enough of a wake-up call, that when the next guy gives him a chance at a job, he takes it seriously."

"I appreciate your candour. I will certainly take your comments and your willingness to defend him into consideration. I still have two other candidates to follow up on, but I must admit, on paper, he seems to be exactly what we are looking for...for the most part." I bit my tongue as the phrase slipped out. "Sorry." I laughed nervously. "I didn't mean it the way it might have come out." He chuckled as I thanked him and hung up.

Reading between the lines, I'd say Jason was a party boy. He was gregarious, fun loving, knew how to schmooze. His boss said he had to let him go because he was downsizing, but leaving a back door unsecured during an evacuation, being overly susceptible to catching the bourbon flu, and missing work had clearly factored in.

Bonnie thought her sister's love of the mystery genre might be behind her insinuation that the museum had been robbed during the evacuation. She must know the museum was up for sale. Maybe she was just trying to make her remaining time at work a little more exciting, by feeding me that story.

After my call to 4SiteSecurity, I considered my next move. According to Bonnie, Jason packed up and left his bill unpaid at the apartment where he had been living, but I didn't know if Jason still lived in the area or had really moved on. I checked the phonebook; he wasn't listed. Next, I googled the Haywood Court apartments. They were located on the east side of town.

As I sat there debating whether to continue my search for Jason or return another day, my phone rang. My heart skipped a beat.

"Hey, Donna. How are you doing? Everything okay?"

"Jorja. You're not going to believe this. Someone broke into my place. You know the key I found in my dad's jacket? It's gone."

THIRTY-ONE

I drove back to Calgary and stopped at Donna's to get an update. Someone broke into her place through the patio doors. It was obvious when she got home that someone had been in her home. Drawers were left partially open, clothing on closet shelves shifted.

She called the police, but not much could be done. Nothing of value was taken. But after the police left, Donna went upstairs to the spare bedroom, where her father's things still lay on the bed while she decided what to do with them and discovered that the key was gone.

I advised her to contact the major banks in the city, let them know that her father had passed away and she was searching for her father's banking records and will, which could be in a safety deposit box.

"You might want to tell them his place was broken into, and that the safety deposit key was stolen. Perhaps they'll apply more stringent due diligence to confirm the identity of whoever shows up with it...assuming someone does show up with it. Meanwhile, the banks should be able to tell you if your father banked with them."

It was already going on eight o'clock by the time I got home. Mike was enroute to Montreal. I caught him while he was waiting for his flight at the airport and gave him an update.

"Tell me I'm not making too much out of these connections I've found between Howard, Guy Palermo, Jeff Nickleson, and Milt Landen."

"You're definitely on to something," Mike replied. "If this object Palermo had in his possession is worth as much as you say it might be, it's motive enough to kill. Not just the owner, but anyone else who gets in the way."

"I still don't know who Howard was working for. Palermo's daughter didn't hire him, and neither did Nickleson's ex-wife. Makes me wonder if Howard figured out who took the statue and was going after it himself. Or maybe he and Jeff Nickleson were working together."

"You need to find this Milt Landen, talk to him."

"I left a message for him this morning, but whether he calls me back is another issue." This time I used my real name and number and said Palermo's daughter had asked me to track down a pre-Columbian jade jaguar that her father had owned.

"Well, if Landen's involved in its disappearance, you may have just put yourself in danger. Watch yourself."

"I will. I've found a PO box number for him, or rather for his company, Traders of the Lost Art, but everything else has been a dead end. If I don't hear back from him soon, I'm going to need some help to run him down."

"Do what you have to do. Donna and I are covering the costs. So, unless you're planning to fly down to look for him in South America, go for it."

"Thanks, Mike. I really need to get some boots on the ground to look for him while I follow up on some other leads. I've got someone in mind."

"I'd help if I could. This task force assignment couldn't have come at a worse time."

"Don't worry, I've got it. Speaking of help though, any way you can find out who the responding investigators were to Guy Palermo's death on the sixth of September?"

"I won't lie—that's going to be a tough one. I'm not working on anything for CPS right now. Poking around asking questions will come under scrutiny immediately."

"I know. I thought I'd ask anyway."

"Why do you want to know who investigated Palermo's death?"

I swallowed. Did I really want to open this can of worms? "A cop buddy of Nickleson's says he'd been obsessed with finding evidence, something concrete, to nail a cop he knows at CPS whom he thought was dirty. He told me Palermo's death wasn't a suicide."

"Oh man, Jorja, I don't like this."

"I know, I know. I still think Palermo's, Nickleson's, and Howard's deaths most likely have something to do with this yet-to-be-seen, possibly priceless artifact that's disappeared. But after hearing that Nickleson thought there was a dirty cop on the CPS payroll, it made me wonder why Palermo's death was ruled a suicide so quickly. Why didn't the cops care to investigate this pricey statue he supposedly owned that is missing. Like you said, if it's worth a couple million—that's plenty of motive for murder."

"Hindsight is everything. Didn't you say Palermo's own daughter didn't even know its worth. So how were the cops to know? I'm sure the ME has her reasons for listing it as a suicide. You know CPS has come under fire for numerous indiscretions as of late. You've heard the Chief of Police publicly declare that racism, bullying, exerting undue pressure, and of course anything illegal or that doesn't follow strict protocol won't be tolerated. I'm sure all ongoing cases are being scrutinized, even more so than before. They can't afford any worms in the woodwork."

"This worm has apparently managed to stay hidden for over three years." A sudden thought occurred to me. Could the cop Nickleson had been trying to prove was on the take, be his former partner from Winnipeg Police Services?

"Or maybe Nickleson was wrong."

I sighed. "Well, like I said, it's not my first premise."

"Promise me you're not going to start poking CPS."

"I can't do that. But...I can promise you I won't unless I've exhausted all other leads."

"God, you're stubborn."

"That's why you like me...we're like twins."

"You know, twins are often portrayed as good and evil, in the movies."

I laughed. "I suppose you think you'd be cast as the good one. Well, maybe that's true. Okay, I'll do my best to stay away from CPS...at least for now."

After disconnecting, I pondered my next move. Speaking to Milt Landen was top of my list. I'd also like a word with Milt's former security guard, Jason Gray. I needed to check the Drumheller News' archives for any mention of the fire or a theft at the Landen Museum.

I knew Nickleson's buddy, Eli Yardley, knew a lot more than he had revealed. Could Nickleson's old partner have also transferred to CPS a few years after him? It would explain why Eli refused to tell me more, and why Nickleson left CPS but was still obsessed with proving one of Calgary's finest was dirty. But I just promised Mike I wouldn't go there. A promise I was already regretting.

THIRTY-TWO

THE STARBUCKS WAS BUSIER than usual this morning, all the inside seats taken as well as those on their small patio. I decided to wait outside. Keeping one eye open for Sal, I focused the other on the patrons, hoping one of them would leave. Ten minutes later, I managed to snag a table inside. Still no Sal, but she wasn't exactly the most punctual person I knew. She'd blame it on transit, as she didn't own a car. Sadly, I suspected her consumption of alcohol might have more to do with it than transit schedules.

The door opened and a woman stepped in, pausing to survey the surroundings. She wore a tan trench coat that had seen better days. She had managed to miss the top button on the left side of her coat, and it ended up being hiked up to meet the right side. Several strands of grey hair escaped her plaid bucket hat. I raised my hand and waved.

Sal limped over and slid into the chair opposite me. "Hey, doll. Nice doo."

I reached up to touch my recently cut hair. "Thanks, Sal. You're looking good. Your knee still bothering you?"

"Doc says I need a new one." She shook her head. "Everyone wants to throw stuff away. I told him my knee might be a bit rusty, but it still works. It only hurts if I let it stiffen up. Gotta keep movin'."

Sal was a big recycler. She believed the planet was suffocating under all our garbage. I'd seen where she lived, and she might soon be suffocating under all the garbage she was trying to keep out of the landfill. She was edging toward hoarding.

"What can I get you, Sal?"

She peered at the chalkboard behind the counter while wrestling an arm out of her coat. The T-shirt she wore underneath was emblazoned with *A Good Planet is Hard to Find*. She turned back to me.

"You payin'?"

"Of course, Sal. Order whatever you like."

I met Sal when she signed up for my *So You Want to be a PI* course—a three-day course I had built to supplement my meagre income early in my career. It outlined what a PI's job entailed, what's necessary in terms of knowledge and skills, and the requirements for licensing. We spent one Saturday in the field, focusing on surveillance techniques. Sal was a natural. Her vagrant-like appearance discouraged people from paying her any attention or making eye contact for that matter.

"Get me one of those caramel macchiatos, doll. With extra whipped cream. In a mug, not one of those damn disposable cups. A couple of breakfast sandwiches, a slice of banana loaf, and...yeah, some kind of square, or a scone."

I got up and put in our order. I brought the food back to the table and went to pick up our drinks. Sal was shoving in the last of one of the breakfast sandwiches by the time I got back.

"So, this a social visit or you got something for me?" she said around a mouthful of her bacon, gouda, and egg sandwich.

I had used Sal a few times before to do surveillance for me or run a piece of information to ground. She always came through, although I suspected the techniques she used didn't always fall on this side of the law.

"A bit of both, Sal, but yeah, I have a job I think you'd be perfect for."

Sal took a sip of her macchiato, which left a line of whipped cream clinging to the fine hairs lining her upper lip. She unwrapped her second sandwich and looked up expectantly. I was going to mention the whipped cream, and then decided to wait until most of her drink was gone, figuring I would just have to repeat the process each time she took a sip.

"I need you to find someone for me. Might take a while. I mean, like a week or two."

"Longer is better than shorter." She winked at me. I suddenly felt like she was alluding to something else and shook off the image of Sal during coitus that immediately filled my mind.

"I don't have much to go on. A post office box number in a small town is all. You still have a valid driver's licence?"

"Sure. Renewed it a few months ago. Cost me fifty-two bucks."

I took a piece of paper out of my purse and slid it over to her.

"Beiseker? There's not much out there. Who does the box belong to, or is that what I'm supposed to find out?"

"It's the address for a company called Traders of the Lost Art. They buy and sell art and antiquities."

"Ha ha," she cackled. "Good one."

"I'm trying to find a guy named Milton Landen. Traders of the Lost Art is one of his companies."

"Art and antiquities, huh?"

"That's what his business card says. He also owns a little museum in Rosebud—the Landen Museum. But he's not involved in its day-to-day operation. I called the number on his business card, but he doesn't want to engage. I've left him a couple of messages, but he hasn't responded. I want to know more about an ancient jade statue that may factor in a few deaths. He might know something about that. But first I have to find him. Apparently, he's a recluse."

"Can't blame the guy. Being social is exhausting."

"You're going to have to figure out a way to not raise suspicion. Probably not many newcomers hanging around Beiseker."

"Leave it to me, doll. You got a vehicle for me, or will I be hitchhiking?"

"I'll rent you one. Probably best to go with a pickup."

• • • • • • • • • • •

After lunch, we drove to JumpIn Jalopies, where I leased all my vehicles. I asked for their most popular truck being leased in rural Alberta. Luckily, they had 2009 Dodge Ram available in their short-term rental fleet. Like all of JumpIn Jalopies' vehicles, it was mechanically sound but had some minor peripheral issue that, given the age of the vehicle, didn't warrant fixing.

Sal and I circled the truck for a closer look. It was a dull burgundy colour with a 4x4 drivetrain and an eight-foot truck bed with a homemade wooden toolbox mounted in back. It had an automatic transmission and came with a gun rack, but no air conditioning. The windshield wipers worked on one speed—super fast—and came on intermittently by themselves. I prayed she'd never use the strip of twelve LED strobe lights mounted on the cab roof.

Sal seemed pleased with it.

I gave her fifty dollars in cash and a preloaded credit card with six hundred on it and watched her drive away. She veered sharply as she exited the parking lot and almost took out a light post. Nineteen feet of burgundy aluminum grinded and lurched as it disappeared from view.

I now realized that instead of asking her if she had a valid driver's licence, I should have asked her if she still remembered how to drive.

I went back inside and bought the optional insurance package for $12.99 per day.

THIRTY-THREE

AFTER SAL DROVE OFF, I noticed I had a missed call from Luis. He hadn't left a message. I checked the clock. As curious as I was about the call, it didn't warrant me interrupting him at work.

By the time I got home, I had another missed call. This time he left a message. It was short notice, but did I want to meet him for a drink after work at Nathan's, a rooftop patio overlooking the Bow River?

As much as I just wanted to sit and mull over what I'd learned in the last two days, I really wanted to see him, too. I missed him. I had the decency to feel slightly ashamed of myself when I realized a part of me saw it as an opportunity to find out more about Jeff Nickleson. Luis might have known him. He had after all, been with CPS for several years before becoming a security guard. I pushed the feeling aside and sent Luis a text, in the affirmative.

I barely had time to jot down some notes and make two phone calls before I had to get ready to leave. I jumped in the shower, towel dried my hair, and pulled on a pair of distressed black jeans and topped it with an emerald-green sweater. I outlined my mouth with a peachy lipstick, added some eyeshadow and mascara, and locked up.

Nathan's was crowded as usual. After checking text messages to see if perhaps Luis beat me here and had already snagged us a table, but finding none, I wove my way though the crowd looking for signs that someone might be getting ready to leave. Twenty minutes later, I had a table for two in the back corner, next to the elevator, which most people didn't use. I sent Luis a text telling him where I was seated and ordered a glass of red wine.

Twenty minutes later, still no Luis. He hated being late, so I knew something must have come up at the last minute. I checked my phone...no message. I looked across the patio toward the river. The patio railing obscured all but the tops of the trees along the river, some already bare. The sun was already low on the horizon, and a server moved through the space, turning on the patio heaters.

A bearded man stood up from a table. My breath caught in my throat, until I realized it wasn't the same man I had seen at the museum. A minute later, I spotted Luis weaving his way through the tables toward me. I raised my hand in a little wave. He didn't see me, or if he did, he didn't return my smile.

A few women checked him out as he passed their table. My stomach lurched. How was it possible that this gorgeous man was interested in me? He arrived at our table, leaned over to kiss me on the cheek, and sat down.

"You're looking sombre," I said. "Tough day?"

The waiter appeared and took Luis' order for a Holy Grale beer and a plate of wings for us to share.

After he left, Luis reached across the table and squeezed my hand. "I'm glad you could make it tonight. Sorry I'm late."

"It's such a beautiful evening—I don't mind." I knew something had happened at work; I could sense it in his mood. He was trying to be present, but I could see in his eyes that he was somewhere else.

I told him about my trip out to Rosebud and Wayne—not all the details, of course, or even why I was out there. "Apparently the Rosedeer Hotel is haunted."

Luis laughed. "I don't understand why people are drawn to places like that."

"Maybe it's because they'd like to believe that we're not all alone in the universe, that there's something or someone out there."

"That's only comforting if that something or someone is benevolent."

"I suppose. Although if it wasn't benevolent, then why hasn't it destroyed us or taken us over by now. God knows we've provided reason enough."

Luis grinned and squinted one eye. "How do you know it hasn't taken us over."

We ordered dinner and chatted about all the crazy theories people believed in. I finally told him I was on the hunt for a cursed statue.

"Why would you want to *find* a cursed statue? Don't you already attract enough bad luck into your life."

I threw my napkin at him. "It's true—I attracted you."

I told him about Guy Palermo, his string of bad luck, and then his fall from a downtown office tower. "His daughter says the statue is missing. Considering its age and its possible checkered history, it could be worth millions."

"Is there a finder's fee?"

"No."

"Now why do you think that is?" Luis asked.

"For starters, his daughter doesn't know its potential worth. Sure, it could end up just being an old statue someone's Nona found hidden away in a basement. There's been a lot of weird stuff happening since Palermo died that makes me think the statue might be worth something or that it is somehow related to his death."

"I take it you're now thinking someone helped him off the top of that building."

"No. I mean, yes. What if it is worth millions? There is a lot about Palermo's death that doesn't add up."

"Like what?"

I swallowed. Here was the opening I was looking for.

"Well, for one, homicide showed up immediately even though the security guards at the building called it in as a suicide."

"So?"

"Then the security guard at the building was killed a week later, supposedly a hit-and-run."

Luis' eyes had grown hard.

"And a friend of Mike's, an ex-cop who was a private investigator, also died the same day the security guard did. Another so-called accident."

"You think one of them had the cursed object and that's why they died?"

"No." I sounded annoyed even to myself. "They didn't believe Palermo committed suicide." I had nothing to back up my statement, but I just wanted a chance to run the scenario past Luis, get his reaction. Now I was on shaky ground. "The security guard told his buddy, a cop in CPS, that he saw something that made him think Palermo didn't leave the building without help. You might have known him, the security guard. He used to work for CPS. His name was Jeff Nickleson."

Luis shook his head.

"Nickleson told his cop buddy that he knew of a dirty cop on the force. He was obsessed with finding enough hard evidence to nail this guy."

"Jorja." The disapproval was crystal clear in his voice.

My stomach tightened. "What? It wouldn't be the first time a cop was found to have interfered or withheld evidence in an investigation." I remembered the second newspaper article Nickleson dropped in my car that day at Glenmore Landing. "I was just reading about a case where charges were stayed against some drug dealers, because proper police procedures weren't followed."

"Really? I don't recall anything like that happening here in Calgary."

I looked away, then shook my head. "No, that didn't happen in Calgary. I'm just saying..."

"Stop. Look, Jorja, if you have something, take it to CPS through the proper channels. Don't sit here and essentially accuse one of our detectives of doing something illegal, or...what exactly are you saying?"

"What if he was there? What if this cop that Nickleson had info on, info that maybe implicates him in something...well illegal, was the cop that showed up at the building where Palermo died? I mean homicide detectives don't just usually just show up at accidents or suicides. Maybe Nickleson saw something, he wasn't supposed to see. Maybe that's why Nickleson was killed too."

Luis shook his head. "Do you have any idea how ridiculous this sounds."

I sat back and crossed my arms. Why did he have to take everything so seriously? Couldn't he tell I was just trying to bounce some possibilities around? I realised I was clenching my jaw. I reached for my drink and took a sip. "I wouldn't say it if I didn't think there was some truth to it."

"Then take that truth to the proper channels—don't use me."

"I'm not using you. I'm just telling you something."

"If there is any truth to what you're saying, can't you see how this could put me in a bad position? I'm not your go-between. Stop trying to drag me into your affairs." He sat back and threw his napkin on the table. "This is why..." His sentence dropped off. For me, it triggered months of pent-up frustration.

"This is why what? You don't want me hanging out with you at your cop events, or events with media presence. Worried that standing too close to me might tarnish your squeaky-clean, boy-scout image. Or is that just a façade as well?"

I was peeved. And yet, deep down, I was angry with myself. Why had I said anything? But something from my childhood kicked in. An uncontrollable urge to see someone lose their cool, because that would make me the winner. That's how it had always been between my father and me. It was the only way I felt in control of the situation—by making him lose control. But in the end, both of us lost.

"Well okay, if you don't want to know more about a potential dirty cop on your payroll. Makes me wonder why you're so eager to dismiss my views, yet you'll champion and defend them without question."

"That's enough, Jorja. If you have something concrete, bring it forward, otherwise don't be saying anything that you..." The waiter appeared. Luis' eyes were hard, his face taut, a small muscle jumped in his cheek.

Luis paid the bill, then stood up. Without waiting for me, he walked away. Tears stung my eyes.

THIRTY-FOUR

The office building was deadly quiet, the small café on the main floor not yet open. I trudged up the stairs to the second floor, the flickering hall lights unable to chase away the gloom. I hadn't slept at all last night.

I had followed Luis out of the restaurant last night. He had walked me to my car, but other than a curt goodnight, he didn't say a word. I hadn't, either. I had wanted to apologize, but I knew the minute I opened my mouth, it would unleash a tsunami of tears and a wave of incoherent blithering babble. I should have anyway.

The night spiralled; I drank half a bottle of scotch once I got home...and then was sick. I knew I had blown it with Luis, and it left me feeling empty, discombobulated. I went through the entire cycle of mourning as I thrashed my way through the night. First, disbelief that a few lousy comments could destroy an entire relationship, then denial that it was over.

Then I told myself I was overreacting, expecting the worst, like I always did. Luis would forgive me; he just needed time to cool off. Then anger. Anger, as I remembered all the times he hadn't been there for me, his dismissal of my work, the way he would drift away or ignore me in the presence of anyone he deemed important to his career, his image. His withdrawal of affection as an attempt to control me, what I said, what I did.

Then as the deepest darkness of night gave way to growing light, the reality of my loss hit me. Even though a part of me had always known our relationship was destined to end, I didn't want it to end now...or maybe ever, for that matter. I almost called him at four in the morning. To tell him I was sorry, that it was all my fault. But something held me back. Maybe I just couldn't accept that we were breaking up, for surely that's what was coming. Maybe if I avoided ever talking to him again, it wouldn't become official, a reality.

A foggy despair settled over me, broken by flashes of painful clarity. I was mortified. My frustration with the case and my inability to find anything concrete that would provide answers to Donna, to Mike, to Jeff's wife had dissolved into a childish bid for information. And when I didn't get my way, something triggered in me, the tactics I had used as a child came roaring out, and out of my mouth flew something just one level up from schoolyard taunting.

My face was burning in humiliation as I unlocked the office door, turned on the lights, and settled myself behind the desk in the interior office. I opened my laptop, desperate for the distraction of the case. I couldn't let one lousy night distract me from the task at hand. People had died, and their loved ones deserved an answer. Somehow, telling myself that didn't make it one bit better.

I stared at the notes in my file. I added some bits of information I had gleaned in the last few days. Was it only forty-eight hours? My trip to Rosebud and Wayne seemed so long ago.

Had Palermo taken his jade statue to Milt Landen? Had Landen recognized the statue as one of the Vanderburg Jaguars but lied to Palermo, saying it wasn't worth much? What about the jade statue he had intended to display at his museum? Surely, he couldn't have been planning to display Palermo's statue, claiming it was one found by his grandfather, decades ago. Pretty ballsy move if that were the case.

My mind drifted back to Eli's story. Nickleson must have spotted or noticed something to make him think Palermo had been killed. Why else would Eli have said, "Guy Palermo's death wasn't a suicide." Nickleson must have told him more.

Was the cop Nickleson thought might be on the take one of the investigators that night? It's the scenario I presented to Luis last night. Was the cop his former partner? It would make sense in terms of him leaving the force and not making a formal complaint. He told Eli he had learned his lesson in Winnipeg and wasn't eager to make the same mistake. But he couldn't let it go. Eli said Jeff Nickleson was obsessed with finding evidence to prove the guy was dirty.

I rubbed the back of my neck. Luis was right—I had nothing concrete. And if Eli knew more, he wasn't going to share it with me, or anyone else. Maybe he didn't have anything concrete either, just hearsay from Nickleson, and he was smart enough to keep his mouth shut. Unlike someone I could mention.

All the bits of information, conversations, facts and figures fed to me by Dr. Garret, supplemented by my research on the internet, swirled around in my head. I couldn't seem to grab onto anything long enough to even figure out how it all fit in—or if it even did.

My phone shook me from my reverie. I didn't recognize the number. I felt a stab of nervous excitement as I answered.

"Jorja Knight here."

"Ms. Knight," snarled a raspy voice. "I'm returning your call."

He didn't have to tell me who it was. "Mr. Landen. Thanks for calling me back."

"I want you to stop calling me. I'll give you five minutes. What do you want?"

"I'm investigating the death of a friend of mine, Howard Bergman. I believe he was looking into the death of Guy Palermo. Last year, Palermo acquired a pre-Columbian jade statue. His friend, a professor of archaeology, thought it might be one of the Vanderburg Jaguars found by Friedrich Vanderburg in the 1800s. The statues were rumoured to have ended up in Hitler's possession but weren't among his possessions at the end of the war. The professor gave Guy Palermo your name and phone number, as he thought that with your expertise in pre-Columbian art, you might be able to assess the likelihood of Palermo's find being one of the Vanderburg Jaguars."

I paused, hoping he would jump into the conversation.

"Four minutes left."

"After Guy Palermo died, it was discovered that the jaguar was not among his possessions. His daughter contacted me to try find out what happened to it. She believes that my friend, Howard Bergman, was looking into her father's death, which may not have been a suicide. I found your name and number noted in Howard Bergman's appointment book, not once but twice. I want to know if Howard Bergman contacted you. I'd also like to know if Guy Palermo contacted you about the statue." I remembered my blunder with Luis last night and added, "You're my last hope at finding this statue, Mr. Landen. Palermo's daughter has suffered enough loss. I'd like to see her at least recover the statue that so…intrigued her father."

"I can't help you. I don't know where the statue is."

"Did you see it? Did Palermo show it to you?"

After a long pause he spoke. "Yes, I saw the statue."

My heart beat faster. "And?"

"I gave him my honest opinion. The statue was a fake."

My heart sank. "You're sure?"

"I'm sure it's my opinion," he snapped.

"Did...uh...you run tests on it?"

"What kind of dumbass question is that? It's a fake. A good fake, but a fake, nevertheless. That's what I told Palermo when I gave it back to him, and that's what I'm telling you."

"Okay. Thank you. What about Howard Bergman?"

"What about him?"

"Did you ever talk to him?"

"I never met Bergman. He phoned a couple times, pestering me, like you are now."

"What did he want?"

"What else? He wanted to know where the statue was."

"Wait a minute, didn't you say you gave it back to Palermo?"

"My patience is wearing thin, Ms. Knight. That's exactly what I said. Seems the statue went missing. I gathered Palermo hired Bergman to find it."

"Wait, let me get this straight. Are you saying the statue went missing after you returned it to Palermo? That it went missing or was stolen before Palermo died?"

"What? You figure Palermo hired Bergman *after* he took a swan dive off a forty-two-storey building? You're wasting valuable time here, Ms. Knight."

"No...no, of course not." This changed things. Or did it?

"Do you remember when you returned it to him?"

"Mid-August. One minute, Ms. Knight."

"I was out at your museum a few days ago. I noticed an empty case there. The brochure said it was to hold a rare jade jaguar, thought to be one of a pair made for a tribal chief or king, around one thousand B.C. Perhaps from the Lost City of the Monkey God."

"Do you have a question, Ms. Knight, or are we done?"

"Was that case built for Palermo's jaguar?"

"My initial inclination is to grace your rudeness with an answer to mind your own business, but I understand a friend has died and you feel obligated to look into the matter. You might not have noticed it yet, Ms. Knight, but I don't care for people. Perhaps it's why I've chosen to deal with fossils, ancient objects, art."

He sighed.

I could hear the exasperation in his voice as he continued, "Palermo wanted me to sell the statue for him. If I were to do that, I told him it would be best if we put it on display for a few months, get some publicity going around it. The case was built while I ran my diagnostics. I concluded the statue was a fake. There are a lot of fakes out there, Ms. Knight. Selling stolen, looted, or fake antiquities is a six-billion-dollar annual business. I have a reputation to maintain. I cancelled plans for the display and gave Mr. Palermo back his statue. It was too late to reprint the fall brochure."

"While I was out at your museum, I noticed the recent grass fire. I hear it was deliberately set."

"I'll repeat myself. I don't particularly care for people."

"One of the security guys who used to work at your museum no longer works there. He no longer works for 4SiteSecurity, the company who employed him. Would you happen to know why?"

"That's a question his former employer needs to answer, not me."

"There are rumours that he didn't secure the museum properly the day of the grassfire. That several items were stolen from the museum."

"Time's up, Ms. Knight. Goodbye."

THIRTY-FIVE

This morning I woke with the last conversation I had with Luis still running through my head. I showered, got dressed, and stared into the bathroom mirror.

"You are a strong, intelligent woman. You have value. You are loved," I announced to the woman in the mirror as I stared into her eyes. Her eyes blurred with tears. I ran a comb through my hair then fluffed it back up with my fingers. I looked like hell. Good thing I wasn't seeing anyone today.

Thoughts of Howard's death and the darn statue kept interrupting my attempt to meditate. My phone rang, pulling me away from my mental chaos. I looked down at the screen. *Crap.* I had forgotten all about Sal.

"Hey, Sal. How are you doing?"

"Great, doll. Just great. I found 'em."

"That's great." I forced some enthusiasm into my voice. "I don't know how you do it."

"Piece of cake."

"Where are you?'

"Got my eye on the place now. 'bout fifteen clicks southeast of Beiseker. Wait till you see the place. I thought it was a damn hotel. There's pyramids everywhere."

"Pyramids?"

"Yeah. There's four of them on the front lawn. One of them's gotta be twenty feet high. There's a bunch more on the roof of the house, which is the size of the Smithsonian. There's even a few out back by the helipad."

"A helipad? I heard the antiquity business is lucrative, but wow. I wonder what's with the pyramids?"

"Landen's mansion is on top of a hill, the highest hill around for miles. The locals tell me the hill is some kind of energy vortex. The pyramids are a focal point for this energy, a healing energy. Maybe there's something to it. Maybe it's what pulled me here, and my knee hasn't felt this good in years." Her cackle ended in a fit of coughing.

Milt Landen might be a rich eccentric with unorthodox beliefs, but he hadn't given me any reason to keep tabs on him. He admitted to evaluating Palermo's statue and claimed he gave it back in August and that it was later stolen. He also said Palermo had hired Howard to try and find it. Maybe Palermo had offered Howard a large reward. Maybe that was what Howard was referring to when he told Donna that he was going to make sure she didn't want for anything. I was going to have to cut Sal's surveillance short. I re-engaged. She was still talking.

"It's all mumble jumble to me. And there's other weird stuff going on that makes no bloody sense."

"Weird like what, Sal?"

"Vehicles arriving in the middle of the night. This morning, they hauled in an excavator."

"Interesting."

"Makes you wonder, doesn't it? Looks like they're getting ready to dig a huge hole. Want me to stay on him?"

I had already talked to Landen, but I still needed to get my shit together and figure out what I wanted to do about this whole mess I had uncovered.

"Yeah, Sal. Maybe just one more day. It might be useful to know where he goes, assuming he leaves the place, or who comes to see him. Let's touch base tomorrow."

"Wilco, good buddy, over and out."

I'd try to catch up with Mike later, but first I had to figure out what I would tell him. I didn't really expect Sal to come up with much, and I might have to swallow the cost of having her out there for an extra day, but I was fine with that. Sal loved surveillance; she loved digging into people's lives, including their garbage. She was a natural nosy parker with a porcupine personality that cleared the way for her intrusion into their personal lives. Besides, I needed the extra day to come up with plan B—or was it plan C? Or conclude that this investigation was over.

I skipped breakfast, figuring I'd pick up something to eat along with my venti coffee at Starbucks, and headed downstairs. I thumped the hood of my Taurus and a cat shot out from under the car. Throwing my bag onto the passenger seat, I climbed in.

I felt kind of bad. If the cats were seeking out my car for its fish odour, they might be hungry. I had talked myself out of bringing food down to the garage—knowing it would also attract mice, magpies, and maybe even a coyote or two. There were other options though. Maybe I should be setting a trap and taking the poor things to a feline adoption centre. I gave the horn a light tap and when no other felines popped out, turned on the ignition.

By the time I got to the office, I was feeling better. Eating helped and so had the coffee. I settled behind my desk and checked my phone. Of course, there was nothing from Luis. The ball was in my court, and I was afraid to make a move. There was, however, a voice mail from Donna.

She'd left a message saying Howard's safety deposit box had been located and she would be checking out the contents this morning. I was hoping for a thumb drive with all his computer files, but having spent hours sorting through Howard's handwritten notes, pages of printouts, and annotated news clippings, I wasn't really expecting there to be one.

A sharp pain shot through my head. I might as well face it, unless Donna found something noteworthy in Howard's safety deposit box, I might be at a dead end.

My mind spiralled into a dizzying stew of people and places, dates and timelines, facts and speculations, until I was interrupted by my phone ringing. It was Donna again. I looked at my watch, shocked to see two hours had passed.

"Hi, Donna. Have you been to the bank?"

"There's a thumb drive," she said by way of greeting.

We arranged to meet. I locked up the office and rushed back to where I had parked my car. Why was I feeling like the worst was yet to come?

THIRTY-SIX

Donna inserted the tiiumb drive she had recovered from her father's safety deposit box into the port on her laptop and angled it so we could both see the screen.

"I don't know what I'm looking at. Must be from one of my father's cases, something important enough for him to store in a safety deposit box."

"Was this all that was in the safety deposit box?"

"Well, no. There was this…" She got up and retrieved a cylindrical object from the kitchen counter and handed it to me.

I turned the black object around and squinted at the markings. "I know what this is. It's a gun magazine for a 9mm gun." I looked up at Donna. "Did your father carry a gun?"

Frown lines appeared on her forehead. "I don't know. I suppose he might have."

I laid the magazine down on the table. There had been no signs of a gun, no holster, no ammo at Howard's apartment. No weapon had been found on his body.

"Could it have been stolen?" asked Donna.

"I have no idea. Might be worth mentioning to the police. They could check to see if he had a gun registered. Let's hope the thumb drive tells us what he was working on."

Donna turned back to her computer and opened the file. "There's not much there. I watched it earlier."

A grainy video started to play. It showed a building lobby. A threesome crossed the lobby floor. An older man came into view and headed to the bank of elevators barely visible on the screen's right and entered an elevator, along with several others. The video clip stopped.

The next video clip was dark, making any object almost indiscernible. We watched as a shaft of light penetrated the darkness; a figure came through the door. The backlight from the open door made any features obscure. The figure looked over his shoulder and ran forward, disappearing off the screen. I noted the timestamp at the top of the screen: 07-09 10:18 p.m.

Now I noticed the video was of a screen, not a direct feed from the camera capturing the images. A blur as someone moved from behind a structure. The face was turned away from the camera, but this time I could see the hair was dark. The figure darted forward. A dark coat shrouded details of the figure's build, but I got the impression it was a man. Something about the way it moved.

Donna and I watched, mesmerized. There was a distinct break in the video and the next image showed a man walking through a lobby. He was wearing a black car coat and had short dark hair. The video was too grainy to see much of his facial features. My eyes flitted to the top of the screen—the timestamp said 10:24. He disappeared from view.

The next video images showed a police officer in uniform entering the lobby. Time on the video was 10:31. The man we saw earlier, the one wearing a black car coat, entered the screen behind the police officer. The video ended.

"What does it mean?" asked Donna.

"I don't know…" But I think I did know. I looked at the time stamp. The clips were taken the day Guy Palermo died. I was betting they were from the Ventura Tower, where Palermo plunged to his death. Which meant we just saw Guy Palermo seconds before he jumped. And there was a second figure there, one who was partially hidden by some kind of structure on the roof.

Donna and I watched the video file again.

"You think this has anything to do with my father's death?"

"It might. I've always wondered if there could be a connection between his death and Guy Palermo, the man who fell to his death at the Ventura Tower downtown. Yesterday, I contacted an antiquity dealer, whose name your father had in his appointment book. He told me your father had been hired by this Guy Palermo to find a rare pre-Columbian artifact that had been stolen from him—before he died."

Donna gasped. "Oh my god, Jorja." Her hand flew to her mouth. "If my father was looking for this artifact, then maybe he was getting close to whoever stole it. My father really was murdered, wasn't he?" She turned; her eyes focused on me with unwavering attention.

"The fact that this video was in Howard's possession makes me more certain of it, Donna. Or at least that someone caused his death. This video is the most concrete evidence we have. I just need to figure out what it means, what it proves."

I left Donna's house with the thumb drive tucked away in the front pocket of my jeans. My head was buzzing. I needed to find a safe place to keep the thumb drive. I surveyed the street. Nothing caught my eye, but I felt someone watching me. I jumped into the Taurus and tapped the horn.

Several things struck me as odd. The first was that there might have been a second figure on what I assumed was the roof of a building. Just a blur, but enough to raise the idea in my mind. The second thing that struck me as odd was the dark figure's behaviour on the roof. If it was Palermo...well, who runs to their suicide?

So, who knew about the jade statue? Someone who didn't know Landen had declared the statue to be a fake could have stolen it believing it was worth millions. The list was short: Palermo's daughter, Dr. Garret, Milt Landen. Or at least these were the three who admitted to knowing it existed. Palermo's daughter seemed genuinely shocked when I told her the statue could be valuable. And considering she was using the proceeds of the sale of her father's possession to pay off his debt, I hardly think she would have killed him for the privilege of doing so.

Could Palermo have shown it to someone else? There was the newspaper reporter who interviewed him, but she provided no details on the statue other than to say it was pre-Columbian and that Palermo thought it was cursed. It would be a big leap for someone to have read the article and assume it was the Vanderburg Jaguar or something that could be worth millions. There could easily be others though. People who worked with or for Landen. Maybe even Jeff Nickleson. He worked in the building. Maybe he knew Palermo and they got to chatting. Palermo could have told him about the statue before he found out its real worth.

I reached the office and thanked the universe for guiding my car here while my brain was fully occupied with Howard's case. For the first time since I started looking into Howard's death, things were coming together. I was once again pursuing my favourite premise, that Guy Palermo, Jeff Nickleson, and Howard had all been brought together by a cursed statue, and all of them had died as a result.

THIRTY-SEVEN

I DASHED OFF A quick email to Mike and attached a copy of the video file Donna found in her father's safety deposit box. I also sent myself a copy, which would now be stored in the cloud. Then I watched the video seven more times, which didn't leave me much wiser.

I made a mental list of what I needed to do next. First, I would visit the Ventura Tower to see if the lobby I was seeing in the video matched. While I was there, I'd stop at the security desk and ask if anyone who was working the night Palermo died would be willing to talk to me. Then I needed to ID the people in the video.

One of the men in the video wore a police uniform and although the other man was dressed in street clothes, I couldn't help but wonder if this could be the dirty cop Nickleson had been obsessed with. If I could confirm the video was of the Ventura lobby, I would reach out to Nickleson's ex-wife, or his friend Eli, to see if they could ID any of the men seen there.

I locked up the thumb drive in the small built-in safe in my office and then headed downstairs. The wind caught my hair as soon as I stepped outside, and I pulled up the collar of my jacket. The blue skies and sunshine had led me into thinking it was warm outside, but the cool breeze reminded me that snow was right around the corner.

I headed east until I reached Fourth Street, then turned and made my way through the underpass that connected my side of the tracks with the downtown corridor. Twice I turned, sensing someone following me, but each time it turned out to be just another pedestrian.

The Ventura Tower was one of Calgary's newer high-rises. The bottom twelve floors were dedicated to offices and commercial space and the upper thirty floors to condominiums. The work-life model appealed to some, but I preferred some space between the two. Perhaps because my office was a dive. It did, however, get me out of my pyjamas and offered up the illusion that I had somewhere important to be.

I entered the Ventura Plaza, just a concrete space punctuated by benches and large polyethylene tubs made to look like stone, filled with shrubs and flowers. I entered the lobby through one of the three sets of revolving doors and made my way to one of several long leather benches that stood against the lobby's towering windows. I sat and surveyed the space.

This was definitely the lobby in the video. I felt my heart start to race. I pulled out my phone and snapped a few quick photos.

A security desk stood across from me, the expanse of marble floor in between gleaming in the sun. To the left of the security desk, a set of turnstiles led to a bank of elevators. To the left of the elevator bank, there was a concierge desk for the residents of the condos.

I glanced to my right. A small café with several tables outside its door anchored the opposite wall. Next to the café, a large poster advertised units still available in the building for lease or purchase.

Now I wondered if Palermo not only worked in the tower, but maybe lived here, too.

I made a plan, put away my phone, and sauntered over to the concierge desk.

"Hello. I was supposed to meet Guy Palermo here in the lobby. But he's not shown up. Is there anyway you can call up and let him know I'm here? My name is Anne Beddingfeld."

She looked down at her computer screen, punched in a few letters, and frowned. "How do you spell that?"

I spelled out Palermo, already suspecting what the answer would be.

"Sorry, I don't have anyone listed like that."

"Oh. I must have gotten it wrong. I assumed he lived here but maybe he works in the tower." I looked around. "I guess I'll check with security."

I could feel her eyes on my back as I walked away. Several people stood at the security desk, and I waited my turn. Finally, a young woman motioned me forward.

"Oh hi!" I flashed her my biggest smile. "I'm wondering if Jeff Nickleson is in today. I'm his cousin. I just came in today and I'm staying down the street at the Westin. I want to surprise him; he doesn't know I'm here. If it's not too much trouble, I'd love a minute with him." I clasped my hands in front of me and mouthed "please, please," while trying to make those puppy eyes Mike always accused me of making when I wanted him to do something for me. Usually something that might be frowned upon by my cop boyfriend.

She looked around frantically. "A cousin?"

"First cousin once removed. I'm a tour guide with Sunward Adventures. I've just come back from a six-week tour of South America. Even though it was my third time, I was still blown away."

She leaned forward. "You haven't heard, then?"

I wiped the smile off my face and grew serious. "Heard what? Has something happened?"

"Oh my." She looked around again. "Wait just a moment, please."

I watched her walk back to talk to an older grey-haired man with a protruding gut. After a few words, they both turned to look at me. It wasn't hard to look worried, because if this didn't work, I'd be back to square one.

Finally, she came around the side of the desk. "Let's go sit over there," she motioned to one of the leather benches on the opposite side of the lobby. "I'm afraid I have some rather bad news."

I followed dutifully. "Bad news? What is it?"

She motioned me to sit. "I don't know how to tell you this...I've never had to tell someone. I'm sorry." She took a huge breath. "I'm just going to say it. I'm afraid your cousin died."

"What? No. That can't be." I shook my head and thought about poor Mr. Whiskers, a dear old cat I had as a child, who died. Tears filled my eyes. "What happened? I can't believe this. When? How..."

She leaned forward and put a hand on my arm. "I'm sorry. It happened about two weeks ago. It was a hit-and-run accident."

"Here? In front of the building?" My eyes widened and I swivelled my head to look out onto the street.

"No, thank god. We've had enough...I mean...I didn't...no, he died near the Glenmore Reservoir—that's in southwest Calgary. About five kilometres from here. Sorry. I just...we had a man die here in front of the building a few days before Jeff was killed." She shuddered.

"Oh gosh." I clapped my hand over my mouth. "Were you working that night? Was Jeff?"

She nodded. "We were both on duty that night. It was awful. The poor man...threw himself off the building."

"Oh god." I turned my head away in mock horror for a second. "Has...did your company provide you and Jeff with any counselling? I mean, to see something like that..." I let my words taper off.

"No." She glanced back at the grey-haired man who was watching us. "They should have. Jeff was pretty shaken up about it. I'm still having nightmares."

"Do you think it might have caused Jeff to...you know."

"Oh no. His death was an accident. Several witnesses saw Jeff run into the street and then a car hit him."

I pulled out a Kleenex and dabbed at the corner of my eye. "I can't believe it. Poor Jeff. It wasn't like him to not pay attention. I wonder if his mind could have been elsewhere. You say this man died just a few days beforehand. Did Jeff know him?"

"We both did. Well, we recognized him when we saw him. Hard to believe."

"I guess we never really know what's going on inside a person. I wonder if Jeff took it hard because it brought back memories or flashbacks. You know he used to be a police officer."

"Yes. I could see it bothered him a lot. Jeff kept looking at the video feed from our security system. I told him he had to quit doing it—that it would just make it worse. But being a former cop, I guess he couldn't help himself."

"Did he think there was anything wrong with the video, that it might have been altered in someway?"

"I don't know. One of the police officers sat in the back room and watched the CCTV video files from the whole day. They didn't notice anything out of the ordinary. At least, I don't think so." She looked back at the desk. The grey-haired man motioned to her with his head.

"Sorry, I've got to go. My boss is a bit of an ogre."

I stood up as she did. "I guess somebody called 911 that night?"

"Yes, I did. We heard people scream outside. Jeff ran outside to see what was going on. He ran back and told me to call 911." She swallowed. "A cop from homicide arrived first, and then several police cars."

We were at the desk now, her boss positively glowering.

I wiped away a fake tear for his benefit. "Thank you so much for telling me. I'll have to give his ex-wife a call with my condolences. Thank you again. This wasn't easy for either of us."

She nodded and walked back to her post behind the desk.

I walked out of the building, certain her boss was making sure I left the building for good and wouldn't be bothering his staff. It's possible the time gaps on the video meant nothing. Perhaps the whole point of the video was to show that the dark-haired man in street clothes, who entered the lobby with the uniformed police officer, was also seen in the lobby seven whole minutes earlier.

THIRTY-EIGHT

THE MIND IS AN amazing thing. Mine had a habit of shooting away from the present and conjuring up either a disastrous future or rewriting the past. By the time I reached my office, I had already concocted a scenario where the man in the car coat, seen in the lobby of the Ventura Tower first at 10:24 and then again entering with a constable at 10:31, was the homicide detective that the security guard mentioned to me. Furthermore, that this homicide detective was the dirty cop Jeff Nickleson had told his friend Eli about.

As soon as I was back in the office, I sat down at my computer to look at the video file for the umpteenth time. I noticed that the first time the man entered the video he came from the left side of the security desk. He would have been coming from the bank of elevators. The second time he was seen, he appeared to have entered the lobby from the main doors.

Usually, 911 calls are dispatched to street patrol, and they would be the ones who called in homicide if anything looked out of place. Of course, there could be a half-dozen good reasons a homicide cop could show up at the scene first. Assuming the man in the dark coat that I was fixated on was even from homicide. He could merely be a witness. Maybe he just came down to the lobby and had seen something while getting onto the elevator. Could he have seen someone go up to the roof? Even if it turned out that he was a homicide cop, he could have been in the building because he lived in one of the condos or was there on other business.

My earlier excitement began to drain away as I came down off my imaginative high. What was I thinking? That a homicide cop had killed Palermo? Why? To steal a statue? How or why would he have even known about it? Besides, Landen had told me the statue had been stolen weeks before Palermo's death. Otherwise, why would Howard have been calling Landen, pestering him for information?

I watched the video clips again. Definitely a second person on the roof. A killer? Or a witness? I wondered if there was other CCTV video that would provide a clearer view. I stared hard at my computer screen. The video clips I was looking at were captured off a device, not the actual video data itself. How did Howard get this? An obvious answer was that Jeff Nickleson had given Howard the video clips, but now I wasn't sure.

Nickleson's co-worker said he watched the video footage from that night over and over. If he thought something was wrong, why hadn't he said so? And if he didn't think whatever he was seeing on the video was enough to bring up to the police formally—why was I barking up that tree?

I rubbed my forehead. Now I wasn't sure of anything. Except that it was getting late, and I hadn't eaten all day. I called Eli and left him a message, saying I had found something I wanted to share with him, something that might be related to Jeff's death. Then I called Jeff's ex-wife and left her a similar message.

I suddenly sat up and looked at my watch. It was already six-forty. I told Sal I'd touch base today. No point in her sitting in the countryside somewhere watching Landen's mansion.

My call to Sal went immediately to voice mail. Even though she had finally broken down and bought herself a smart phone, she often turned it off at night and forgot to turn it on in the morning. I told her she could just mute the darn thing, but Sal was Sal. I left her a message to call. Then I packed up and headed home.

I was steps from my car when I noticed it. A black SUV, with its motor running, sitting across the street from the small parking lot where my car sat. This wasn't just a black SUV—it was the same one that I had seen on several other occasions. I reached my car, paused with my hand on the door and stared over my shoulder at the SUV. Getting into my car, I shivered. Whoever was following me wasn't bad at surveillance—they *wanted* me to know I had a tail.

THIRTY-NINE

Evening found me at home, pouring out my worries to Jack Daniel's. I still hadn't heard from Sal, and I was getting worried. If I didn't hear from her by morning, I was going to have to look for her. Now I was questioning everything, for the umpteenth time. Someone was out there still looking for something. It had to be the statue. *Or the video file.*

I cursed and poured myself another two fingers, telling myself this would be the last. Or maybe I should keep drinking until I passed out—at least that would end the circus in my head. All the questions I had been asking myself remained unanswered.

I switched gears. What did I have to do to wrap up this case and get whoever was following me to go away? I had to make it clear to someone that I was no longer interested in pursuing answers to whatever the hell this was. That might not happen if I had to go looking for Sal. *Maybe she found something that would provide some answers.* I shook off the thought.

Mike called at ten. Which meant he was up late. He had watched the video I had sent him.

"You don't recognize any of the guys in the video, do you?"

"Afraid not."

"Have you been able to find out who the officers were who showed up at Palermo's suicide?"

Mike sighed. "The ME was called out by the patrol officers, but she wouldn't give me the constables' names."

"Oh. So, she wasn't called out by homicide. Is that normal?"

"Yeah. She usually attends to suicides, although most not as spectacular as this one. But after speaking to the cops on scene, witnesses who saw him falling, and the security guards inside who called 911, she had no reason to believe it was anything but a suicide. Later, after confirming the victim's identity and learning of the recent emotional and financial blows he suffered, it seemed to make even more sense."

"What about the video?"

"The door to the roof is alarmed. Unfortunately, it had been going off several times a day all that week. When the security personnel went up to check, they found the doors locked. They filed a report and were waiting on someone to repair the system, so when the alarm went off for the second time the day Palermo jumped, they weren't concerned."

"Someone could have been tampering with the door all week, for this very reason."

"Or," said Mike, "the exit door alarm was simply faulty. Not everything is a sign that an evildoer is at work."

"Okay but listen. I've been giving this a lot of thought. Why would Palermo hire a detective to try to find the statue if he had already been told it was a fake? I realized that when I talked to Landen, I was the one who told him that Howard was a detective, that he was dead, that I had found his name in Howard's appointment book, and that I thought Howard might be looking for this cursed statue of Palermo's. What if Landen lied to me? What if the statue is worth millions? I only have his word that he returned it to Palermo. What if Palermo did hire Howard, but it was to try and get his statue back from Milt Landen?"

"I can see where you're going with this, but if Palermo believed the statue was worth a lot of money, cursed or not, why hire a detective? Why not go to the police and report it stolen?"

"Maybe there is something bigger going on. Maybe Landen is dealing in stolen goods and Palermo somehow found out. Maybe that's how it ties to Jeff Nickleson, and Jeff noticed this dirty cop at the building the night Palermo died. Maybe Landen is paying off a cop to look the other way."

"Jorja, that's really stretching it. I wouldn't be uttering the word 'dirty cop' unless I was darn sure of my facts."

That was the second time I had been told to be careful about implicating the police without concrete proof, by two different men in my life, both, of course, with ties to policing, but still.

"Okay, okay. I know."

"When there's a rotten apple in the barrel, it sometimes takes years of complex undercover work to find the cop and enough evidence to make such allegations stick."

"I get it, Mike."

"So dead end?"

"It's starting to look that way. Depends on how much further you want me to go with this."

"Do we have anything definitive to go on? By that I mean, definitive enough to take to the police and have them open up an investigation?"

I did a mental inventory. Howard's apartment and car were broken into, stuff stolen, a police report filed. The ME found nothing suspicious. All I had was a piece of video but no one on the video was doing anything that looked illegal, and I didn't even know why or how it came to be in Howard's possession. *Time to drop it, Jorja.* The message was delivered to me by one of my inside voices. Intellectually, I understood, but my gut was telling me this was all wrong. After all, Donna's place had been broken into as well, Howard's safety deposit key stolen. And someone had been tailing me since I started this case.

"Dead end, I guess," I said reluctantly. "I have a few things to tie up and I guess we can tell Donna I couldn't find anything that would counter the idea that he slipped, fell, hit his head, and drowned. Even if someone had been chasing him, it doesn't exactly make his pursuer a murderer."

After our call, I poured myself yet another drink. The little critic that lives in my head was now questioning if I was even cut out for this kind of work. I carried my drink back to the couch and sat down, curling my legs in under me.

What did this mean with respect to Jeff Nickleson's death and what Eli told me? Maybe this cop who was Nickleson's nemesis *had* shown up at the office building. I heard Luis' voice in my head. *"So what?"*

So what, indeed. I had already thought of three or four perfectly innocent reasons for him being at the scene. But there was so much still unanswered. Howard told Donna to contact Mike if anything happened to him. Nickleson was calling his ex-wife to make sure she was engaging her home security at night. And what about Howard's neighbour seeing someone who looked like a cop entering Howard's apartment hours before Donna was even contacted about her father's death? His place was definitely broken into, his computer stolen, his files trashed, but they didn't get his appointment book. There had to be something in there he wanted to keep hidden.

I reminded myself not to hammer things together that I had no proof of. Howard might have seemed fearful because of a new case he had taken on. A case that brought him to the shores of the Glenmore Reservoir. It's possible he did slip, hit his head, and drown.

Could that new case have had something to do with Jeff Nickleson? Possibly. I had no proof of that, either. Or it may have simply been a coincidence that both men had been at or near the reservoir on the day they died.

I felt sick. I had hammered all these bits together when they could be entirely innocent and separate events and then essentially told Luis he had a dirty cop in his shop. I had messed up my relationship with Luis—because I was insecure and childish.

And stupid, the little voice in my head added.

I got up and got ready for bed. What I really needed to do was call Luis, apologize, and get my life back on track.

·····●··●····

The sun was already high in the eastern sky by the time I woke up. I swung my feet around and sat up, sending the room spinning for a second. At least I hadn't lain awake all night. I stood up and staggered into the bathroom. Did I call Luis last night? Oh god...I did, but it wasn't last night—it was early this morning.

I banged my head lightly against the mirror above the sink. *Think. Think.* It was all coming back to me. The conversation started off well enough—well, except it was a bit one sided. How long had I blithered on?

I remember apologizing. I do remember telling him I should have never made those comments about a dirty cop or hinted he might be somehow involved or covering it up. That I had absolutely no proof of anything I hinted at that night, and I was way out of line. That I said those things because I'm emotionally immature, frustrated with the case I was working on, and I really needed to work on keeping my frustration in check. I asked him to forgive me. My hand flew to my mouth. I watched my eyes in the mirror widen in horror.

And then I said, "I love you."

Shit shit, shit. I banged my head a little harder.

He hadn't said it back.

I tried to recall what he did say. I remember him saying something like *it's early* or *it's late*. That we should have this conversation some other time. *Damn.*

No going back now. Que será, será. I looked the woman in the mirror in the eye. *You idiot.*

FORTY

I HAD CALLED SAL a few times last night, but still hadn't heard back from her. Sal had a habit of going dark on me, when it suited her, and I had overlooked this little annoyance because she always came back with the goods. After trying her several more times this morning, I decided that if I was going to keep using her, I needed to let her know this was unacceptable. My most recent try was met with a recorded message telling me her voice mailbox was full. I had already sent her a couple of text messages and an email. Now I was getting seriously worried.

My plans for the day were simple. I needed to write up my report, tie up some loose ends, and get back to Donna to let her know I just couldn't catch a thread to pull that led to anything bigger or more concrete about her father's death.

I was about to leave for the office when Edith, Jeff Nickleson's ex-wife, returned my call. Edith was on my list of things to wrap up. I wanted to give her a quick update and let her know I hadn't found anything substantial about Jeff Nickleson's hit-and-run accident, either. I had almost forgotten I had called her to see if she could ID the man in the video. An insatiable curiosity took over.

"I'm at work, but you can swing by if you only need a minute," she said.

Edith worked at a women's clothing store in Britannia. It took me less than twenty minutes to get there. She was serving another customer when I arrived, so I browsed. I was fondling a knee-length herringbone poncho trimmed with a rich brown faux fur when she appeared at my side.

"That would look so good on you. It looks great with jeans and boots. Perfect weight for fall."

I checked the price tag. Did I have an extra one hundred and sixty dollars? But the vision of myself wearing it wouldn't go away. I made the mistake of trying it on. This insatiable curiosity of mine was going to cost me.

I followed Edith to the front counter and while she rang up my purchase, I pulled out my phone and opened the video file. While we waited for my credit card to go through, I handed her my phone. "Have a look at the guy who comes into view. He later comes back into view with a police officer, so there's a better shot of him the second time he appears."

I watched Edith as she viewed the video, frown lines forming between her eyes.

"Do you recognize him?"

She shook her head.

"Are you sure?"

"Not really. This video is quite grainy." She watched the video again. "No, I don't recognize him. Who is he?"

"That's what I'm trying to find out. I wondered if he might be a cop. Someone your ex-husband worked with."

Edith shook her head slowly. "No, sorry. I didn't know a lot of his cop buddies. Can't say I've ever seen this man."

"What about his old partner in Winnipeg? I met with Eli, and he told me about Jeff being ostracized after he reported his partner doing something that didn't meet scrutiny. Eli thought it was the impetus for your move here to Calgary."

Edith let out a loud sigh. "I don't know much about what happened. I do know Jeff never liked his partner from the get-go. I know I shouldn't have, but there are times I wondered if maybe Jeff was looking for something to pin on the guy."

"Do you remember his name?"

She looked off to her right, chewed on her bottom lip, and slowly shook her head. "I think...Ace. That's it...Ace. I'm sure it's a nickname, but that's all I remember. Eli might know."

"I already asked Eli, but he's not comfortable sharing that with me...you know, since he's still active."

"Yeah, the old bro code. I've got your back and you need to have mine."

I sort of got it. I mean, if you had to trust your life to someone, you'd want to trust them unconditionally.

I put my credit card and phone away, thanked Edith, and left with my new fall wrap.

I had hoped to talk to Eli, see if he could ID the man in the video, but since he hadn't yet returned my call, I was pretty sure I had seen the last of him.

· · • • • • · ·

As soon as I got to my office, I knew something was wrong.

Leaving the outer door open, I slid into the small reception area, where Gab used to work.

"Hello?" I called out.

The inner office, where I normally worked, remained dark, silent. The light switch to the inner office was located inside, to the left of the door.

I looked at the reception desk. Gab had left behind a small fake cactus. I picked up the pot. It wasn't heavy but might be a distraction if I needed to turn and run.

"Anybody here?" I took three steps forward and slid around the reception desk. I could now see into the inner office, and part of my wooden desk. Most of the office remained hidden behind the half-open door. I was positive I had closed the inner door when I left.

I slid closer to the door and, holding the cactus in a ready-to-throw position, nudged the door with my foot. It swung open. No screaming banshees, poltergeists, or bearded men appeared.

I reached in and flicked on the light switch. I pushed and the door swung open all the way, hitting the wall behind it. I peered in and, seeing no one, stepped inside and blew out a sigh of relief.

Everything was as I left it...or was it?

I surveyed the scene. My chart papers still hung on the wall. Stacks of Howard's papers lay on my desk and the small round table tucked up against the window in the back corner of the room. I opened the wall safe; the thumb drive still lay inside, along with an extra cartridge for my Walther BB gun and a copy of the office lease.

I took a deep breath and let it out in a whoosh. After locking the safe and closing the door to the hallway, I sat down at my desk. My eyes swept over the piles of papers on my desk.

The pages were no longer perfectly aligned. Someone had rifled through the piles of paper on my desk, I was sure of it.

FORTY-ONE

It was already late afternoon when I stopped kidding myself. Sal was in trouble. And if she wasn't, I was going to wring her neck. I had been to Sal's place once before but it took me a while to remember the way back.

I parked and walked back to the small run-down 1950s split-level that hadn't seen a lick of work done on it since it was built. I had no idea who lived in the house, all I knew was that Sal rented a room in the basement and had her own entrance in the back.

I followed a crumbing sidewalk around the side of the house and stopped. The yard was a mess. A rusted washing machine and a pile of lumber lay against a crumbling fence, which leaned precariously toward the neighbour's house, which didn't look all that different to this one. The knee-high weeds were punctuated by piles of discards, old tires, a stack of bricks, an old swing set. I searched along the back of the house and found a set of crumbling steps leading down into what I presumed would be the basement.

I found a wooden door at the base of the steps. It was pushed tight into the doorframe, but I could see it wasn't closed properly, let alone locked. I knocked and when no one answered, I shouldered the door open.

Pulling out my phone, I turned on the flashlight and shone it around the space. *Holy crap.* The yard was only the appetizer to the junk smorgasbord inside. I spotted a path between a wall of boxes stacked to the ceiling and a park bench loaded with bags on the other side. I slid past a row of old bicycles and squeezed by a ghostly white cylinder which looked to be a functioning water heater.

Moving aside a shopping cart pilfered from some grocery story and loaded with bags of who knows what, I crept forward, looking for the entrance to Sal's room. The air was musty, a stifling combination of wet cardboard, dust, and possibly sweat. I was in someone's basement, all right. I looked back over my shoulder, the door I had entered through no longer in sight. Inching forward, I spotted another wooden door.

Sal had told me the homeowner ran a home business repairing small appliances, but now I considered the possibility that Sal's recycling efforts had gotten out of hand. I picked my way through the last couple feet of junk and reached the door, this one locked. I knocked.

"Sal? Are you in there?"

Nothing. I heard something scurrying behind me and turned in time to see a squirrel beat a hasty retreat. At least, I hoped it was a squirrel.

I knocked louder. "Sal? It's Jorja. Open up."

A scurrying sound behind me made me eager to get out. I knocked once more and then picked my way through the stacks until I was back outside. I made my way around to the front. Two basement windows were half sunken into the dirt. I crouched by one to have a look. Something was stacked up against the glass. I walked over to the other one, but a few decades of grime didn't let me look inside. Whatever Sal was paying to live here was ten times too much. Actually, no one should live here.

I stood up and looked around. Now I realized I hadn't seen Sal's truck on the street, and that little beauty was hard to miss. I made my way back to my car, climbed in, and rolled down the window. The musty basement odour had followed me.

I glanced backward as I prepared to pull out of my spot and screamed. The cat hissed, barred its teeth, and took a swipe at me. I put the car in neutral and jumped out. A mangy orange thing shot out and disappeared under someone's car. I stood there with my hand over my thudding heart until my brain caught up. *Just a cat.*

My heart was still thundering against my chest as I climbed back into the car and pulled out into the street. I drove in ever-increasing circles around Sal's neighbourhood until I convinced myself the truck I'd rented for Sal was nowhere near. I told myself that it was a good thing. Maybe Sal had decided to overnight it in Beiseker or one of the small towns out that way. But my heart wasn't buying it.

Finally, I drove home, sick with the knowledge that something bad had happened to Sal. And it was my fault.

FORTY-TWO

AFTER A QUICK STOP for coffee and a breakfast sandwich, I pulled down my sunglasses and settled in for my drive out to Beiseker, less than an hour's drive away. I had assumed Sal would be spending her nights at home, but it didn't look like that was the case. I had cruised past her place once again this morning, but there was no sign of Sal or the truck. Finding her was my number one focus.

By the time I reached the Beiseker turnoff, the carbs and coffee had kicked in. I slowed to the requisite thirty kilometres per hour and drove down the main drag. The small shops and businesses lining the street and the angled street parking brought back memories of the small town in Ontario where I had grown up.

I drove past a café on my right and a no-name brand grocery story on my left. I circled a few more blocks, then pulled back onto the main street and stopped outside a small café. I got out and went inside.

Three of the ten tables were occupied. Four men sat in a back corner booth drinking coffee and discussing something which, by the tone of their voices and arm gestures, had left them agitated. A young woman approached with a menu in hand.

"Sorry, I'm not looking to be seated." I looked around. "I'm looking for a friend of mine, a woman. She's older, mid to late sixties, grey hair, walks with a slight limp. Have you seen anyone like that in the last few days?"

The woman shook her head.

I got the same response at the other restaurant in town. Of course, there were a half-dozen or more small towns all within twenty minutes of each other out here, so she could be buying coffee or eating at any one of them. Or, knowing how cheap Sal was, she might be buying food at a grocers' and making her own sandwiches and pocketing the rest of the per diem I paid her for expenses.

I tried a few shops, and this time I also asked for directions to Milton Landen's place. I told them I had lost the directions out to his place, but knew he had a huge house with several pyramids and a helipad in the back, about fifteen kilometres southeast of Beiseker. All it got me was strange looks. I found the town's administration centre and got lucky. The woman at the front desk didn't know who owned the house I was looking for but knew where it was.

With a rough description of how to get there, I climbed into the Taurus, checked for stray cats, and set off. I made one wrong turn, which took me into a riding stable, but after turning around and doubling back, found the railway tracks the woman had mentioned. I followed the road running parallel to the tracks until I came to a set of mailboxes at a T-intersection and turned south.

I passed a string of large homes, set well back on their acreages. It was peaceful out here, the rolling hills now golden brown, the small stands of trees here and there breaking the monotony of prairie farmland. I rounded a corner and the sun glinting off something blinded me. I slowed to gawk at a monstrous building, which stood on top of a knoll. Even though the house was set far off the main road, I could see Sal hadn't been exaggerating. The place was like a castle, except this one was modern looking.

I checked for cars behind me and, seeing none, I slowed as I passed the entrance into the property. A small, paved lane wound its way up to the house, if one could call it that. I continued past, noticing the building wrapped around the knoll exposing an entire new section of house, including what looked to be a four-car garage. Several large pyramids stood out on the lawn in front of the house and a large pyramid-shaped tower rose from the centre of the building.

There was no way to get close without driving up the winding front drive and I had noticed a closed gate not far up the drive. I spent the next hour scouting for spots which might afford me a closer look. Finally, I crossed over a small stream and turned down a dirt track that may have been created by locals driving their vehicles down to the water's edge.

I slowed and followed the track to a flattened area which could hold three or four vehicles and parked. My car was the only one here. I checked Google Maps, grabbed the binoculars out of the glove compartment, and followed the creek back.

An hour later, hot and tired, I scrambled up the embankment and found myself in a pasture with about a hundred cows. A few curious cows ambled over. A man on a tractor worked the fields to my right. The land continued to rise in the direction I was going. I ducked back down into the creek cut and continued to a stand of maple trees I had spotted just down the hill from what I assumed was Landen's property. Twenty minutes later, I was standing in the small grove of trees looking up the hill at the house.

The place was obscene. I pulled out my binoculars and adjusted the lens until the house came into focus. The windows were shuttered, all twenty-four of them. I focused in on the tower in the centre of the building. The pyramid-shaped dome was made of glass. Maybe Landen owned his own private observatory.

One of the doors to the four-car garage stood open. I refocused my binoculars, and the open door came into sharp view. A man in grey coveralls was moving around inside. After watching for about twenty minutes and seeing nothing, I asked myself what I had expected to find. I looked around the small grove of trees I was standing in. There was no sign that Sal or anyone had been here recently; none of the grass at the base of the trees was flattened. I watched for another hour. At least the bugs weren't bad now that we'd had a couple frosts.

The man inside the garage closed the door. No sign of other life. My feet had grown cold and the wind picked up, sending another stream of leaves to the ground. I looked up. The clouds had been building while I stood here watching, and the air had cooled. It looked like we might be in for some autumn rain.

I found my way back to the creek and slid down the small escarpment to the strip of dirt edging the water. That's when I saw it.

An old hat was lying in the mud. I found a twig, bent down, worked the twig under one end, and lifted. Mud sprayed in my face as it came free. I pulled the stick toward me. A brown plaid hat like the kind Sal wore. I looked closer. A Green Party campaign button was pinned to the side.

It was Sal's hat.

FORTY-THREE

I scrambled out of the creek bed and ran along the top of the embankment, not caring who saw me now. I tripped as I scurried across a field of stubble, the uneven ground slowing my progress, the short dry stalks of the recently harvested crop scratching my ankles. I spotted the main road and slowed, breathing hard. No chill in the air now. I was sweating.

I knew Sal had been out here; she's the one who told me what the place looked like. Why had finding her hat thrown me into a panic? She could have dropped it and not noticed it missing until later. I crossed the highway and found the small track leading down to the creek. I exhaled in relief when I found my car, still the lone vehicle parked there.

I stripped off my jacket, slid in, and checked my phone. No messages, nothing from Sal. *Nothing from Luis, either*. I started the engine, edged my car around, and drove up the gentle embankment and back onto the highway.

Now that I was starting to think again, I knew why I had panicked. Sal had not just dropped her hat and left it there. Sal was on a one-woman mission to clean up the planet. She once spent three days looking for a mitten she dropped. She wasn't going to leave behind a perfectly good hat without a reason. Certainly not with her political party's campaign button pinned to its side. Yes. Sal was part of the one percent of Canadians who voted for the Greens.

Now I wish I hadn't bolted. I should have looked to see if there were any signs of a struggle, or anything else that might tell me where Sal went next.

By the time I hit the QEII I had calmed even further. Sal could be home already. Or she was sick and lying in a hospital, I quickly reminded myself. Why did my mind always jump to the negative? Maybe she was holed up somewhere with a lover. More likely, she lost her phone and hadn't had time to get another. I reached the edge of the city and traffic slowed. Of course, it was rush hour. I was exhausted from trying to think up plausible explanations for Sal's silence. There was no good explanation. Sal was really missing.

FORTY-FOUR

I CLEANED UP AND had a bitc to eat, but I couldn't sit still. I couldn't just sit here waiting, hoping Sal would turn up okay. I locked up, went downstairs, jumped back in the Taurus, and spent a couple hours looking for Sal.

I checked several of Sal's favourite haunts; the bottle depot on Tenth Avenue, the shops along Fourth Street where she often picked bottles to supplement her PI income and whatever meagre pension she received from the government. If she received a pension. I drove past the community garden in Hillhurst then over to Sunnyside. Not much activity there this time of year. I checked her place again and spoke to the neighbours. No one had seen her.

Several recent murders in Calgary rolled through my mind. A woman's body had been found in an abandoned trailer on the side of the road, body parts found in black garbage bags behind a dumpster, remains found in a field east of town. I did the only thing I hadn't yet done. I drove down to the police station.

I parked my car and entered the station. A police officer was trying to calm a man who appeared drunk and was shouting. I turned left, took a number, and sat down in the small waiting area where six or seven people already waited. Half an hour later, a young man, who looked to be about twelve but wore a CPS uniform, called me up.

"Yes, what can we do for you?"

"I'd like to report a missing person."

"Was this person last seen in our jurisdiction?"

It was the last place I had seen her, but she would have likely been seen by someone else afterwards, near or around Beiseker. I swallowed. "Yes. I last saw her here in Calgary three days ago. We had been in touch by phone but then all communication stopped two days ago. I haven't been able to reach her by phone or email. I checked her apartment, she's not there. I've checked some of the places she likes to hang out at. No one has seen her."

"Okay, ma'am. I'll get you to start on the missing persons form and I'll let someone from our Missing Persons Team know you're here."

"Thank you." I took the clipboard he handed me and sat back down. I knew the Missing Persons Team was part of the Special Crimes Unit. Luis Azagora's unit. Then I reminded myself that CPS was undergoing a reorganization, so maybe that was no longer the case. I really didn't need to run into Luis tonight, not here. I started in on the form.

I was almost done when a constable from Missing Persons arrived. She introduced herself as Constable Sheila Macrae. I followed her down a maze of corridors and found myself in a small meeting room on the second floor. She took the form from me. I had managed to fill in the entire form, other than the questions for which I had no answers. She went over the questions and my answers.

"You haven't checked the hospitals yet. What about family members?"

"As far as I know, she has one daughter somewhere in Nova Scotia, but they're estranged."

"You don't have a recent picture of her?"

"No. I don't have any picture of her."

"I see here she's retired."

The question had given me reason for pause. Should I have mentioned she was working for me? Hard to admit to since I was paying her under the table. I decided not to complicate things and had answered yes.

I was able to provide her cell phone number, the make and type of phone, who her service provider was, as well as her home and email address. All the information regarding which bank she used, credit card information, passport number and its location, and family members and their contact information were blank.

"I see you've given us a description of the truck she was driving. This her truck?"

"No. It's mine. I mean, I rented it. She borrowed it."

She looked up at me, her eyes on mine. "What was she planning to do with your truck?"

"Umm...well...she collects things. You know...salvages stuff. Like last year she heard about a place that was going out of business and had all these empty plastic jugs they were...I don't know, giving away? Or selling for next to nothing. Sal picked up about fifty of them and turned them into hanging planters. She sold them at a local farmers' market." At least that part was true.

"I see. And this time?"

"I'm not sure." What I was sure of was that Constable Macrae could tell I was fibbing. "She mentioned something about someone having these wooden pallets that they wanted to get rid of. I don't know what she planned to do with them, but she's a big recycler, so I'm sure she has something in mind. I think they were at a farm somewhere east of here. Beiseker maybe?"

"Okay. You indicated here no one has heard from or seen her in over forty-eight hours."

"That's right. We were going to touch base two days ago, but I never heard from her. I called her, but she didn't answer. Since then, I've been calling her several times a day but she's not answering. Her mailbox is full. I've sent text messages and emails, dozens of them. I went to her apartment, but it's locked up and there's no sign of the truck anywhere. I'm worried that maybe she's had an accident, or something has happened to her."

"We have a standard assessment tool we use to assess the missing person's potential risk of imminent harm. It guides us on how many and how quickly resources should be deployed to their case. We look at risk factors posed by things such as age, their physical and mental health, lifestyle factors such as gang involvement or drug use, and if they were involved in any suspicious or dangerous activities. I'd like to go through that assessment with you if that's okay."

I wanted to scream, *Her risk is high, it's high, just go find her.*

I answered the questions as best I could. The fact that she lived alone in a run-down, illegal basement suite and sort of hoarded and bottle picked to supplement her income, helped raise her risk factor. I wondered what the risk factor would be if I had told her I was investigating three deaths and had sent an unarmed and unskilled older woman to hunt down someone who just might be somehow involved in one or more of these deaths. I hoped if we found her alive, she'd never find out I hinted at emotional instability, hoping to raise the risk factor higher as a mechanism to compensate for my lack of truthfulness.

I was almost at the elevators when I spotted him. Azagora was in a meeting room with five or six others. Several charts covered the walls. The new chief constable stood at the front of the room. I recognized him from newspaper photos and from the charity gala Adan held, which now seemed eons ago. I willed Luis to not look my way, but that's not how the universe works. He looked up and his eyes met mine. My face burned red as I slipped into the elevator.

FORTY-FIVE

The next morning, I was up early and out the door before seven. Feeling only slightly better now that the police would be looking for Sal, I couldn't just sit back and hope it happened. I thumped the hood of the Taurus, threw my backpack on the floor behind the driver's seat, and climbed in.

I should really talk to my neighbour, Mrs. Wilson. She was as prickly as a cactus, but she was a cat lover, and so was I. Maybe she'd be interested in helping me capture a few of the raggedy cats hanging around the garage and finding homes for them. I'd take one in, but my lifestyle wasn't conducive to having pets, at least not ones that needed to be fed and watered regularly.

A thought had occurred to me as I lay awake last night. What if Sal had driven out to the Landen Museum? She might have followed Milton out there. And based on what I saw of her driving skills, she could have missed a curve and ended up in the in the trees. The roads out there were not well travelled now that peak tourist season had passed.

I tried not to feel sorry for myself on the trip out, but the vast barren fields, devoid of humans, the leafless trees that occasionally dotted the landscape, and the cold blustery wind fed my mood. My two best friends were off living their lives happily elsewhere while I skewered my relationship with Luis and lost an operative and had nothing consequential to show for ten days of work. I shook off my self-pity. Sal was out there somewhere and might be hurting worse than I was.

I stayed consistently fifteen kilometres over the speed limit and got to Rosebud in no time. The hamlet had a different feel today, with the weekend visitors gone and many of the shops closed. I drove down the deserted main street, reminding myself that although I couldn't see them, a few souls lived here all year round.

I reached the grain elevator at the end of the street, turned right, and continued to the Landen Museum. It, too, stood closed. Today there were no cars in the parking lot. I parked and made my way up the sidewalk. Dried leaves skittered across my path, the wind swirling them into little mounds against the few low Bird's Nest Spruce that lined the walk.

I climbed the few steps and read the notices posted on the front doors. There was no mention of the museum being permanently closed or anything to indicate that the museum was up for sale. Of course, commercial businesses were bought and sold every day without notice to their customers. The new owners might even keep the name of the museum and be quite happy to run it as is.

I glanced back at the parking lot and now I noticed a lane branched off from the main parking lot and ran past the museum and around to the back. It must not go very far back as the rear of the museum was set into the side of the hill. It's probably why it seemed so dark inside when I was last here...and cool.

I descended the steps, returned to the parking lot, and found the entrance to the small lane. I skirted around a gate that kept cars from proceeding further and walked the two hundred or so metres to where the hill rounded its corner and dipped into a gully.

I stopped and scrambled for the hillside, the adrenaline already coursing though my body. A black SUV was parked below. Did the SUV belong to the museum? To Landen? Why the hell had it been following me?

I listened for sounds and, hearing none, crept forward and peered down into the gully. A set of metal doors stood open, doors leading into the side of the hill. Bonnie, the woman who used to work here, had mentioned that the museum had a workshop and storage area for archived items below the main level. She said it's where Milt Landen occasionally came to prepare new artifacts or stored ones no longer on display.

I ducked back as a bearded man came out of the storage area and walked around to the back of the truck. He pulled a flat crate from the back, hoisted it up on his shoulder, and carried it to the entrance.

I turned and crept back uphill to the main parking lot and ran back to my car. I was surprised he hadn't heard me drive in, but perhaps he had been inside when I drove up. Now I was nervous about starting the car, but more nervous just sitting here.

I turned the ignition. For one brief second, I thought the engine wouldn't start. As soon as the car rumbled to life, I backed out and crept out of the parking lot, keeping one eye on the rear-view mirror. When I reached the main road, I accelerated and let out my breath.

Why would the SUV have been tailing me? The question kept bouncing around in my head. I checked my rear-view mirror again, turned off onto the driveway leading to the grain elevator, and pulled around the back.

Grabbing my binoculars out of the glove compartment, I made my way along the old railway tracks until I reached a clump of trees. I didn't have to wait long before the black SUV appeared. It slowed at the T-intersection and turned down main street. Focusing my binoculars on his back plate, I repeated the licence plate number over and over as I ran back to my car.

I jotted down the plate number, started the car, and exited the parking area in a flurry of dust. I kept an eye open for the SUV but didn't see it. I reached the junction to Highway 72 and had a decision to make—left or right. I hadn't seen which way the SUV had gone, and I had to assume it wasn't parked somewhere on a side street in the tiny hamlet. I chose left.

Ten minutes later, I spotted a black vehicle ahead of me but with the distance separating us, I couldn't tell if it was the SUV or not. I closed the gap slightly but had no desire to catch up. I was suddenly aware how little travelled this secondary road was in the middle of the week.

I was sure the SUV I had seen at the museum was the same one I had noticed on other occasions and now I had a plate number. A few turns and twenty minutes later I found myself in familiar territory.

I slowed at the intersection to Highway 791 and turned north. Milt Landen's mansion was only a few kilometres down the road. I gunned it until his property came into view. By the time I reached the driveway into Landen's place, the SUV was pulling around to the side of the building.

There was nothing suspicious about the SUV having gone from the museum to Landen's place. Milton did own the museum. What didn't make sense is why the SUV had been following me in Calgary.

Without giving myself another minute to talk myself out of it, I turned in to Landen's driveway.

FORTY-SIX

I rounded a small curve in the driveway and swore. A man stepped out of a small pyramid-shaped structure next to a single-arm steel gate that barricaded the road. It took me a minute to realize the pyramid housed the property's security guard. Perhaps all the pyramids had a function other than decorative ones.

The guard wore a long-sleeve brown shirt and had a sleek headset strapped over his closely shaved head.

"Morning, miss. How can I help you?"

"I'm here to see Milton Landen."

"You'll have to make an appointment."

"But I'm here already."

"Mr. Landen doesn't see anyone without an appointment."

"Oh." Two men now stood beside the SUV at the top of the hill, watching me.

"Could I speak to one of those two men?" I pointed in their direction.

"This is private property, miss. I'm going to have to ask you to leave now."

I stared at his unsmiling face. "Sheesh. Okay, I'll make an appointment."

I attempted a three-point turn, which ended being a seven-point manoeuvre, and cringed as I drove away, certain they were all having a good laugh.

I wasn't ready to give up on Sal, but I really didn't have any idea what to do next. Thirty minutes later, I found myself winding down the hill that led to Drumheller. I pulled into the Tim Hortons, bought a coffee, and sat to collect my thoughts.

I had sent Sal to find where Landen lived and to watch his comings and goings. She found him, then disappeared. I should have been more forthright with that bit of information when I filed her missing persons report yesterday. I hadn't, so it was on me to follow up since no one else would be. Although I had flip-flopped on the idea that the missing jade jaguar had something to do with Howard's death, a growing unease told me Milt Landen was up to something, something that may have gotten Sal in trouble.

At one point, I had considered searching for Jason Gray, the security guard who had been on duty at the museum the day of the grass fire, hoping he could tell me more about the empty case standing in the museum. Landen told me he meant to display Palermo's jaguar to raise its profile and awareness with possible collectors, but that when he determined the statue was a fake, he obviously wasn't going to put it on display. But why lie and represent it as an item his grandad brought back from his expeditions to find the Lost City of the Monkey God? Is that what Dr. Garret meant when he said he didn't approve of Milt Landen's ethics?

The gal working at the museum said several articles were missing from the museum once it reopened after the fire. Jason Gray had been let go by his employer. What if Landen lied and Palermo's statue had been stolen from the museum? What if Gray was somehow involved or knew something about that?

Bonnie, the woman who manned the museum's front desk the day of the fire, had given me the name of the man who managed the apartment building where Jason Gray lived. I looked up directions to the address I found, started the car, and drove there.

Haywood Court was made up of eight separate buildings, each with six townhouse units, each unit with their own entry. I found Unit 102 in Block H. A sign with the words *Rental Manager—Inquire Within* told me I had the right place.

I parked in visitor parking and made my way to the front door of Unit 102. On closer inspection, the building could use a new coat of paint. Fogged up windows indicated leaky seals, and a few were obviously cracked.

I knocked on the door. A small dog barked, and someone moved inside. A thin man with a deep tan and shaved head opened the door.

"Hi. Are you Devlin?"

He looked out at the parking lot nervously. The funky smell of marijuana was prevalent. "Yes. Are you here about a rental?"

"No. My name's Jorja Knight and I'm a private investigator. A friend of yours, Bonnie, gave me your name. I'm trying to track down Jason Gray. I understand he used to live here."

"Got any ID?"

I dug out my PI and driver's licences and handed them to him. He glanced at me and the photo on my licence, handed them back, and stepped outside, closing the door behind him.

"If you find the little ferret, tell him I'm looking for him, too. He owes me two months' rent."

"I take it you don't know where I could find him."

"He's split. I haven't seen him around town lately. His girlfriend might know, but she's not talking."

"A girlfriend is a good start. Do you have a name or an address for her?"

"Her name's Candace. Candy. I don't know her last name. She works at the Broken Spoke."

"Is that a bike shop?"

He looked at me as if I were nuts. "No. It's a bar. In Carbon."

"Oh. Thanks." I didn't have the nerve to ask him where Carbon was, but figured it was somewhere nearby.

I climbed back into my car and checked Google Maps. Carbon was a mere forty kilometres west of here. Everything was forty kilometres from where I was.

I phoned Jason's former employer, 4SiteSecurity, and told them I was with the management company that looked after the Haywood Court apartments and that I had a cheque for Mr. Jason Gray and did they have a forwarding address for him. They did not.

I figured the Broken Spoke might not be flush with patrons at two in the afternoon, so I had lunch and, with several hours left to kill, drove back to Rosebud. I asked around at the few places that remained open during the week if they had seen Sal. A woman at the café in the Mercantile Block thought she'd seen someone who looked like Sal a few days earlier, but she couldn't be sure without seeing a photo.

I kept checking my phone, hoping for a text from Sal, a phone call, anything. The sky darkened. My mind kept taking me places I didn't want to go. I had to face the possibility that I wouldn't find Sal. That she might be dead.

FORTY-SEVEN

I ARRIVED IN CARBON shortly after seven. I took a drive through town and circled back, a trip that took six minutes. The Broken Spoke sat on the edge of town, a reddish one-storey building with the name posted on a large sign above the door, and above that an old Coca Cola sign. A sign on the heavily nicked and gashed front door proclaimed the Broken Spoke as best country music bar in Alberta. I entered.

The place was dimly lit, always an appreciated feature in a drinking establishment. A large dance floor ran down the middle of the space, with tables set on either side. A rough-hewn fence made of unfinished wooden planks strung between wagon wheels separated the seating areas from the dance floor. A wide stage, raised a foot off the floor, ran across the entire back of the building. The ceiling was low, and half of the acoustic tiles were damaged or missing entirely.

There were three people in the place, a middle-aged couple and a lone man nursing a beer. I turned left, stepped up to the seating area, and sat down at a table.

Glassware clanged. Muffled voices drifted from out from somewhere out back. A waitress backed out through a set of wooden swinging doors, carrying a tray of drinks. She dropped off two beers at the man's table, several glasses at the couple's table, then crossed the dance floor to where I was sitting.

"Hi hon. Do you want a menu?"

She wasn't wearing a name tag. I should have asked Devlin for a description.

"Yes, please."

She grabbed a laminated menu off her tray and plunked it down in front of me. "How about a drink?"

I looked around at the dozen or so neon Budweiser signs. "I'll have a Budweiser, and a glass of water."

"You got it." She hustled back to what I assumed was the kitchen. I looked down at the menu, although I wasn't hungry at all.

The waitress came back with my drinks, and I ordered the deep-fried zucchini appetizer and a burger with onion rings. She came out with my order twenty minutes later and set the plates down in front of me.

"Uh...you wouldn't by any chance be Candace?" I asked.

"No. Whatcha want with Candace?"

"I'm actually looking for a friend of mine, an older woman, mid to late sixties. Last I heard she was planning to drive out to Drumheller to visit her nephew or maybe it was her nephew's son. She told me her nephew was dating or staying out there with someone named Candace. Anyway, she's gone missing, and I can't locate her nephew either. I was hoping that she managed to connect with Candace, and that she said something to her about where she was going next, or something that might help me to find her."

She looked around the bar and grill, which was slowly filling up. "I have a break coming up in about a half hour. I'll come talk to you then."

I didn't want to get my hopes up, but any information right now was better than none.

The burger was decent, and the onion rings out of this world.

The band was setting up on stage by the time Nyomi, the waitress, joined me.

"One of the girls called in sick, so I only have a few minutes," she said.

"Thanks for giving me some of your time. Do you know how I can contact Candace?"

"She's gone. She went off somewhere with her boyfriend."

"Jason?"

"Yeah. I don't mean to be disrespectful to you or your friend, but Jason's trouble."

"Oh. How so?"

"He parties way too much, gets into fights. He's always cooking up some scheme or other to make money. They've all backfired. He's a cheater, too. Candace deserves better."

"You think they've left Drumheller? Where would they go?"

"I don't know." Her eyes grew concerned. "Look. I don't like the way Candace left."

"What do you mean?"

"She left in a hurry. No goodbyes or anything. Just didn't show up for work one day. I went by her apartment. The super said she'd moved out, but she left a lot of her things."

Sounded like she and Jason both left in a big hurry. Now more than ever I wanted to talk to one or the other of them.

"I don't know what they've got themselves into but I'm betting dollars to donuts it's trouble."

"You wouldn't know where they could have gone? What about friends, family?"

"Candace grew up in care. She hasn't stayed in touch with any of her foster families. I don't know anything about Jason's family. You probably know more than I do if your friend is his auntie."

Too bad that wasn't true. "Can you think of anyone else I could talk to, who might know where they went?"

"You could try Skyla. She's just a kid, still in high school. Candace took a shine to her, maybe because Skyla is a foster kid. She used to take her places, you know, like shopping in Drum, or to get their nails done."

"How do I find Skyla?"

"Well, there's only one high school around here. She won't be hard to miss. She's got long purple hair, a tattoo on her neck, and usually wears black lipstick."

Nyomi headed back to work. The first few twangs of a Fender Player Telecaster sounded as the band warmed up. I stayed for another ten minutes or so, then paid my bill and left.

The evening had cooled considerably now that the sun had set, and a thousand stars had exploded in the sky. I gazed up in wonder. Each of those stars had been born, existed, and would die. Maybe that's where our energy went when our bodies gave up. A coyote yipped in the distance.

"Sal, where the hell are you?" I whispered into the darkness.

FORTY-EIGHT

Nyomi was right—Skyla wasn't hard to spot. I had overnighted it in Drumheller and drove back to Carbon this morning. Kneehill High was the only secondary school in the area and not too hard to find. Skyla was sitting on the top bar of a bike rack that stood off to the right of the two-storey red-brick building.

Long, purple hair framed her face below a beanie. Her black rimmed eyes matched the colour on her lips and nails. She wore a short-sleeved green T-shirt over a long-sleeve black polo and tan cargo pants. Now that I was closer, I could see the T-shirt had a cannabis leaf on the front with the word *Addicted* below. She ignored my approach and blew out a stream of thick white vapour from her e-cigarette.

"Hi. Skyla?"

She looked over at me and blew out two small vapour rings in succession.

"You don't know me. My name is Jorja. I'm a private investigator. I'm looking for a friend of mine, and Nyomi thought you might be able to help."

"Who's your friend?"

"Her name is Sal. She's an older woman, late sixties. She's missing." I gave her the same story I gave Nyomi. "I'm hoping Jason, or your friend Candace might have seen her. I'm hoping she told them where she was planning to go next."

She stared at me for a full minute, then took a drag off her e-cigarette and jumped down from the bike rack. "How do I know you haven't made all this up?"

The question took me aback because she was right on the nose with her comment. Why should she believe me?

"Here is my ID." I pulled out my PI and driver's licence. She took both, looked at them, and handed them back, her pursed lips twisted to one side.

"Okay, I'll level with you. Sal sometimes does surveillance work for me. I sent her out to locate Milt Landen for me. Ever hear of him?"

She shook her head, but I could tell I had caught her attention.

"He's an eccentric millionaire who owns a museum in Rosebud, among other things. Jason Gray worked as a security guard at the museum. There was a grass fire there and afterwards a rare artifact, which was supposed to go on display, was pulled back. Or...it was stolen."

"Let me guess. This rare artifact is worth a lot of money, right?"

"Possibly. It's a matter of authentication. It may turn out to be a fake and not the real thing at all."

She laughed. "That would be just like that idiot's luck."

"You think Jason lifted it?"

"Don't you?"

"Yeah, possibly." She was an astute young lady, hiding her cleverness behind a fuck-off attitude. She got points for that in my book.

"Is there a reward for it?"

"No."

"Then why do you care what happened to it?"

"I don't. I care about Sal. It's like she's dropped off the planet." I shuddered at my own words. "I'm worried that something bad has happened to her. I don't know much about this statue or Milt Landen, except that a friend of mine, another PI, was killed, and he had Milt Landen's name in his appointment book. So, two people I know who went to find or talk to Landen have ended up missing or dead."

She was shaking her head now. "I told Candy that asshole was no good."

"When did you last talk to her?"

"Like, two weeks ago. She came by to tell me she might have to go away for a while."

I took a deep breath as a shiver ran down my spine. "What else did she say?"

"Nothing. She just wanted me to know…so I wouldn't worry."

I didn't say anything for a minute. If she hadn't been worried about Candace's need to go away for a while back then, she probably was now.

"If Candace is in trouble, where would she go? Or Jason, for that matter?"

"Do you carry a gun?"

The question surprised me. "Not usually."

"If you're going to look for Jason, you might want to."

My fingertips started to tingle. I took a deep breath. "Okay. Duly noted."

Skyla told me Jason liked to go hiking in Horsethief Canyon. Candace had gone with him a couple of times. They spent the night in an abandoned cabin Jason liked to imagine he owned. He took weapons out there and did target practice. He also had a stack of supplies out there—Jason saw himself as a survivalist. He said if anything happened, like a foreign invasion, or a meteor struck the earth and wiped out most of the population, he was prepared to survive.

Unfortunately, she didn't know the location of this cabin, other than it had taken Candace and Jason a few hours to get there on foot and Candace had fallen, ripped her best jeans, and after freezing her ass off in an unheated cabin, swore she'd never go back there.

But things look different when you're running for your life.

FORTY-NINE

I didn't like the idea of going out to Horsethief Canyon on my own—or unarmed. If Jason Gray and Candace were holed up in Horsethief Canyon, they were hiding from someone. If Jason had the jade statue something must have gone horribly wrong. Who steals a pricey artifact then hides out in no man's land? And if the jaguar statue was worth anything, why hadn't a reward been offered for its return? Whatever Jason had or knew, something had him and his girlfriend running for their lives.

I needed a plan. One that wouldn't result in my death or disappearance as well. I was already halfway to Calgary when my phone rang. I switched on Bluetooth and answered.

Static crackled and a man's voice replied, "Mr. Landen asked me to call. I understand you would like to speak with him. He can see you now."

It took me a second to find my voice. "Okay. Thank you." My eyes flew to the clock on the dashboard. "Uh...I'm on the highway. It will take me thirty minutes to get there."

"Fine. I will let Mr. Landen know."

I wondered what precipitated this turn of events. Five minutes later, I was turned around and heading back toward Beiseker. Twenty-five minutes after that I arrived at the entrance to Milt Landen's property.

The gate leading up to the house was locked, and no security guard appeared to be on duty. I spotted an intercom set on a small post next to the gate. I got out of my car, walked up to it, and pressed the button.

Static crackled and a man's voice replied, "Yes."

"Jorja Knight. I'm here to see Milt Landen."

"Leave your car where it is and walk up."

Seriously? I looked around. Landen probably had security cameras everywhere. I retrieved my purse and phone from the car and began walking. It was farther than I thought.

I reached one of the larger pyramids. It was made of some sort of semi-translucent material that shimmered in the light. I wanted to touch it, but I knew I was being watched. I looked up at the building in front of me.

The house—if one could call it that—was four storeys high if you counted the ground level parking garage as level one. No sign of the SUV today. I climbed the steps and crossed a ten-foot span of concrete to the massive front doors.

Beware all ye who enter here. The phrase, from some book or film, popped up from the dregs of my memory. I lifted the large brass door knocker and let it fall.

The door opened. I don't know what I was expecting, maybe a butler or someone dressed like a medieval knight, but a man with a white handlebar mustache and greying hair, wearing a plaid flannel shirt tucked into jeans, stood there.

"Ms. Knight, I presume?"

I nodded.

I followed him through a towering foyer. A chandelier made of four or five wagon wheels hinged together hung overhead from invisible wires, the lightbulbs fashioned as miniature lanterns at each spoke. Below the chandelier stood a golden horse. One foreleg was raised and its head thrown back, the luxurious mane carved to look as if the horse was running into the wind.

"Wow." I couldn't help myself.

The man turned to me. "You'll see several spirit animals in the house. The horse, especially the wild horse, symbolizes strength and an appetite for freedom."

He led me into a large room panelled in mahogany. A thick Persian carpet muted the sound of our footsteps. I stopped.

"Spectacular, isn't it?"

The room held twenty or thirty wolves, some perched on ledges jutting out from the wall, others crouched on the floor ready to spring, their eyes gleaming in the dim light.

"The wolf is one of the most striking of the spirit animals. The power of the wolf spirit comes from its intelligence and cunning instinct. When a wolf shows up in your life, Ms. Knight, pay attention to what your intuition is telling you." With that he turned and left the room.

I could feel all my internal organs vibrating at a low frequency. *Was that a warning or some sort of threat?*

"Well, don't just stand there gawking."

I jumped. The gnarly voice came from one of four wingback chairs set in a semi-circle in front of a massive fireplace. I hadn't noticed him there, half hidden in the dim light.

It was hard to tell how tall he was as he sat hunched in his chair. A nondescript septuagenarian, with white hair and thick dark rimmed glasses that hid half of his deeply lined face. His gnarled fingers rested on the end of short cane—perhaps used to help leverage his frame from the chair when it was time to do so.

He waved the stick to one of the chairs and I sat.

His voice was still strong as he spoke. "What exactly do you want from me, Ms. Knight?"

"The truth."

"Ahh...whose version of the truth would you like to hear?"

"Yours, of course."

"I see. You didn't like the truth I gave you earlier on the phone, so you've come looking for another version. One that more suits your fancy, is that it, Ms. Knight?"

"Well, no...yes."

"Spit it out, Ms. Knight. What is it you want to accuse me of?"

"I...uhmm, I'm not accusing you of anything, Mr. Landen. Several people with connections to Mr. Palermo are dead. A statue he thought might be valuable is missing."

"Yes, yes, of course. You think I lied to you. You believe I recognized Mr. Palermo's statue as a valuable artifact worth millions and yet told him it was worthless. That I didn't return it to Mr. Palermo, but instead planned to keep it for myself."

That's exactly what I had been thinking.

"Let's play this little scenario of yours out. I keep the statue, then what? I planned to display my stolen statue to the public? Realizing my foolish mistake, I hired an arsonist to burn down my museum and faked the robbery of the statue. Then when Mr. Palermo hired your friend to find the stolen statue and got too close to the truth, I killed or hired someone to kill both. Do I strike you as a foolish man, Ms. Knight?"

"No, you don't."

"Would I have told you Mr. Palermo hired your friend to find the statue if I were trying to cover my tracks? Why would I have planned to display a statue, one of such possible cultural significance, if I had indeed stolen the statue from Mr. Palermo? Wouldn't it have been better for me to kill Mr. Palermo and just quietly take the statue? Why would I have allowed Mr. Palermo such an opportunity to prove me a liar and a thief?"

"But things were taken from the museum during the fire."

"Yes, they were—several small, rather insignificant items. The fire may have been set as a diversion." He held up his hand. "Yes, Ms. Knight. Young Jason Gray, my former security guard, may have seen an opportunity to make some money and snatched a few items on his way out."

"Did you report the stolen items to the police."

"For what purpose? The police have their hands full with real criminals. Should the police immediately start patrolling the pawn shops or monitor the hundreds of online shops that deal in such items, most of which would never question the historical lineage of the items in someone's possession?"

I was starting to feel foolish.

"But he's missing."

"Missing? You mean because he and his girlfriend have moved on. Young people do that nowadays, don't they? Besides, there's an arson investigation he might be wanting to avoid."

I nodded. "Who is the bearded man who drives the black SUV, the one in your garage?"

"I'm an antiquities trader, dear. I have items going in and out of the country all the time. My clients are all over the world. He picks up and delivers all my packages and shipments. Or do you think he works for me as a hired assassin?"

Shit. Landen was reading my mind and shooting down one rather unsubstantiated theory after another.

"I've seen him in Calgary. He's been following me."

"Have you not been doing the same?" His voice sharpened. "Call the police if you like. You can explain how you found me, my private home. You call me, accuse my employees, accuse me of stealing, of drowning your friend, and yet you're troubled when I have you checked out? You're barking up the wrong tree, Ms. Knight. Are you sure you know what your departed friend was up to before he died?"

I startled as the man in the plaid shirt who had let me in earlier materialized at my chair.

"I didn't make the first move, but I am calling checkmate. Now, unless you have further accusations to levy, Charles will see you out."

I did have one more accusation to levy. I wanted to know what he or his delivery men had done with Sal, but I knew any suggestion he was involved in her disappearance would be met with more mockery disguised as conversation.

I left, feeling somewhat like a child who had been given a pat on the head by a forgiving uncle for having broken a cherished but inexpensive bauble.

I was at the edge of the Calgary city limits when I realized Milton Landen was lying to me. *No, it couldn't have happened that way.* The first time I had spoken to Landen, he told me he gave the statue back to Palermo in mid-August and told him the statue was a fake. Assuming that were true, why would Palermo have hired Howard to find a statue that was essentially worthless if it had gone missing shortly afterwards? For him to have hired Howard to find it, he must have come across something that made him believe the statue was worth something, otherwise this didn't make any sense. Or maybe Howard hadn't been hired by Palermo at all. I only had Landen's word that he had.

By the time I reached the city, another thought occurred to me. Why did Landen know or care enough to know that Jason Gray and his girlfriend were missing or had skipped town? And I had never mentioned anything about Howard having drowned.

FIFTY

THE BURGER I PICKED up on my way home did little to dispel the hollow feeling inside. That void could not be filled by food. I eyed the bottle of scotch, half-empty from my last binge, and felt queasy. I called Constable Macrae to see if there was any news on Sal, although I knew if there had been she would have contacted me. The news wasn't good. Sal's cell phone was turned off, no longer pinging nearby cell phone towers. The last time her phone had been detected was near the Calgary airport, four days ago.

I should have told Macrae I found Sal's hat a mere half-kilometre from Milton Landen's place, but I knew by now it would likely be gone. Landen seemed to be one step ahead of me. Even had I picked up Sal's hat and taken it to the police, I'm sure Landen would dismiss any implied accusations by claiming I was harassing him, that I'd shown up at his private home uninvited, and that I had hired Sal to spy on him, which of course was true.

Landen had beaten me to the punch and outlined the very scenario that had been running though my mind. Which meant he had been prepared for me, had pre-emptive answers to questions I didn't even get a chance to ask. The man was cunning, like the wolves he so admired.

The scenario we hadn't explored in too much depth was the one that had Jason Gray and his girlfriend Candace running for their lives. I think Milton had told me some truths. I do think he told Palermo the statue was worthless. Maybe he even told him the statue had been stolen along with the few other items taken but that he didn't file a report because the items were not worth much.

My phone pinged. I lunged for it, hoping to see a text from Sal. Instead, I had one from Luis.

"We should talk."

No preamble. No *How was your day?* Straight to the point, a sharp stab to my heart. I typed back. "We should. Do you want to meet tonight?"

"Can't tonight. I have to attend this thing…an event."

I stared at the message. The man was infuriating.

"Tomorrow?" I typed back.

"Maybe on the weekend."

What the hell? I felt the anger building inside of me. Even though I had overstepped the bounds, I had apologized, I had asked for forgiveness. This was classic Azagora. He was making it clear to me he was controlling the situation. The ball was in his court. This did not smack of forgiveness. This was a reminder I played second string in his orchestra and should be grateful when and if he threw me a bone. I tossed my phone down. I was so damn mad I was mixing my metaphors.

My phone rang. I snatched it up.

"What?"

"Somebody's having a bad day."

"Oh. Hi, Mike. Sorry. I thought you were someone else. And yes, I'm having a bad day."

I decided to come clean. Besides, I needed this off my chest.

"Remember about a week ago, when I told you I could use some help, some boots on the ground, when I was still chasing after the jade jaguar and thinking maybe that Jeff Nickleson's death was re-lated—which then opened up this whole question about a dirty cop he was obsessed with?"

"I do."

"Well, she's missing, Mike. Something bad has happened to her."

"Who?"

I didn't mean to let the flood gates open, but I did. I told him how I had sent Sal out to find Landen. This, of course, being before Landen told me he believed the jaguar to be fake and that he'd returned it to Palermo. That Sal had found him. That we agreed to connect the next day and how I couldn't get a hold of her. When yet another full day passed with no response to any of my texts or phone calls, I filed a missing persons report. Now it was day four and there was still no sign of her.

"Jeez. This is serious, Jorja."

"I know, Mike. I feel just horrible. What if...what if she's dead?"

"Now, don't go there. There could be other reasons you haven't heard from her."

"Really. Like what?"

"Maybe she's been in an accident. Or she's had a stroke and is in a hospital somewhere. Or maybe she had a family emergency and she's jumped on a plane and in her haste left her phone behind. Or lost it."

Mike didn't offer up a plausible explanation I hadn't yet thought of. I knew she hadn't had a family emergency or jumped on a plane.

She could have lost her phone, but there were phones everywhere she could use to contact me.

I brushed away a tear as my eyes filled again. I was about to tell him I found Sal's hat out at Landen's place, but that would open up all sorts of discussion I really didn't want now. Besides, I had sent Sal out to find Landen. Finding her hat out there really didn't prove much more than the fact that she had located his residence.

"I talked to Landen today. He's lying, Mike."

"How do you know he's lying?"

"You know the SUV that's been following me around? It's one of his. Landen said he gave the statue back to Palermo—that it wasn't worth all that much. Then the statue apparently goes missing. Whether it was stolen from Palermo or Landen lied and it was lifted from his museum during the fire, doesn't really matter. There's a lot that still doesn't make sense."

"Okay. Shoot."

"Why would someone have tossed Howard's place after he died? Why would Landen have sent one of his men to follow me? I saw a bearded guy I swear is the one who works for Landen slip into Howard's memorial service. He was gone by the time the officiant made closing remarks. He was looking for who was there, who might know something. Why did someone search Donna's place? Why take a key? Why follow me? If the statue is a fake, why all this interest in it now that it's disappeared?"

"Could the guy you saw at Howie's memorial service have just been another guy with a beard? Did you get a good look at him, Jorja? Good enough to pick him out of a lineup?"

"I don't know. No."

I don't know why I couldn't tell Mike that Landen had all but said Howard hadn't merely been looking for the statue but that he was somehow involved. Or had I misunderstood when he asked if I knew what my "departed friend" was up to before he died?

Now the redacted insurance policy I had found in Howard's apartment came to mind. It stated something about no one item being insured for more than two hundred thousand dollars. I hadn't followed up on it. Could Palermo, standing on the brink of losing everything, have faked the statue's theft, to try and cash in on the insurance? Then why no police report? And Dr. Garret said insuring an artifact like the jade jaguar would require authentication. Besides Palermo didn't seem like the kind of guy who would commit fraud. The insurance policy must not be related to this case.

"You need to extract yourself from all of this. Even if you're right and Landen is behind all of this, people are dead. You did the right thing to report your friend missing. Let the police do their work."

"And if Jason Gray or his girlfriend turn up dead?"

There was a long silence.

"You can't save everyone, Jorja. Like you said, it doesn't really matter who stole the statue, if it has been stolen. Maybe Palermo binned it. Maybe Howard was working on something completely different. What I'm saying is, I don't think we've uncovered anything that would allow us or Donna to question the ME's ruling that Howard's death was an accident."

I sat quietly. I knew Mike was right.

"You might want to tell the officer handling Sal's case that she was out there doing surveillance for you. Tell them you've been looking into Howard's death, not necessarily to prove he was murdered, but to provide some answers to his daughter as to how and why he might have died. That you had this idea that the statue played into it and that Landen might have some information for you, particularly if the statue was worth something. You can even truthfully say Landen has since told you the statue is a fake but before you could call Sal back, she went missing. At least it would put them in the right area to look for her."

I took a shaky breath. As much as I didn't want to, this was Sal's best chance of being found. The police had resources I didn't have; I owed Sal at least this much.

After my call with Mike, I called Constable Macrae. She gave me a lecture about lying to police. It was the third time in as many days I had been chastised by someone.

After my call, I dug my rather pathetic little Walther BB gun out if its storage place in my lingerie drawer. I got out a CO_2 cartridge, loaded the pellets into the clip, and placed both on my nightstand. Milt Landen was a conniving man, and I had to be ready. Extracting myself from this case wasn't going to be as simple as Mike thought it would be. I needed a day to think about it.

Now, I had one more thing to do.

FIFTY-ONE

I PUSHED THE BIKE along the bike path until I reached the art mural, then turned south. The balloon tires made it heavy, and the wire basket mounted to the handlebars made it ungainly. Two blocks further on, I was across the street from Azagora's condo.

The voices in my head told me this was a bad idea. If he spotted me, it would be an immediate end to our relationship. Of course, this is exactly why I was doing this. I was sure that his "we need to talk" text was the lead-in to the breakup meeting. And what exactly was this *thing* he had tonight that prevented us from getting together to have that conversation.

This wasn't the first time Luis had an event to go to—alone. It had become his standard response, usually when I reached out to see if he wanted to hang out or otherwise spend time with me. Now I saw it as another technique he was using to control the relationship. I saw Luis when Luis wanted me to see him, not when I wanted to see him. And more than anything, I wanted to find something that would allow me to be the one to end the relationship when we did finally have our chat and save some of my dignity.

I looked down at the ratty, stained grey car coat. It was missing buttons and smelled faintly of oil.

Dignity. I didn't have any.

After making several passes by Luis' condo, I parked the bike against the wall of an older ten-storey apartment building and pressed myself into the recessed side exit door. If Luis was planning to take his car or a cab, I would be out of luck. I waited.

The bike, as well as the coat and shearling-lined trapper hat I was wearing, came from the house where Sal rented a room. The bike had been leaning against an old washing machine in the basement, the trapper's hat and coat hanging from a nail on the wall nearby. I shuddered when I jammed the hat onto my head, but the side flaps did a good job of partially hiding my face.

It was already dark when Luis emerged. A cab pulled up and Luis jumped in.

I leaped to action. I mounted the old bike, turned it around, and drove my feet down hard against the pedals. The bike wobbled, then took off. I kept my eyes glued to the cab and pedalled furiously.

"Behind you," I yelled, and veered left as a young couple dodged to their right.

I raced across the street; the cars mere blurs beside me. The cab turned right. I reached the end of the street, the bike leaning precariously as I rounded the corner. I got lucky and the cab caught a light at the next corner. I slowed to catch my breath and ready myself for the next sprint.

The sweat built up under my shirt, which was layered under my own coat and then the wool car coat I had borrowed. The earlier whiff of oil I detected when I pulled on the coat now blossomed, leaving me slightly nauseated. Drops of sweat rolled down my cheek from the shearling-lined hat.

An odd snippet from my high school biology class resurfaced. "Head lice eggs, called nits, are often found in the hair as the warmth and humidity of the scalp are needed for successful hatching."

I momentarily lost him on Tenth Avenue but then spotted a cab in the left turn lane about two blocks ahead. Praying it was him, I tore after it, standing now on the pedals.

I turned on to Thirteenth Avenue and almost died. The cab was parked in front of me; Luis was getting out of the car.

Putting my head down and looking the other way, I shot past the cab and continued at full speed down the street. I imagined Luis' eyes boring into my back.

I turned the corner, brakes screeching as I came to a stop. I threw the bike down on the sidewalk, ran the few steps to the corner of the building, and peered out.

I died a second death. Luis wore a dark suit with a white shirt and tie. With one hand casually tucked into a trouser pocket, he strode toward me.

Leaving the bike where it was, I ran down to the back of the building and into the alley. I turned, back pressed to the wall, waiting for Luis to appear. When Luis didn't materialize at the corner, I figured he entered one of the buildings along the street. With my heart rate now above critical stage, I crept back to my bike, picked it up and, after a cautious glance around the corner of the building, crossed the street.

Most of the shops had closed hours earlier. The windows in the Black Stilt Art Gallery were lit up. I moved forward, pushing the bike along until I was across from the gallery. There was already quite a crowd gathered inside, the women in glittering dress, the men in suits or other evening attire. A limo pulled up and disgorged a woman in a long, red-sequined dress.

I moved down from the gallery, parked the bike by a lamppost, and sat in the doorway of The Cooking Emporium. My fingers felt for the camera cord hanging around my neck. I pulled out my camera and nestled it between the folds of the coat, using my knees to steady it. After firing off a dozen or so shots, I checked the images and shifted the camera slightly to the left.

The party continued. Canapes and drinks were flowing. My butt grew cold on the pavement. At one point, the guests gathered in front of a thin woman in a black dress, diamonds dripping from her ears. The guests clapped as she finished her speech and presented a framed painting to a man wearing a tux. He spoke briefly, then someone relieved him of the painting.

Luis stood next to the woman in the long red dress. I gritted my teeth.

I waited as the night air cooled, now grateful for the grubby coat. A homeless man tried to engage me in conversation. I handed him a five-dollar bill and sent him on his way.

The crowd inside thinned as a steady stream of cabs and limos came and went. I recognized a tall, grey-haired man standing next to the woman in diamonds. Franklin Dirks, the business developer responsible for the new entertainment complex going in north of the city. The woman now looked familiar, too. I'd have to confirm, but I was sure I had seen her with Dirks at Adan's charity gala. Had the gala only been two weeks ago? It felt like months. Back when Luis and I were speaking, even discussing the possibility of a winter weekend getaway.

I blinked back the tears and ran the ratty sleeve of the jacket across my nose, shuddering as I suddenly realized the filthy sleeve had touched my mouth.

Another limo appeared. The driver jumped out and rushed around to open the back door. The woman in the red dress came out, Luis right behind her. I watched her slide into the limo while Luis ran around the vehicle and climbed in beside her.

I stood up. My heart dropped to my boots as I watched the limo drive away.

FIFTY-TWO

Taking off the shearling cap, I flipped my head over and scrubbed my scalp with my fingers. I reminded myself that nits can't survive for long after they've fallen off a warm body. Surely the hat hadn't been worn in months.

The inside of the basement was pitch black. I manoeuvred the bike back in with the light of my cell phone. I made out the faint outline of Sal's door. What if she was inside, in medical distress? I crawled past a stack of wire crates and rattled the door to her apartment. It was still locked. I knocked but there was no reply. The police must have checked her place.

Leaving the coat and bike where I found them, I made my way outside. No lights on in the house upstairs, either. What if they were all dead? I shook my head and called Constable Macrae. She was off for the night, but another officer answered, this one younger sounding still. No news on Sal yet, and yes, they had the homeowner open Sal's apartment, and she hadn't been inside.

I hurried back to my car which was parked down the street from Sal's place. Part of me couldn't wait to get home to shower. The other part of me was furious. I tried telling myself there was a logical explanation for Luis getting into the limo with the lady in red.

Maybe she was simply giving him a ride home. She could be an old acquaintance or a former partner of his, and they were merely going out for a drink to catch up. Or maybe she was 'the thing' that kept Luis busy when he didn't want to see me.

I started up the car and was parked down the street from Luis' condo fifteen minutes later. Yup. I was officially a stalker now. I got out for a better look. The lights in the north-facing corner unit on the tenth floor were dark. I climbed back into the car.

How could he do this to me? Why had *I* been okay with playing second fiddle at every turn? Waiting for him to pay me some attention, like a bloody schoolgirl crushing on her teacher, or someone else totally inappropriate and out of reach.

The anger slowly dissipated, replaced by self-pity. At midnight, I climbed out of my car, now chilled to the bone, entered the lobby, and pressed the intercom link to his unit. If he answered, I would tell him I was here to have that talk he had mentioned. Now. But he didn't answer.

What the hell was I thinking? This "I'll see you later if it suits me" relationship I had with Azagora had to come to an end. At least it answered a few questions. Seems like I did want a real relationship after all. Not necessarily marriage—but someone in my life who could be there for me occasionally, when I needed them. Azagora wasn't it, and I was lousy at playing the open-relationship game. I was a one-man woman—at least, one man at time.

I drove around for a few hours. The city was different at night. Buildings, towers stood empty, with an occasional lonely lit floor or office, signifying someone working late into the night.

I had stopped blaming my father for my failures and disappointments years ago but now I realized it had coloured my life in ways that made it hard to ignore. Men may hold the balance of power on the planet, but that didn't mean I had to accept being treated as a second-class citizen in order to forge a relationship with one of them.

I parked in my underground parking spot, almost too tired to get out. I caught a glimpse of myself in the elevator doors as I headed upstairs and laughed bitterly at the spent, dishevelled woman staring back at me. The woman in red was the type of woman Luis would want to stand beside him as he rose in the ranks. He was married to his job, and I was just the mistress.

I took a long shower, crawled into bed, and lay awake until the first sign of dawn. It wasn't the first time I'd spent a sleepless night wishing I could go back and change what I did, what I said, what I should have done but didn't.

It also wasn't the first time I'd been so engrossed in my inner deliberations that I hadn't noticed a black SUV had been prowling the streets with me.

FIFTY-THREE

The effects of last night's lack of sleep were slowing me down. Why is it that 3:00 a.m. is the time when we revisit all the stupid things we've done or said and rehash all the bad decisions we've made that still haunt us?

This morning I was drawn to the Black Stilt Art Gallery like a moth to a flame. So troubled by my reaction to seeing Luis at the gallery last night, it had taken me a while to remember that the second business card I had found hidden in Howard's appointment book had been from the Black Stilt Art Gallery. Something must have led Howard to the gallery too!

Today, there wasn't much to see. The gallery was closed but would be open to the public between two and four in the afternoon. A quick look through the front window revealed several oil paintings, mostly mountain landscapes, a few showing the beauty of the northern lights against a bleak snowy backdrop. Several carvings stood on display on pedestals, mostly birds and animals—a giant owl with outspread wings, a muskox, a wolf.

I wondered if last night's event was in honour of a charity, or perhaps it was an art showing for one of the gallery's artists. I hadn't noticed anyone leaving with a painting tucked under their arm, but it was the kind of place that would deliver a patron's acquisition to them the following day. Along with flowers or a bottle of champagne.

I went around to the back of the building and ducked behind a large metal disposal bin behind one of the stores. A white cargo van stood in gallery's loading dock. A man came into view, partially hidden by the open cargo van doors. He offloaded a picture frame and carried it into the gallery. He made several trips back and forth and unloaded six frames. Each frame was wrapped in layers of plastic.

Finally, he came out, closed the van, sauntered over to the back wall of the building, and lit a cigarette. I registered a sense of disappointment. It wasn't the bearded man.

·······

Now I was sitting in my favourite restaurant in Glenmore Landing having a late lunch. The day was grey and drizzly, the forecast called for mixed rain and snow tonight. This time of year, the weather could turn on a dime. It wouldn't be the first time we had an ice storm or a massive snow dump in early October.

My chicken wrap arrived along with a tall glass of orange juice and soda water. I placed my phone next to my plate, googled the Black Stilt Art Gallery and read while I ate.

Black Stilt Art Gallery specializes in the acquisition, sale, and appraisal of fine modern & contemporary Canadian art. Please contact us if you would like us to host your private art exhibition or special event, or to inquire about our annual Art-In-Event-ation Gala for our most prominent indigenous and notable Canadian artists.

Our inventory is deeper than shown online. We both offer and seek notable and exceptional art for new and experienced collectors at a variety of price ranges. Please contact us if you are searching for a specific piece, as we travel worldwide for special projects. Appointments can be made at your or our offices for confirmed project engagements.

The website had the usual bumph about promoting art and artists of merit and a statement about adherence to ethical practices. The gallery owner was not named, which I found rather unusual. Instead, it said the gallery was led by individuals whose backgrounds were in museums, business, and art history, and staff had internationally recognized professional designations having completed formal training in all aspects of fine art research and appraisal.

Could Milt Landen be the owner?

The last page of the website listed their latest exhibitions, held at the gallery or other locations such as Art Avenue New York. I scrolled through several pages of the online art. All of the items were modern, contemporary, no old-world art.

I found a section on their website that could only be viewed by an account holder, presumably showing them pieces curated specifically to match their interests. A contact form was provided for anyone wishing to discuss an appraisal or acquisition project. The form ended with the words, "All inquiries are held in strict confidence and without obligation."

I swallowed the last bite of my wrap and wiped my fingers on a napkin. Who knew buying and selling art required so much confidentiality?

I slowly scrolled through photos I had taken last night. Maybe the woman in the black dress and dripping in diamonds was one of the experts extolled on the gallery's website. I googled some of the art shows mentioned on the site.

The woman in black turned out to be Regina Boscovich. The article I found didn't say if she owned the Black Stilt Art Gallery but did mention that she owned an art galley, headed up an art foundation, and lately made herself known on the charity circuit with Franklin Dirks. Now I was certain I had seen her with Franklin Dirks at Adan's charity gala.

Why did Howard have this gallery's business card taped to the back of his appointment book? They didn't seem to deal in antiquities or pre-Columbian artifacts. There had to be a connection to whatever he had been investigating.

What was Luis doing at the gallery last night? He certainly didn't dabble in fine art. The walls in his condo contained a few framed newspaper articles about the biggest cases he and his team had solved, and two large pencil-line drawings—one showing the pieces of a deconstructed magnum and the other an early version of a lie detector—hung over his sofa.

The restaurant crowd thinned, and the server brought me a third refill of coffee. Besides the woman in black, I had identified twelve of the sixty or so guests who had been at the gallery along with Luis.

Franklin Dirks had been there along with a Senator, the mayor, a former oilman known for his philanthropy, and several members of the Calgary Development Committee, just to name a few. The lady in red, with whom Luis left, remained unidentified. My gut grew heavy as I recalled Luis climbing into the back of a limo with her.

I expanded several more photos before I realized what I had seen. I scrolled back and expanded the photo until it became too grainy. I switched to email.

My finger flicked each screen until I found it, the video from Howard's safety deposit box that I'd mailed to myself. I opened the video and watched until the man in the black car coat appeared on screen. I froze the video clip and went back to the gallery photos. It was the same man. I was sure of it.

The dullness that had settled over my brain cleared. I sat up and expanded each photo of Luis. There was the man again, standing and chatting with Luis. They looked like they knew each other.

Was this the dirty cop Jeff Nickleson had been obsessing over? And what about Luis? What was he doing there? Could this be the reason he had flown off the handle when I hinted...okay, not hinted, *accused* him of not being interested in any potential wrongdoing in his department?

FIFTY-FOUR

Any thoughts I might have been entertaining about writing up a final report of my findings—or rather, lack of findings—to give to Donna went out the window once I saw the photo of Luis talking to the man in the video—the video that showed the man in Palermo's office building the night Palermo died. A video file Howard had carefully secured in a safety deposit box.

Maybe I had it all wrong.

What if it was the video clip from the night Palermo died that everyone was looking for, not the statue? Maybe something on that video was so important that someone killed Howard and Nickleson to keep it quiet. Howard obviously thought it was important enough to secure in a safety deposit box.

I pulled open the door to my office building and took the stairs two at a time up to the second floor. I rushed down the dimly lit hallway to my office and unlocked the door. My excitement grew as the lights flickered and bloomed into full light in the inner office. I sat at my computer and waited while it booted up. As soon as it finished, I pulled up the video from Howard's thumb drive. I stopped the video every second to scrutinize each frame. The background in one of the frames caught my eye.

A shot of two people standing by the elevators now had my attention. One of figures was of a man, his back toward the camera, but I could tell by the stoop of his shoulders that he was older. He wore a fedora, a long, belted trench coat, and held a cane in his right hand. I sucked in a breath and peered closer. The image didn't allow me to see more details, but I wondered if this could be Milt Landen. The figure was thin, and I could see he wore glasses.

I looked at the time stamp. This clip was one from the twenty seconds or so of video shown before a large jump in the time stamp. I continued watching until the man I had seen with Luis came into view. Deep lines at both sides of his mouth creased his wide face. He walked with purpose, like he meant business, and this time I noticed the clenched fist.

I compared his image with the one I had taken of him at the gallery. In that photo he was smiling but the smile never made it to his eyes. I needed to know if this man was a cop and Luis sure as heck wasn't going to tell me. I had already asked Mike and Nickleson's wife if they could ID the man in the video, and both said they couldn't. All Nickleson's wife could tell me was that her husband's partner in Winnipeg, the one who caused him to relocate to Calgary, had been called Ace.

Eli Yardley, Nickleson's cop buddy, would know, but he hadn't returned any of my follow-up emails or calls after meeting me to tell me that Jeff Nickleson had been obsessed with a cop he thought was dirty. I tried Eli again, this time sending him the photo from the gallery, the one showing the man I was trying to ID standing talking to Luis.

I had no idea what I would do with the information, if I ever got it, but I needed to know if the man in the video was a cop named Ace.

Could Nickleson's old partner have transferred to Calgary? Is that what Nickleson meant when he told Eli that he learned his lesson in Winnipeg and wouldn't be making the same mistake twice when he noticed something not quite right. If his old partner transferred to Calgary—could that be the reason Nickleson left CPS?

I scrolled through my file on Howard until I came to the list of dates I had found in his appointment book. I sat up as adrenaline shot through my veins. 17 10 21 (bsag). The date was for the night of the private event I witnessed at the Black Stilt Art Gallery. *Bsag—Black Stilt Art Gallery—it has to be.*

I jumped up, unable to sit still. This changed everything. The date of the art gallery event was almost two weeks after Howard died. Why was that date in his appointment book? Something important must have happened last night. And not just me seeing Luis leaving with a stunning woman.

· · · • · • · · ·

The parking lot of Jordie's was packed when I got there. Mike and I had met here several times in the past. It had a reputation as being a cop bar, mainly due to its proximity to CPS headquarters. I opened the door and walked in.

A hostess greeted me and asked me if I'd like a table. I looked past her. Several seats remained empty at the bar.

"I'll just sit at the bar, if that's okay."

"Of course."

I made my way to the bar, slid off my coat, and settled myself on a leather stool. The bartender came right over.

"A scotch, please. Glenfiddich, if you have it. Neat."

He nodded and walked away. I took a minute to scan my surroundings. Most of the tables were occupied by groups of two or three. A larger group in the corner was celebrating something, their noisy, boisterous laughter filling the room.

The bartender returned with my scotch. I took a sip. Every bit as good as ever. I felt a tap on my shoulder and swivelled around.

"Ryker! My gosh. How are you?"

His face lit up with a smile. "I thought that was you."

"You haven't changed a bit. Married life agrees with you. And fatherhood." I dated Ryker once. Now it seemed like an eon ago. We didn't last long. Ryker had been eager to find the one, get married, and start a family. I had been in a post-breakup phase after ditching my narcissistic ex-boyfriend and wasn't looking for anything serious.

"We have two now. A boy and a girl."

"That's awesome. Congrats on baby number two. I can't believe it. The last time I saw you, you and your wife were expecting your first."

"Yeah, well, we didn't waste any time. The kids are fourteen months apart. A bit hectic now, but it will be great when they get older."

I nodded. "Can you join me for a drink, or are you here with someone?" I stared past him to see if anyone was paying us any attention.

"Thanks, Jorja, but I'm actually on my way out. Tana's been with the kids all day, and a quick drink after work is all the time I can afford. But it was great seeing you."

"Great seeing you, too." I meant it. Ryker was one of the good guys. It was nice to see him looking happy. Then I remembered why I was here. "Oh Ryker, before you go, can you look at something for me?" I turned and picked up my cell phone off the bar where I had placed it.

"Sure."

"I'm trying to locate a police officer who knew my client's husband when they worked together in Winnipeg. Her husband died recently, and she thought, since I know some of the members of CPS, that I might know him. This guy." I pulled up a photo of the man I was trying to ID and showed it to him.

He leaned in for a closer look. I prayed he wouldn't question my weak story about why I wanted to locate him. He straightened and shook his head. "Sorry. I don't recognize him."

"That's okay. A long shot—but you never know." I flashed him a smile.

"Well, I better go. Take care, Jorja." He lifted a hand and walked away.

I asked a few other people, including the bartender, if they knew the man in my photo. All said no. I was getting ready to leave when I sensed someone behind me. A man slid into the seat next to me.

The bartender looked over.

"A Jack and Coke. And another drink for the lady." The stranger nodded in my direction.

I started to protest, until I turned and met his eyes.

It was the man I was looking for. I felt suffocated by his presence. His arm, next to mine, was massive. His eyes watched me without a hint of warmth.

"I was just getting ready to leave, but I guess I could stay for one more." My heart was racing so hard it was starting to flutter in my chest. I knew my smile looked tight, frozen.

"I know you from somewhere."

"Oh. Well, I come here occasionally. A friend of mine used to be with the Toronto Police Service. He introduced me to the place."

"No. That's not it."

The bartender set our drinks down in front of us, looked over at the man next to me, and raised his eyebrows.

As soon as the bartender stepped back, the man repeated his question.

"Where do I know you from?" His tone was demanding. A cold sweat broke out on the back of my neck.

"I really don't know. You sure that's not a pick-up line?"

He leaned in closer, his build obliterating my view of anything else. "Why? Would you be interested if it was?"

"Maybe." I swallowed.

"What's your name?"

I tried to keep my voice light. "Jorja. What's yours?" My hand shook slightly as I reached for my glass. I left it lying on the bar, curled around my drink.

"Raymond." He took a drink, set his glass back down, and stared at me. I was getting the full interrogation treatment. I'm sure this worked well for him with his perps. "You got a last name?"

My brain convulsed. Should I give him my real name or make one up? I tilted my head and looked at him from behind half-closed eyes. A strand of hair fell across my cheek. "I'll tell you mine if you tell me yours."

"I think I know you." He nodded several times, as if confirming his own thoughts. "You dating any cops?"

I realized he might have recognized me from one of my too-frequent visits to the cop shop over the last few years.

"Let me guess," I countered. "Are you a cop?"

"Do I look like a cop?"

"Actually, you do."

"So, Jorja. You here looking for someone in particular, or just a good time?"

I tightened my grip on the glass and, with great effort, brought it to my lips and took a sip. I put my glass down and turned to look at him. "How about neither."

"Lady. You don't want to mess with me." He stated it like a fact, but he looked pissed.

I gathered up my phone and purse and turned to slide off the stool.

He threw a couple of bills on the bar, stood up, and put his hand on the back of my neck. He bent his head until his mouth was next to my ear. "I won't tell your cop boyfriend you're cruising the bars looking to be picked up. Our little secret, right?" His fingers tightened on my neck before he let go and walked away.

It took every inch of strength I had to gather up my things in what I hoped looked like a leisurely pace and make my way outside. I glanced around, worried he was waiting for me outside, then sprinted to my car. Not only had he made me, he knew who I was.

FIFTY-FIVE

Too wired to relax after my encounter with Raymond, I went back to the office. Now as the building quieted for the night, I questioned my decision. I got up from my desk, walked out to the outer office, and locked the door. I stood still but couldn't hear anyone outside.

Raymond was clearly the man in the video. Now I wanted to know if he was also Jeff Nickleson's old partner from Winnipeg. I could see his fellow cops nicknaming him Ace. More likely, he gave himself the nickname. I remembered Howard's neighbour's description of the cop she had seen going into Howard's apartment. A big, beefy guy with broad shoulders. Too bad she didn't get a good look at his face.

I sat back down at my desk. What exactly would it mean to this case if Raymond turned out to be Jeff Nickleson's nemesis? Nickleson was so certain his former partner was a dirty cop that he bet his career on it. Could his former partner have later transferred to CPS? Is that why Nickleson became disgruntled with CPS so quickly and retired? Is that why Nickleson's friend, Eli, refused to say anything more.

Nickleson's co-worker said Nickleson had watched the building security camera videos multiple times the night Palermo died. He was the person most likely to have given Howard the video clips from that night. But why? What did he notice or see? And if Raymond was the dirty cop Nickleson was referring to, who was he working for? Landen? Dirks, the real-estate developer? A government official?

Why would Landen need a CPS cop in his pocket? Could he have provided Landen with a falsified report, saying the jade statue had been stolen? I'd be more willing to believe that instead of Landen's ridiculous story about him not reporting the theft at his museum to the police because the artifacts weren't worth the trouble.

I shook my head. It didn't make sense. If Landen had been paying off a cop, it was for a larger reason, not a one-off theft. I looked around for divine inspiration, but all I saw were stacks of paper salvaged form Howard's apartment and a few half-filled flip charts on the wall. It was hard to let go of my current thinking to come up with a different angle.

I glanced at the papers on my desk and pulled over one of the piles. It contained a mishmash of invoices, printed pages from a computer file, newspaper clippings, and handwritten notes. I shifted through the papers, flipping each page over into a separate pile after giving it a cursory glance. I pulled three articles out of the mix, all three containing a hand drawn asterisk at the top of the page. I assumed the asterisk was made by Howard.

Jeff Nickleson had been carrying around two newspaper articles in an envelope when I saw him the day he died. An article about the cursed jade statue and Palermo's death, and the other about a big drug bust that never reached trial because police conduct in the investigation had come into question. A minute later, I had all five articles spread out on my desk.

One of the newspaper articles was about an airport baggage handler who was killed when the ramp to the cargo hold collapsed, pinning him to the ground. The victim's family sued when it was discovered that a bolt on the ramp had sheared. Another article was about a Canadian man who died in a diving accident while vacationing in Thailand. The last article mentioned that a case against a member of The Eastside Bloods, a drug gang, had been dismissed after a waterline leak destroyed crucial evidence in the police station's property room. *How lucky is that.*

I sat back and rubbed the back of my neck. These news articles couldn't just be random stories that had caught Howard's eye. Could they be somehow related to the dirty cop Nickleson had been investigating? Could he have been the one who investigated these cases? But none of the articles mentioned a cop or anyone named Raymond.

My eyes snapped open. It was dark outside, the building eerily quiet. I glanced at my watch. An hour had passed. I must have dozed off. I had been dreaming about something.

I stared at the news articles laid out in front of me. The hair on the back of my neck bristled. My fingers gripped the wireless mouse as I sat up. I scrolled down to the list of numbers I had looked at earlier, the ones I had found in Howard's appointment book.

My insides vibrated as my eyes flew from the newspaper articles in front of me and back to my computer files. I matched one of the numbers to the date of the drug bust mentioned in the article that Nickleson had dropped in my car and a second number to the date the airport handler had been killed. A third number matched the date of the Canadian diver's death. A film of moisture formed on the back of my neck; my face felt flushed. I still didn't know how or why these articles would be so significant to Howard that he made a note of them. But there had to be a connection. And I suspected the connection was to Nickleson's dirty cop.

I looked through the articles again but couldn't find a match for the remaining numbers listed in Howard's appointment book.

I sat back, closed my eyes, and took several slow, deep breaths to calm my mind. It was pointless. I got up and paced my small office. The last date on the list Howard had made—the one with BSAG written after it—was made while Howard was still alive, but the date was for several weeks in the future. Howard must have known about the planned private event that was to be held there. He must have thought something important was going to happen at the Black Stilt Gallery that night. But what?

Another half hour of pacing had me ninety percent certain. The missing jade jaguar, the foiled drug bust in Winnipeg, Palermo's death, the other deaths mentioned in the newspaper articles that Howard had highlighted—they were all connected. They had to be. What if Howard had figured out how they were connected, and someone killed him for it?

Whatever Howard was working on, something had gone wrong. I reasoned that there was a good possibility that Jason Gray had nicked Palermo's jaguar and not just a few worthless artifacts from Landen's Museum the day of the fire. Even if he didn't have the statue, his behaviour afterward was cause for concern. Why else had he and his girlfriend Candace gone into hiding?

I sat down and pulled up a map of Horsethief Canyon. Candace told her friend Skyla she had to go away for a while, and Skyla told me that Jason liked to hang out in an old, abandoned cabin in the canyon. Jason Gray and Candace could be hiding out there.

The little voice in my head, the cautious one, screamed at me, *Are you crazy? You're not going out there, period.*

But this could be it, I argued back. This could be my chance to wrap up this case, find out what's been going on. Find out what really happened to Howard.

Later, I would wish that I had listened to the voice of reason.

FIFTY-SIX

I ARRIVED HOME AFTER midnight and spent the next few hours tossing and turning while I picked apart my relationship with Luis. Why had I told him I loved him? Did I love him? I'd never felt like this about anyone before—but was it love? Or just good old lust. I drifted off into a shallow sleep, waking several times before the phone woke me.

I scrambled for the phone and found it on the floor next to my bed. It was already nine in the morning. A CPS phone number was on the screen. My stomach sank.

Constable Macrae told me Sal's truck had been located. A farmer spotted it parked behind the barn on his neighbour's property. He found it odd, since his neighbours were attending a niece's wedding in Mexico and then planned a two-week holiday afterwards. He had been checking on their place while they were away. The truck hadn't been there three days earlier, so he called the RCMP.

"Where was it?" I asked.

"Just outside Brooks."

"Brooks?" That was an hour and half southeast of Drumheller. What was Sal doing out there? "No sign of Sal?"

"No. The truck's not damaged, no sign of anything amiss. It was left locked up behind the barn. There were no personal items in the truck, no cell phone, purse, coat, or anything that would indicate she left in a hurry."

"What happens next?"

"We're having it dusted for fingerprints, and we're checking the street cams in Brooks to see if any of them captured the truck entering town. Of course, it could have come in from one of the secondary highways and not gone into Brooks at all. We're trying to contact the owner of the property to see if there's a connection between them and your missing friend."

As far as I knew, Sal didn't know anyone in Brooks. Then again, I had never had a reason to ask her if she did. I thanked Constable Macrae for the update.

My relationship troubles with Luis faded into the background. Sal wasn't in a coma in some hospital. She hadn't gone on a bender and forgotten to call me. Someone had locked up the truck and hidden it behind a barn. Where the hell was Sal?

The call spurred me into action. I showered, dressed, then packed my Walther BB gun away in my day backpack, along with a bottle of water and a warm sweater. I grabbed my jacket, laced up my hiking boots and headed downstairs. First on the agenda was a visit to JumpIn Jalopies. I should have switched vehicles as soon as I noticed the black SUV tailing me.

I had studied Google Maps for over an hour last night. The map showed several trails leading into the canyon bottom. There were two or three structures, which might be old cabins, visible on the satellite images of the canyon.

I had nothing to indicate that Howard could have been tracking down Jason Gray. But he could be the missing link, the unexpected something that pushed bigger plans, whatever they were, off their intended track. Even if Jason didn't steal the jaguar, maybe he knew or saw something that made him run.

My trip to JumpIn Jalopies took less than twenty minutes now that rush hour was over. I walked in to find my favourite leasing agent behind the counter.

"Neil. Good to see you! How's business?"

He tossed back his head. The swatch of black hair falling across his face flipped back and briefly revealed a thin face and dark kohl-rimmed eyes before it once again settled across his cheek.

"Oh my gosh—Jorja! Hugs and kisses." He feigned giving me a kiss on my right cheek, then the left. "How's the old Taurus been treating you?"

"Good. But lately I've attracted some attention to it, if you get my drift."

"Ahh yes." He turned to his computer screen. "You need something...a little different. Now, let's see." He ran a finger down the screen. "Oh, here's one. It's perfect."

I turned in the Taurus' keys while Neil contacted someone to bring the vehicle he selected for me out from the back. He pursed his lips as he updated my file.

"You still have a pickup truck out with us," he commented.

"Yes. And yes, it's still intact."

He leaned forward and whispered conspiringly, "I know it's not you...it's the job."

Twenty minutes later, I was driving out of the lot in a white van. All of the windows were tinted, which was a nice feature. The shag carpet covering the ceiling and walls in the back, not so much. Everything in the van was manual—the transmission, the windows and doors, outside mirrors, standard radio. No Bluetooth, no GPS, no heated seats. Neil claimed no one would be expecting me to drive this kind of vehicle. He was right about that.

I offered up a prayer to the powers that ruled the universe that Sal would be found alive and well, and I headed east to Horsethief Canyon. If I didn't find any answers out there, I was done.

FIFTY-SEVEN

It started to snow once I got out of the city, little pebbles of ice at first, then a deluge of white stuff which blew horizontally across the road. So much for the hope of a long, dry, mild fall. I was out of the snow squall in ten minutes, but ominous grey clouds told me there was another one up ahead. I wondered if the van had snow tires. Probably not.

I tried not to think about what lay ahead. Getting out on the highway left me feeling like I was leaving all my worries about Sal, Luis angst, and this crazy case behind. I knew it was a temporary illusion, but a welcome one for the few hours or so that it would last.

I passed through two more mini snow squalls before I reached Drumheller. The roads in town were wet with melting snow and the sun was struggling to make itself seen. After a quick stop to pick up a bottle of water and a sandwich, I followed the signs to North Dinosaur Trail. I passed the turnoff to the Tyrrell Museum and continued north.

The van's engine laboured as it climbed out of the Red Deer River valley. The meagre traffic I had encountered on Highway 9 was now nonexistent. Other than the climb in elevation, Dinosaur Trail was like any other quiet countryside road.

I crested the hill and spotted a small sign pointing me to the Horsethief Canyon lookout. I followed the gravel lane into a parking lot. One other car was there. I parked at the far end of the lot, got out my daypack, and locked up. I made my way across the gravel and stepped into a grassy field. A family of four were taking pictures at the rim of the canyon.

I crossed the grassy flat and stopped. A network of narrow valleys winding their way through steep canyon walls materialized mystically from the flat prairie landscape around me. The view was overwhelming and unlike anything Google Maps prepared me for.

I hoisted my daypack higher on my shoulder and pulled my ballcap down firmer. A faint breeze took away any warmth from the sun struggling to make its presence known, and I was glad to be wearing my fleece hoodie. The family moved on, the two children racing each other back to their car.

I had read that none of the paths into the canyon were marked, so I followed the rim until I found one. I paused to stare at the steep walls, eroded by thousands of years of rain, raging rivers, and harsh weather. The walls were barren, and the canyon deeper than I imagined.

Multicoloured layers of sediment formed prominent stripes in the canyon walls and mirrored the horizontal layers of grey-streaked sky. Bands of yellow and rusty orange outlined the canyon floor, a sharp contrast to the grey and pale-brown colour of the surrounding walls.

I started down the path, the loose pebbles and recent skiff of melting snow making for a treacherous descent. Now that I was in the canyon, the breeze I had felt at the top no longer existed. I paused after a while and scanned the path ahead of me.

The canyon was known for its rich fossil beds but was also home to a variety of snakes. I peered closer at a small ledge jutting from the canyon wall. Most of the snakes were harmless, except for the Prairie Rattlesnake, which was venomous and hard to spot because of its dull, brown-grey colour. They'd be on the move now, slithering through rocks and around boulders as they moved from their summer digs to their winter dens.

I stopped again, halfway down, where the path diverged. Unzipping my hoodie, I reached in for my map. The path leading to the right wound around the canyon wall and led me deeper into no man's land. I looked up; the walls seemed even steeper looking back from this vantage point. A prairie falcon swooped high above me.

The difference in the weather was remarkable. The wind was nonexistent down here and now that the sun was out, it was bordering on hot. I stripped off my jacket, tying the arms of the hoodie around my waist, and continued on.

The path was dusty, dry, and soon my boots were covered in a fine reddish powder. How the canyon came to be called Horsethief Canyon was still somewhat of a mystery. Local legend believed that horse thieves and cattle smugglers had once used the canyon to hide their pilfered livestock.

An hour later, I spotted it. A crumbling shack of rough-hewed boards, the walls leaning at a precarious angle. The air was deadly still now. I paused to catch my breath, my thumping heart the only sound in my ears. A chill ran down my arms, standing the hairs up on end. I shuddered and continued down, stepping sideways so as not to slide on the loose material.

I continued toward the shack. As I got closer, I could see the roof had caved in, leaving a gaping hole open to the sky. This couldn't be the cabin Jason Gray and his girlfriend were using as a hideout. I thought about the warning Skyla had given me, that Jason stored a hoard of firearms somewhere in the canyon. I stopped and pulled my Walther BB gun from my daypack, realizing that it would be pointless against Jason's arsenal of weapons.

Something moved to my right, and I jumped back, raising my gun. A garter snake slithered into a dusty mud-cracked crevice. My heart beat faster. I looked up at the wall of banded rock above me. Climbing out of here was going to be a challenge.

I continued down the path, the gun held loosely at my side. The cabin wasn't completely on the canyon floor, but in a flat spot where the canyon walls began to widen. I could place my feet more surely now—the path was broader, not as steep.

Something shifted under my boot. I jumped back, a scream clawing its way up my throat. I looked down, expecting a rattle snake, my heart hammering against my chest.

What the hell?

I reached down and picked up a wrinkled, dusty leather square. I flipped it open. Howard Bergman's face looked up at me.

FIFTY-EIGHT

I FOUGHT THE URGE to turn and run. Howard's driver's licence was visible through the plastic window on the left. Two credit cards remained in the leather slits on the right. I pried the wallet open further; two twenties sat in the money compartment along with a small, folded piece of paper.

My hand shook as I pulled at the paper, and it dropped to the ground. Squatting to pick it up, I unfolded it. The numbers looked like a series of map coordinates, written in pencil. I put my gun back in the daypack and pulled my phone from my jacket pocket, hoping to find the location of the coordinates. No signal. I returned the paper to the wallet, stood up, and scanned the canyon walls.

What the hell had Howard been doing out here? Had he come out here, like I did, looking for Jason Gray? Had he found something to make him believe Landen's former security guard had the jade jaguar and was hiding out here? What happened to make him drop his wallet?

I looked at the fold of leather again. It was well worn from years of use, the brown colour already worn off the edges. Now it was covered in dirt, and the way the plastic window had stuck when I first opened it told me it must have lain out here in the rain and sun for days.

Snapping a few pictures of the cabin and the path where I had found Howard's wallet, I debated my next move. Mostly, I wanted to turn and run, but I had spent over two and a half hours getting down here and it would be foolish to not at least check the cabin out.

I zipped Howard's wallet into the front pocket of my daypack and moved forward. Donna's voice came back to me. *"My father wasn't in all that great shape."* I looked over my shoulder. What would have made him come down here?

I closed the distance to where the cabin stood and caught a whiff of something foul. I moved closer, my arm now raised across my mouth and face. The odour I smelled a few minutes earlier had grown stronger. It was indescribably vile. A mixture of rotten meat, feces, and sickly-sweet overtones that I'd never experienced before, but I knew immediately what it was. It was coming from the cabin.

I moved closer and gagged.

My phone was still clutched in my left hand, and I turned on the video, still twenty feet from the cabin entrance. What once may have been the door lay in the dirt to one side. Something lay on the floor inside. Not a dog, not a stray cow that made its way into the canyon. I felt my legs go weak. I didn't need to move any closer.

I turned, retching repeatedly as I staggered back up the pathway, while the compulsion to look back overwhelmed me.

I stopped, my heart ready to explode as it careened wildly in my chest. I gulped in air in great heaves as I stared at the cabin below. The words *"It's not Sal,"* repeated over and over in my brain.

The phone was still clutched in my hand, now slippery with sweat. I checked for a cell phone signal. Still none. I looked up at the canyon walls, towering over me. Could I even get myself out of here? Dark clouds were moving in, the sun no longer visible. I turned and continued to climb.

I moved up the path on autopilot, each step timed to a loud ragged breath. My mind was a million miles away. Had there been two bodies down there? Was it Jason Gray? If so, where was his girlfriend, Candace?

I looked back over my shoulder; the cabin now hidden behind the curve of the canyon wall. I couldn't be completely sure who the grotesque, faceless blob was, but the clothes looked like they belonged to a man. I zipped my phone into my daypack pocket, next to the wallet I found, and continued climbing.

Halfway up, another thought intruded. What else would the police find down there? Could Howard really have come out here? What happened to Jason Gray's great arsenal of weapons? Now I realized that Skyla may have told me about Jason's weapon stash to scare me off, not go looking for him or Candace. What if Howard found Jason Gray with the statue in his possession? I shook off the next thought. No way would Howard have killed Jason. And no way would a gun-toting survivalist have stolen the statue and simply handed it back when Howard showed up.

I paused, resting my hands on my knees, struggling to pull in a full breath. Despite months of kickboxing, my thighs still burned. Not bloody likely Howard climbed in and out of this canyon. Another voice argued, *He could have, if he took his time.*

I shook my head and pressed on. Maybe Howard's wallet had been left here by someone else. Was someone trying to frame Howard?

Was I being set up? Now another kind of fear took hold of me. I looked up at the cliff of rock above me. Someone with a good rifle and scope could pick me off any time they wished.

I moved closer to the canyon wall. Something slithered next to my face. I screamed, staggered back. My hands clawed at the hardened earth as I slid off the path and down the canyon wall.

I pressed down the toes of my boots and felt my hands grabbing at the few grasses that clung to the hard sediment. My toes found a crevice and I clung to the wall, terrified to move.

After a long while, I looked up. I couldn't see the path, just the banded wall of rock above me. I couldn't look down. I scanned the wall, looking for a crevice, anything to dig my fingers into. I reached up, wrapped my hand around a small knob of sediment, and tugged. It didn't crumble in my hand. I shifted my weight and pulled myself forward.

I lost track of all time. Now I realized that a bullsnake, coiled on a ledge next to the path, had caused my stupid panic. The ugly, dull-brown snake was huge, though I knew it wasn't venomous. But I hadn't had time to recall that fact, I just reacted.

I looked up. I could see a break in the slope now, where the path was. Slow and steady, I reminded myself. I had slipped back a few times, losing precious time and distance, and I was too close to making it out of here to risk another misstep.

My hands and fingers were streaked with blood, and I felt the pressure under my fingernails from the dirt and silt packed under each one. I reached the spot where I had gone over and hoped the snake, as harmless as it was, had moved on.

I reached up. A hand grabbed my wrist. I felt myself being dragged up the last few feet. And then everything went black.

FIFTY-NINE

My fingertips tingled. I felt a fluttering in my chest. Something was wrong. Every cell in my body was vibrating in waves—dizzyingly fast, then slowing, only to speed up again. I couldn't breathe.

My eyes snapped open and peered into a dense blackness. *Oh my god...I can't see.*

I lifted my hand. It came up against something hard. Scattered thoughts raced through my brain, none making sense. My heart rate reached dizzying speed. I turned my head and spun out of control. I pressed my hands to the side, to stop my freefall into a black vortex. My throat closed. A dark heaviness tightened around me.

The blackness rolled to a standstill. My laboured breath puffed against my face. Something was covering my face, my mouth, making it hard to breathe. My fingers dug into something soft. I was rocked to the left. We were moving again. I was in a vehicle. My fingers grasped the material beneath my fingers, and I pulled. Shag carpet. I was in the back of my van. I started to shake. The tightness in my chest deepened.

A sharp pain shot through my head. Everything went still.

· · · • · • · · ·

I lifted my head and it touched something smooth, hard. My arms flew to the side and hit something rigid. I tried to move my legs, but they were wedged in. We were no longer moving. Where was I?

My chest heaved with fear. I turned my head, searching for a speck of light. Anything. There was none.

My hands reached up and pressed against something solid. I slid my palms back and forth, feeling the roughness of wood. I lowered my hands and slid them along each side of my body, each breath now quick and ragged.

Please, god, no. No. No. No.

The depth and power of the hopelessness that gripped me frightened me more than death. I jerked up in panic, smacking my head. I clawed at the wood; I kicked frantically. *Oh Jesus.* Would anyone hear me if I screamed? Was I already underground? I screamed over and over again until I couldn't scream anymore.

Oh god. Luis, Mike, where are you? How long was I unconscious? How much air do I have left?

My breaths were quicker now, shorter, each breath a sob. A cloak of despondency settled around me...so dark...so deep. I was going to die.

Stop. Oh please. Oh god. Maybe I wasn't six feet under. Maybe they were going to cremate me. I focused on my breathing—I was wasting precious air sobbing and screaming. *Slow. Slow.* I tried to calculate the volume of the space and how much oxygen would be in here, but my brain refused to make the computation.

Did anyone know where I was? Would anyone be out looking for me? *No.* By the time anyone noticed me missing, it would be too late.

I built a picture of the coffin in my mind. It was a coffin, not a casket. It was unlined and narrower at the bottom than the top.

I ran my hands along the rough wood above me and then slid them slowly down the side. I felt down an inch or two from the top. No seam. No fancy lining.

The centre of the lid would be the weakest.

I scrunched forward and lifted my legs to kick, but the space was too small to lift them any height. I kicked my legs out in anger. Something shifted. I kicked again and again. Now I was certain I wasn't already six feet under. A sob of relief escaped from my lips.

I lay exhausted, sweat drenching my body. The added effort was using up my precious oxygen. Each breath took effort to pull the thinning oxygen into my lungs. Soon I'd slip into unconsciousness.

I opened my mouth, but no air went in or out. I willed myself to breathe with every molecule of strength I had. My movements were slow now, my body already shutting down as I drew in lungful's of air with only traces of oxygen left.

I kicked out furiously, over and over again, until I couldn't.

A sliver of light appeared. *Go toward the light.*

Where was I?

I had momentarily blacked out. Now it all came crashing back.

I kicked again, slowly, one kick at a time. My mouth gaped open, and my neck strained with the effort to draw in a breath. The light expanded in size.

I felt a cool touch on my cheek.

Mum? My lips moved as I tried to say her name, but no sound came out.

My body shook as I scrunched myself lower. Anchoring my hands against the wood beside my head I pressed my feet against the end of the box. The gap widened. The muscles in my legs spasmed as I pressed harder.

I lay gulping quick, shallow breaths, but the air wasn't reaching my lungs. I closed my eyes and breathed. After a while, I kicked again, and the end of the box gaped open.

I turned, scrunching my shoulders to make it around, pulled my knees in as far as I could and lifted. My back strained against the wood. It gave an inch, then inched out further.

The box broke open. I lay in my scrunched positioned, too weak to move.

Something cool touched my face. My mother called my name.

SIXTY

I SAT BACK ON my knees and looked around, gasping in air. Strange objects hung all around me in the dim light, but their names wouldn't come to me. I looked down at the floor of the wooden box and struggled to get a leg over the edge. My leg flailed in the air and I tumbled over, taking the wooden box with me. I hit the floor hard and lay there, totally spent.

"Jorja."

I pushed up on my arms. *Mum?* The room spun. Nothing made sense. I wanted to say something but couldn't form the words.

"Doll...I'm...over here."

I struggled to sit up. "Sal?" it came out as a whisper. Tears welled up in my eyes.

"Over here, doll."

A lightness bubbled up my throat, a warmth radiated through my body. I peered around the dimly lit room. "Sal! Where are you? Sal? Are you okay?"

"I'll...fine."

I looked over at the box, which now lay tipped on its side on the floor next to two wooden workhorses. A simple rough-hewed wooden box. *A coffin*. A flash of memory returned...the canyon...a hand closing over my own. Then nothing.

I looked up. The ceiling was crisscrossed with steel beams. I struggled to my knees but couldn't stand up. A row of wooden crates and pallets stood next to me. An enormous table at the end of the room had one lit florescent light dangling above it. A figure sat propped up next to the table.

"Sal?"

Too weak to stand, I crawled toward her.

Sal was sitting with her back against one of the square wooden legs of the worktable. She clutched her left arm against her chest and her lips were dry and cracked, her eyes sunken.

She gave me a half smile that was more like a grimace. "That was...some...entrance, kid."

Sal was struggling to talk; her breathing was slow, shallow.

"Where are we?"

"Basement...museum."

I pulled myself up using the table. The effort exhausted me. Snippets of memory came back. I shuddered as the images flooded my brain. The wooden shack, the decomposing body.

I looked down, noticing that a chain tethered Sal's ankle to the table. I patted my pockets and looked around me. No phone, no sign of my backpack. "Sal, hang in there. I'll get you loose." My eyes searched for something I could use to break Sal's chains. Getting Sal out of here might be impossible, but I had to try.

"No time," Sal croaked. "You've got to get out."

I spotted a sink and stumbled toward it. "I'll get you some water, Sal."

I grabbed a mug standing by the sink, rinsed it, took a sip and, finding no odd taste or smell, gulped down a few mouthfuls. I refilled it and brought it back to Sal.

I lowered myself next to her and helped her take a few sips. Her left arm lay motionless across her chest.

"Thanks, doll. You don't have much time. They'll be back soon."

"I'm not leaving you." I set the cup down and looked at the chain tethering Sal's ankle to the table leg. Each link in the chain was about an inch long. The clamp around Sal's ankle was held together by two long metal pins.

"I've got to find bolt cutters...or something." I muttered.

"No...just go. Only reason I'm still alive...bait, they knew you'd come lookin'."

"No, Sal. I'm not leaving without you." I rummaged around the worktable area for anything I could use to cut Sal free. How were we going to get out? I glanced at the tall metal door to my left. Another section of the basement extended to my right. It was darker there and I couldn't see much of anything. I staggered forward, keeping an eye open for a light switch but didn't see one. I spotted a crowbar, lying on top of one of the crates.

Lugging it back to Sal, I stretched out the chain on the concrete floor and pounded the chisel edge against the links. Sweat poured down my face. I had to stop after every few thrusts, shocked at how fatigued I was.

Finally, one of the links bent enough to separate it from the rest. I helped Sal to her feet and we both stood, leaning against the table, breathing hard.

"We need to open the garage door," I gasped.

Sal lifted her hand and pointed. "...power."

"Okay. I'll check it out."

I left Sal leaning against the table and stumbled to the metal door, tall enough to accommodate cargo vans and transport trucks, wide enough for two cars. I located a box next to the door, a large button prevalent in its centre. I pressed it. Nothing happened.

I looked around for a switch or electrical box, or anything that looked like it might control the power. My eyes followed the line coming out of the box next to the door. It disappeared into the ceiling.

My brain re-engaged. Automatic garage doors usually had an override mechanism in case the power went off. I looked up. A red handle dangled ten feet over my head. My eyes searched for something to stand on. Would I even have the strength to open it if I could reach it?

I made my way back to Sal. We weren't going to get out. Even if we did, it was a long hike to town.

Sal turned, grimacing in pain.

"Sal. Are you okay?" It was a stupid question—she wasn't okay.

"I'm fine. Might have a broken arm, is all."

I looked into the black interior to our right. "There must be another way out of here."

I thought back to my time in the museum. There had been an alarmed exit door off the main exhibit hall. It would be locked from this side, of course, but maybe we could open it or trigger the alarm.

Sal voiced the very thought going through my mind.

"You go, doll. You got a better chance of getting help without me."

She was right, but I couldn't risk that help would arrive back here too late.

"No, Sal. We're sticking together."

I rummaged around the work area. Ignoring the rock saw, a small centrifuge, and an assortment of sieves and scales, I headed to the chemicals. My previous work as a lab analyst was my superpower now.

I scanned the various bottles and flasks. A pinkish-white streak of material on the table caught my eye. I touched it and rubbed my two fingers together. It felt grainy, sandy. I lifted my finger up to my nose and sniffed. It smelled slightly like gasoline and something else...something sweet. I touched my finger with the granules to my tongue. *Bitter*. It left a burning sensation.

Cocaine.

SIXTY-ONE

Soon I had our little arsenal ready. A bottle of Sodium Hydroxide, a small spray can of epoxy glue, and a retractable X-Acto knife. Personally, I'd rather have my eye splashed with acid than Sodium Hydroxide, which destroys cells on contact, leaving little chance of recovery after washing it out.

I also found a small flashlight, the batteries weak from use, and some strapping material, the kind used to secure items stacked on pallets, which I fashioned into a crude sling for Sal.

"Come on, Sal. We're not going down without a fight."

Sal shuffled stiffly to my side and took the spray can of glue from my hands. "Let's roll."

We snaked through a bank of storage racks containing wooden trays filled with artifacts. It was darker back here and I considered turning on the flashlight but decided to keep it off until the blackness became so thick we couldn't walk.

"What happened, Sal? How'd you get here?"

"After I found Landen's place and called you, I went in…for a closer look. I left the truck on a side road with the hood up and ducked through the neighbour's field. Damn cows were making a racket. I found a good spot to watch the house. But those darn cows are more curious than magpies. They way they were carryin' on, I should have known someone would come looking."

I had no trouble picturing what Sal described. "You were watching the house from that stand of trees by the little creek?"

"You psychic or something?"

"Not exactly. When I couldn't reach you, I went looking for you. Found your hat in the mud down by the creek."

Sal's voice edged up a notch. "You keep it?"

"Sorry, Sal. One of their guys spotted me, so I hightailed it out of there."

"Well, now that I know where it is I can go back and get it."

Assuming we get out of here.

We manoeuvred through a narrow aisle packed with flat crates on either side and entered another room, almost the same size as the one we had been left in. I turned on the flashlight, its small beam unable to penetrate more than a few feet of darkness. Sal jumped. "Holy Jezus."

I swung the light beam in her direction. A decayed mummy lay in its sarcophagus next to us.

"Now that's one old broad," huffed Sal as we passed.

"I just want to live to see fifty. So, you were watching Landen's place," I reminded her.

"For a bit. The damn cows were clustered at the corner of the property, my feet were wet, and I got a cramp in my back, so I figured I'd go back. Then one of the garage doors opened and out drives a bobcat. It comes down the hill toward me. I was ready to run when it stops and starts digging." Sal stopped to take a breath. "I'm freezin' my ass off and thinking its going to be dark soon, but the damn hole is getting big, and I know they're not planting no tree."

"What were they doing?"

"When I'm pret-in near frozen solid, they drive a car out of the garage and into the hole and start piling the dirt back in over it."

I glanced back. "A car?"

Sal shook her head. "Some people have way too much money. The engine sounded good, but the windshield and front end were smashed."

I stopped and Sal ran into me. I heard a sharp intake of breath.

"Sorry, Sal. Are you okay?"

"Yeah, yeah, other than feelin' like roadkill."

"What kind of car?"

"Sporty...grey or silver, newer model."

I tried to process what Sal just told me. She was still talking.

"I heard somethin' behind me. I thought it was one of those damn cows, coming down to the creek. Then I see this big guy. Arms like a gorilla. I figure maybe it's the neighbour, pissed cause I'm trespassing. He grabs my arm and twists it behind my back. I figure that's when my arm got busted. That's all I remember. Then I wake up in the garage. Chained to the table like a dog."

"God, Sal. I'm so sorry." It was all my fault; I had put her into this situation.

"Now, don't go feelin' all guilty. I took the job; no one put a gun to my head. Well, not till later."

There was only one reason anyone would bury a car. I couldn't help but wonder if it was the car that ran down Nickleson. Maybe Landen had kept Palermo's statue and killed or had someone kill him and then later kill Nickleson. That would mean he or the killer suspected Nickleson saw something incriminating. Could Raymond, the man in the video, be what set Nickleson off? But if any of this was what had transpired, why would this cop be helping Landen?

Now the museum basement was black as sin. I strained my ears for sound.

"When I didn't hear from you, I knew something bad must have happened. I went to your place and checked around, but no one had seen you. I filed a missing persons report on you. Hopefully the cops find you...us."

"Wouldn't count on it, doll."

"I found some powdery grains on the worktable back there." I nodded in the direction we had come from. "I'm sure it's cocaine."

"The gorilla and another neanderthal come here every so often. They let me have a piss and something to eat and drink. They've been bringing in these flat crates, with paintings inside. I watched them change out the frames and then they pack everything up again and leave."

I turned on the flashlight. The batteries were so weak it barely lit a path two feet in front of us. We had been feeling our way through a maze of crates and I was totally disoriented.

"Sal, I have no idea where we are. Maybe we should just find a place to rest for a minute. I might need to go scout around. No use following me until I figure out where we are."

Sal tucked herself in behind a large crate and I set the Sodium Hydroxide I'd been carrying in my pocket beside her on the concrete floor. The X-Acto knife was still in my jeans pocket.

The flashlight was almost useless. I shone it at my feet and felt my way around the crates until I came to a wall. I touched the wall, and something shifted. I pulled at the wood and a tray rolled out from the wall. I cursed.

We had somehow wound our way through various alcoves and around stacks of goods and circled back on ourselves. I was sure the wall I was looking at contained the racks of trays we had passed earlier.

Then I heard it. Faintly, the sound of a motor and the garage door rolling up.

SIXTY-TWO

I DIDN'T HAVE TIME to make it back to Sal. I pressed myself into a space next to a display cabinet. The lights in the outer garage area flickered and came to life. The light barely reached the area I was in, but now I could see the outline of cabinets, crates, and stacks of wooden pallets. I held my breath. Angry voices filtered back to me. I tightened my grip on the crowbar.

"Just fucking find them."

Footsteps pounded on the concrete. I raised the crowbar.

He stopped near me, cursing under his breath. I heard a noise to my left, a scraping sound. *Sal.*

He moved forward, breathing hard now. I waited until he passed and swung the crowbar at the back of his head. He crumpled to the ground.

I could hear Sal now, shuffling through the maze of boxes and crates. I turned around. She appeared several feet behind me. She mouthed 'go' and waved me forward.

I crept down the aisle toward the light.

"Hey, Dragon," a voice called out. I pressed myself into the shadows and waited.

"Dragon?" A second man appeared; it was the bearded man. "What the hell? Shit." He pulled a gun from the small of his back and crept forward. I waited, hardly daring to breathe.

A raspy voice call out, "Dragon's having a nap, asshole."

I knew what Sal was trying to do. As soon as the man with the gun moved on, I crept out into the aisle and rushed toward the garage bay area, keeping my weight on my toes. Boxes crashed to the ground behind me and the man let out a string of curse words I'd never heard before. I broke into a run.

Rounding the corner, I flew past the wooden workhorses and toward a van that was parked just inside the garage doors. I reached the van just as another man stepped out from behind a stack of crates. I barely had time to flinch before he brought the wooden rod he held, down on me.

· · · • · • · · · ·

Pain shot through my shoulder. Something rough and cold pressed against my cheek. I opened one eye, then the other. The bile rose up my throat and sent me into a gagging fit, the duct tape across my mouth making it hard to breathe. I felt my body slide and my head bounced on the metal van floor.

I lifted my head. Sal lay crumpled in one corner, her back toward me. A younger woman, her eyes wide with fear, sat near Sal. Her hands were behind her back, her mouth and feet duct-taped. I wiggled my fingers behind me and felt my back pocket. The X-Acto knife was still there. I slowly worked it out of my pocket and into my hand.

Opening the blade, I turned it around and poked at the duct tape. The van was speeding; the cargo box swayed from side to side. I was pretty sure we were in the back of the cube van that had been parked at the door to the museum's basement. I glanced over at the back door. It had a handle built into one of the doors, but no telling if it was locked.

I felt the tape give and pulled my hands free. I sat up and peeled the duct tape from my mouth, sucking in a few mouthfuls of air. I cut my feet loose and scrambled over to the girl. I cut through the duct tape binding her hands, then scuttled over to Sal.

"Oh god, Sal." Her face was grey and her breathing shallow. I slowly peeled the duct tape from her face. They had left her arms free, the one arm still bound to her chest by my makeshift sling. I cut through the tape around her ankles and leaned over to hand the knife to the girl who was trying to unpeel the tape from her feet.

Sal stirred. I leaned my back against the wall that separated the cargo portion of the van from the front and pulled Sal forward until her head was on my lap. I looked over at the girl. Her hands shaking so badly that she was having a hard time cutting through the tape. Finally, she freed herself and handed me the knife, her eyes still fearful.

I realized I had been staring at her. I took the knife and gave her a weak smile. "My name is Jorja."

"Candace," she replied.

I sucked in a quick breath. "Are you kidding? I've been looking for you...and your boyfriend, Jason. I'm a private investigator. I've been following a trail of bodies that seem to be connected to a jade artifact, a jaguar. The owner gave it to the man who owns the

Landen Museum for assessment. I figure the jaguar and some other things got stolen the day of a grass fire. Am I right?"

Candace started to cry.

"No, no, no. It's going to be okay." I didn't believe the words coming out of my mouth. But if we had any hope of getting out of this, we had to keep our wits about us.

Candace stifled a sob.

I nodded my encouragement as she wiped her nose with the back of her sleeve, but tears continued to roll down her cheeks.

"Sorry that you're in this mess. Do you want to tell me what happened?"

"I...I told Jason that it was a bad idea." She pulled in a huge breath and hiccupped. Her teary eyes met mine. "And...now we're going to die."

SIXTY-THREE

Candace told me Jason overheard a conversation Milt Landen had with someone about the jade jaguar. He said it could be worth millions. Landen was planning to put it on display briefly to raise the interest in the statue, then he planned to sell it to the highest bidder in a private auction. Jason saw an opportunity to make himself a rich man.

"It had been so dry all summer that it didn't take much to start the fire. Jason said that's all I had to do. Start the fire. I was worried it could get out of hand, maybe burn down the museum or kill someone inside. He said he'd make sure everyone got out. And because it was early morning, there would only be a few visitors."

"You set the grass fire?"

She nodded miserably. "Jason got everyone out, like he said he would. He managed to get into Landen's office and access the safe. He'd been watching the old man and knew where he kept the combination. I guess Landen didn't trust his memory, so he had it written down. The statue was inside. Jason took it and grabbed some other stuff as well on his way out."

"What was the plan? It's hard to sell something like that unless you know the right people."

She nodded. "Jason knew something funny was going on at the museum. He figured they were bringing in drugs. He saw a lot of shipments coming in and out of the museum, a lot of picture frames. He got curious when he once saw one of the guys drop a frame. It just shattered into pieces. Later he found traces of powder where it had broken. He said it was cocaine."

I nodded. "I found traces of what I'm sure is cocaine in the museum basement. Was Landen making fake artifacts and smuggling cocaine in that way as well?"

"I don't know. Jason thought the jaguar was real—at least at first. But then Landen didn't report the theft of the jaguar to the cops and when there was nothing about the robbery in the papers he started to wonder."

"I thought that was odd, too. Landen told me the jaguar was a fake and that he had given it back to the owner, and that only a few relatively inexpensive items were taken from the museum. But it never made sense to me, because the owner later hired a friend of mine to try to find the jaguar statue."

The van suddenly swayed, flinging us forward and then back. I dug my fingers into the ridges in the floor to steady myself until the van corrected itself.

"You okay?" I asked Candace, who was rubbing the back of her head after hitting it against the wall of the van.

"I'm okay." Candace grimaced and went on. "Afterwards, the fire-fighters and cops were looking into the fire and Jason's company was all over him for not following evacuation protocol. A week later they fired him. His boss told him it was because business was slow, but Jason didn't believe him. By then, Jason figured he was right about Landen's drug operation. That the reason Landen didn't report the jaguar stolen is because he didn't want the cops poking around and finding his drug op. So, Jason changed the plan."

"Landen must have known Jason had taken the jaguar, or at least he must have suspected him."

"I think so too. Jason noticed a guy following him, and then one night the guy showed up at my place. I was terrified. Jason said we had to hide out for a while. He had already bought us tickets to fly to the Dominican Republic. I didn't want to leave the country, but he said it would only be for a little while, until things cooled down."

"What was the new plan?"

"Jason sent Landen a ransom note asking for a million dollars. That if he didn't pay it, word would leak out about his underground operation at the museum."

"Whoa. So even if the jaguar wasn't worth that much, he figured Landen would pay it anyway as a form of hush money."

"Yes. Jason wanted me to do the drop, but I didn't want anything more to do with all of this. He promised me all I had to do was start the fire." She started to cry again.

Obviously plan B had failed, or we wouldn't all be in the back of this van. "Tell me what happened."

"The ransom drop was to happen a week later, to give Landen time to get the money together."

"Where was the drop?"

"At the Glenmore Reservoir in Calgary."

I sucked in a sharp breath. Candace wiped her nose with the back of her hand.

"You agreed to do the exchange."

Her chin quivered. "There's a small path on the south side of the reservoir that runs from the yacht club to Glenmore Landing. Not the main path but a smaller one that isn't as busy. I was to meet Landen at the third bench along that path. Jason was going to be there too but stay hidden. He said I wouldn't be in any danger; he'd look out for me."

"What went wrong?"

"Jason wouldn't give me the jaguar to take to the drop. I was to get the money then after I had the money, I was to call his cell phone. He would tell me where Landen could find the statue. That he would leave or hide it somewhere nearby. I was to take the money and go back to the yacht club parking lot where there would be lots of people around. Jason's car would be parked there waiting for me. He said he'd leave the keys on top of the front driver's side tire. All I had to do was drive away, go to a motel, overnight it, and he'd call me the next day to tell me where to meet him."

I didn't think this was the brightest of plans, but of course, this is usually how things fell apart. "Obviously things didn't go as planned."

Candace sniffled. "When I got there this big, bearded man was waiting on the bench. I was scared. Then I noticed he didn't have a bag or anything with him. For a minute I thought maybe it was just some random guy. I stopped a few feet away and called out, asking if he had something for me. He got up and started walking toward me. Then he reached out to grab me. I turned and ran. He caught up to me and started dragging me into the bush. Then a man stepped out of the trees, an older man. He tried to stop him, and they started to wrestle. He told me to run."

My muscles tightened as I shifted my body toward her. The movement caused a wave of dizziness, then nausea. This must have been

Howard. I shook my head. I needed to hear what Candace was saying.

"I just kept going. Except it was the wrong way." She shuddered as she wrapped her arms around herself. "It took me a long time to circle around and make my way to the yacht club. I found Jason's car and climbed in. I thought I was going to have a heart attack."

"So, then you went to a hotel?"

"I was planning to. I even had a hotel picked out near Chinook Mall. But on the way there I saw a black SUV following me. I made some turns and looped back, and it did too. I just panicked." She put her hand up to her mouth to choke back a sob. "I called Jason, but he wasn't answering."

"What did you do?"

"I know I shouldn't have but I went back to my place. I still had the keys, and my rent was paid up until the end of the month. I figured if I got out of town, he wouldn't follow me. I kept watching him in my rearview mirror but once I got onto Deerfoot Trail I lost him in all the traffic."

"Let me guess. You didn't lose him."

"No. I couldn't sleep. I couldn't reach Jason. I didn't know what happened. I figured Jason would eventually come to find me. Then a few days later, something woke me in the middle of the night. I heard someone coming in through the bathroom window. I ran out the front door and that's when he grabbed me. When I woke up, I was in a small, dark room. It was all concrete and had no windows."

"The museum basement?" I guessed.

"I don't know. They moved me two more times, then tonight, they came and got me, tied me up and put me in the back of this truck."

"So, no money, no statue."

"They kept asking me where Jason was, where the statue was. I told them I didn't know. I *don't* know. Jason was supposed to tell me where it was *after* I had the money. They threatened to kill me. They said they would go after my friends, my family. After a few days, they got rougher. This...this...the man with the beard came into the room with another guy. They unwrapped some instruments. They said they were going to pull all my teeth, one by one, until I told them."

Candace began to cry in earnest. I moved my free arm around her shoulder. Sal stirred in my lap. "I told them about Jason's hideout in Horsethief Canyon. I didn't know if that's where he was, but I figured it might be."

I fought down the panic that was starting to consume me. I was pretty sure they had found Jason. I looked at the back door of the van. Maybe we could jump out when the van stopped or slowed. Assuming we hadn't been locked in from the outside. I looked down at Sal and fought back the tears.

The van slid to the side. Sal moved to sit up, just as the van swerved, throwing each of us against the other. The van leaned to one side then tilted sharply to the other side

"Hang on," I shouted. Candace screamed.

SIXTY-FOUR

A HORRIBLE, METAL-ON-METAL SCREECHING filled my ears as the truck rolled and tumbled. After what seemed like an eternity, the truck came to an abrupt stop, throwing us forward and then snapping us back. Candace lay by the back door. I was now against the opposite side of the van, my arms still clutched around Sal, who was miraculously still breathing.

I listened for sound, but all I could hear was whimpering coming from Candace and my own breathing. I lowered Sal gently to the floor and crawled over to Candace. My heart rate was through the roof and my vision darkened. My chest heaved with each breath. It took me a second to locate the door handle, which wasn't where I expected it to be. I realized the van must be on its side.

"Help me with this door, Candace." I stuck my fingers into the slot and lifted the lever, then pushed it to one side. The door clicked open. I pushed the door with my shoulder, and it tipped open with a loud thud. I winced at the sound, slid across the door, and jumped to the ground.

It was pitch black outside, and cold. I reached for my little X-Acto knife and extended the blade, pathetically small for the task at hand.

Nothing moved up ahead. I made my way cautiously to the front of the tipped van. I felt the van shift as Candace crawled out.

I reached the cab of the van. The passenger window was inches from the ground. I moved around to the front. The windshield was dented—a large impact crater on the driver's side. The glass hadn't broken but was riddled with fractures and smeared with a large red stain.

Candace crept up beside me, then gasped, covering her mouth.

"We need to get away from here," I whispered. "I can't tell if there is one person inside or two. The driver might be unconscious. We need to put as much distance between him and us as possible before he comes to."

I circled the other side of the van, my feet leaving tracks in the snow. Now I recalled that I had driven through several snow squalls on my way to Horsethief Canyon. *When was that?* It must have snowed in earnest as evening fell and the temperature dropped. The roads were probably covered in ice. I peered into the darkness. Where were we? Where the hell was the road? I hurried to the back of the van noticing the back tire lay in shreds. I could hear Sal's voice.

Sal was sitting up.

"The truck's tipped on its side," said Candace, taking Sal's good hand.

"We have to get out of here Sal. How are you doing?" I reached out and touched her face. Her skin was cold and clammy. Her breathing was laboured; each breath that left her body made an odd wheezing sound. I grew even more concerned when I realized Sal hadn't answered me.

"We seem to be in the middle of nowhere. I'm going to try to find the road." The last few words came out wobbly as I shivered in the cold.

Candace began to protest. I gave her the tiny knife. It was all I could do. I followed the marks the van left in the inch or two of snow that covered the ground until I reached the road. We had gone off at a curve. I stepped up onto the asphalt and immediately knew why. Black ice.

I glanced back. No sign of lights anywhere, no vehicles, no sign of a farmhouse or building. I looked at my watch. It was broken.

I slipped and slid back to the van, thankful that I was wearing boots. We couldn't risk the driver coming to. The van was a write-off, and he might not be in any shape to take on me and Candace, but he could have a cell and call for backup. Or his backup might be lying next to him, or in a vehicle just a mile behind.

I considered my options. I briefly thought of climbing up into the cab of the truck to try to find a cell phone, but quickly discarded the idea. Our best bet was to get away from here.

Candace had Sal sitting up in the back of the van by the time I returned.

"Road's up ahead about two or three hundred feet. It's covered in black ice. Following it is our best bet, but we're going to have to stay low, maybe use the ditches along the side. Someone might come looking for the van when it doesn't show up wherever it is that it was taking us."

"I'm not going with you," Sal said, her voice raspy in her attempt to sound defiant.

A second or two of relief ran through me and disappeared.

"Sal."

"No," she cut me off. "You two are our best bet." She stopped, gasping for air. "But...only if...go." She waved me away with her good hand.

I peered back over my shoulder at where the road lay, and then back at the two of them huddled in the van. I couldn't leave Sal behind. There had to be a way. My eyes went to the van door. I briefly considered the possibility of us being able to get it off its hinges to make some sort of makeshift sled. A vein in my neck throbbed with each heartbeat. I clenched my teeth to stifle a scream that threated to explode from my throat. *Calm down.*

Sal needed help. But she was right. She wasn't going to make it out of here even with our help.

"Okay." My eyes filled with tears. I turned away. "Come on, Candace. Let's go."

Candace handed the X-Acto knife to Sal and gave her a hug. She crawled out of the van, giving Sal a small wave.

"We'll send someone back as soon as we can," I managed to choke out.

"Better go...doll." Her voice dropped to a hoarse whisper. "No use standing around dripping crocodile tears."

I wiped the tears rolling down my cheeks, gave her a wavering smile, and turned toward the road. Candace scrambled after me. Several minutes later, we climbed the small embankment up to the road.

"Which way?" Candace gasped.

I peered into the darkness. We had gone off at the point in the curve where the road started to bend back over itself.

"That way." I pointed ahead. Maybe once we got around the full curve there would be signs of a farmhouse. Shivers wracked my body. We were now facing another threat...hypothermia.

Something hit the ground behind us.

"What was that?" Candace whispered, her eyes wide, her hand shaking as she brought it up to her mouth.

"Sounds like it came from the van."

We broke into a run.

SIXTY-FIVE

I noticed a slight lightening in the sky in front of us. Candace and I had been travelling for what seemed like hours. My feet were cold but couldn't be as cold as Candace's sneaker clad feet. Both of us had fallen several times and I was worried hypothermia was setting in. I had kept our pace going fast enough to generate some core body warmth, but I was dog tired and now it was an effort to just get one foot in front of the other.

Candace had fallen behind, but she had turned out to be a little trooper. Even though she was a bit slower than me, I was grateful for her company. I suspected the body I had seen at Horsethief Canyon was Jason, but I hadn't mentioned it to her. I bent over, placed my hands on my knees, and waited for Candace to catch up. My lungs ached from the cold air. Each raspy inhalation sent a sharp pain through my shoulder and down my right arm.

"Can we...rest...for a minute," she panted as she reached me.

"Of course." My inclination was to keep moving, but I'd had my minute of rest and she hadn't. I swallowed, the saliva thick in my throat. "We have to be getting close to something," I said, although part of me questioned whether it was true or not. Even though we had been walking at a good pace, I figured we had travelled less than fifteen kilometres. Even if there were farmhouses nearby—set back from the road, I questioned whether they would be visible in the darkness.

We both turned. Two pinpricks of lights came into view. Headlights. Still far away but travelling from the direction we had come from. My heart lifted, then dropped. I was tempted to wave it down. It could just be a trucker passing through—or it could be someone out looking for us. Someone who wanted us dead. We looked at each other, turned, and ran into the ditch.

We hadn't come this far only to risk being caught by someone who had come out to see what was holding the van up.

A truck passed. I popped up my head up just enough to see the taillights growing smaller. We waited another minute until they disappeared and continued on.

"It's getting lighter out." I nodded at the growing grey streak low on the horizon. I was hoping the truck belonged so someone who was up early, heading off to work and that we would spot a house soon, or a town. An image of Sal, hurt, lying in the cold dark, flashed through my mind for the hundredth time. I begged the universe to keep her alive.

We crested a small hill and stopped. A small square of yellow light hovered in the darkness ahead of us. I turned to Candace.

"Look, a farmhouse." I hoped it was a farmhouse and not a light near a pumpjack, tank farm, or one of the many other oil and gas facilities that dotted the Alberta landscape.

Candace held back. "Wait. Jorja."

I turned.

"This is all my fault," Candace said.

"No, it's not. Why do think that?" I walked over to put my hand on her shoulder, suddenly realizing that I couldn't feel the tips of my fingers. Candace's nose looked waxy, the skin on her cheeks bluish-white. This wasn't the time to debate whose fault it was, nor question how willing she'd been to participate in what was clearly a crime.

"None of this would have happened if I hadn't kept harping at Jason. I wanted out of Drum, and I told him I wasn't going to waste my life on someone who didn't have a plan in life. That I didn't want to cut out coupons so that we could make do with his paycheck, especially if we were going to have kids."

A tsunami of emotions washed over me. Suddenly I wanted to laugh hysterically or weep. "Candace, you know he could have made other choices. Theft and blackmail aren't the only way out of poverty."

She nodded. "I scoffed when Jason told me the statue was cursed. I teased him about it. But it is. I hope it's buried somewhere, where no one can find it."

We stood there for another minute. Our breaths, little puffs of white, coalesced in the predawn light and drifted away.

"Well, cursed or not, we're still not home free." I looked over my shoulder and nodded at the small square of light. "Let's go see if our luck is any better over there."

SIXTY-SIX

THE SMALL SQUARE OF light Candace and I had seen turned out to be a farmhouse, and they called the RCMP. Now Candace and I were sitting in a small meeting room in the RCMP detachment office in Torrington, which was about a hundred kilometres northwest of Landen's Museum. The RCMP in Drumheller had been contacted and they were out looking for the van and Sal. I had done my best to give them directions as to where we went off the road but couldn't accurately estimate the distance we had travelled until we came upon the farmhouse.

We hadn't had time to tell the RCMP much when they arrived at the farmhouse, except that we had been abducted, held at the Landen Museum, then—bound and gagged—found ourselves being driven somewhere when the van went off the road. And that our friend Sal was badly hurt and still out there.

Candace was sitting next to me. She had a towel wrapped around her hands and occasionally rubbed her cheeks with it to try and warm the skin on her face. Someone had scrounged up a few blankets, coffee, and a box of donuts and muffins.

The tips of my ears were burning. My fingers were starting to thaw, and the tingling sensation hurt like hell. I had been relieved to discover that my fingertips were red and not a deadly white color or black. They still felt ice cold to the touch, even though my hands were wrapped around the coffee cup.

Finally, an officer walked in, Corporal Percy. "How are you ladies doing?"

I sat up. "Any sign of our friend Sal?"

"Sorry, no. We alerted all of our offices in central Alberta. Things might go quicker now that the sun's come up and people are out on the highway again, after last night's storm and freezing rain. There have been reports of dozens of vehicles going off the road, but no signs of a cube van yet." She pulled out a chair and sat down across from us. "If you're up to it, I need you to tell me what happened. And I have some questions for you as well."

I nodded. Candace stared vacantly into her coffee.

There was no easy way to do this, but I couldn't just sit here and talk about Howard, the missing jaguar, the museum, and all of that while a body lay at the bottom of Horsethief Canyon.

"Uh...I can start. I want to start. There is something I need to tell you."

The officer and Candace both looked at me.

"Uh...yesterday, I was at Horsethief Canyon." *Was it only yesterday?* "At least I think it was yesterday, but that was where I was abducted and I was unconscious for a while, so... You know where Horsethief Canyon is right? Near Drumheller?"

Corporal Percy nodded. I felt Candace stiffen next to me. "Well, when I reached the bottom of the canyon, I found an old, abandoned cabin." I swallowed hard. "There's a body in the cabin. A dead body."

Candace let out a sob. Corporal Percy pushed back her chair.

"I didn't have a chance to call police. My cell phone was out of range and then, when I managed to climb out of the canyon, someone nabbed me."

"Oh god," Candace sobbed. "It's Jason. And it's all my fault. I killed him." She folded her arms on the table and dropped her head onto them, muffling her sobs. I looked over at Corporal Percy, who was standing now. "She meant that...at least I don't think she killed him."

· · • • · • • • · ·

Candace and I were separated and taken into different rooms to give our statements. Sergeant Ibsen took mine. Four hours later, they had the whole story. I told them I had been trying to find out what Howard had been working on right before his death and then learned about Palermo's death and then Nickleson's. How I thought the missing jade statue might be the trigger for all that had transpired since, and how I had traced it to the Landen Museum, then learned that items may have been stolen during the fire evacuation. How my search for answers had taken me to Horsethief Canyon to try to find Jason Gray, and how Sal had been sent to locate Landen. I ended up telling him I had filed a missing persons report on Sal in Calgary before going missing myself.

It was now past noon. Someone had brought in more coffee and sandwiches. Then Corporal Percy entered the room, looking grim.

"Sal?" I asked, my heart in my throat.

"She's been found."

I dared not breathe. "Alive?"

"Yes. They've taken her to the hospital in Olds."

I flopped back in my chair, tears prickling my eyes. I closed my eyes for a few seconds, then sat up, swiping away the few tears that managed to escape. "Olds? Is she going to be okay?"

"Seems the van you were in failed to manoeuvre the corner where Highway 806 bends right before it intersects with Highway 583. Olds is closer from that point than Drumheller."

"But is she going to be all right?" I asked again, knowing Corporal Percy couldn't possibly know the answer.

"She's in good hands. They are assessing her now."

"The driver?"

She shook her head. "He didn't make it. Do you need a bio break or anything? We need to go over a few things in your statement again."

It was late afternoon before they finished with me. This time there was a lot of focus on the Black Stilt Art Gallery—how I heard about it, who I had seen there. I cringed as I gave up Azagora's name. I also mentioned the other nine or ten guests whom I had been able to identify and mentioned that I had returned to the gallery the next day in time to see what looked to be picture frames being delivered to the gallery by two men. I recognized one of the men as one of the three men we had tried to outsmart while being held captive in the museum basement. The second of the three men was the bearded man who had been following me. I told them that he was employed by Landen. I didn't recognize my third captor. I assumed one of them had been driving the van and was now dead.

After being warned by both Azagora and Mike to keep Nickleson's theories about a dirty cop to myself and treat them as the hearsay it was, I didn't mention that part to Sergeant Ibsen but did tell him about the short series of video clips back at my office, taken the night of Palermo's death from the lobby of the Ventura Tower, where he fell.

Sergeant Ibsen asked me if I had anyone I wanted to call. Since Mike was still out east, and Gab was in Paris, I said no. I certainly had no desire to see Azagora under these circumstances. I hoped like hell he had only been an innocent guest at the Black Stilt Art Gallery.

Sergeant Ibsen offered to have one of their constables drive me into Calgary. I wanted to see Sal, see how she was doing with my own eyes, but it would have to wait. I had no phone, no money, my hair was matted, my face and clothes filthy. So, I accepted the ride.

Candace was being held overnight. It finally sunk in that she wasn't just a victim in all of this, that she might be facing charges as an accessory to theft. Maybe even blackmail.

I was quiet on the ride home, no energy left for small chit chat. The constable let me sit silently in the back seat, staring blankly at the passing scenery, until he let me out in front of my building.

I buzzed the condo manager to let me in since my keys were gone. He took me up to the eighth floor and let me in. Mrs. Wilson, my crusty old neighbour, paused in her evening walk of the floor as the condo manager and I arrived at my door. "Well, look what the cat dragged in," she announced gleefully.

As soon as I got into my condo, I located my burner phone and called the Olds Hospital. Sal was not in ICU but was sedated for the night. I drew in a deep breath and closed my eyes. All I wanted now was someone to hold me.

I called Mike.

SIXTY-SEVEN

I parked my new rental, a bright-red, 2013 Chevy Spark in the hospital parking lot, and made my way across the parking lot. The snow that had fallen a few days ago had melted, but the air was crisp, heralding the fact that soon more snow would find its way here. The last two days were a blur. As exhausted as I was, Mike and I talked for over two hours the night the constable drove me home. His committee was taking a break, sending everyone home for a much-needed weekend off, and I was looking forward to seeing him.

I had let JumpIn Jalopies know my van had been stolen but was happy to report that the vehicle Sal had been driving had been found and was now in a police impound lot. After leasing the Chevy Spark, I methodically went down my to-do list and arranged to have the locks on my condo and office doors changed, purchased a new phone, and contacted my bank and all credit card companies, assuming I was never going to get any of it back.

Anxious to see Sal, I stepped through the main doors and found my way up to the second floor. I had driven out to the Olds Hospital twice in the last two days, but each time Sal had been in a deep sleep. This time I found Sal awake and sitting up in bed.

"Sal. You're awake!" I rushed into the room.

"Yeah. I figure thirty-seven hours of sleep is enough. Besides, a body's gotta eat."

I leaned over and gave her a hug, careful not to crush her arm, which was in an arm sling, or disturb the IV which was stuck in her other arm.

"Did you have breakfast?" I asked.

"Apple juice, a thimble of Greek yogurt, and a piece of toast. Hardly worth waking up for. You didn't bring coffee, did you, doll?"

"No, but I'll get you one from downstairs before I leave. I'm so happy to see you. How's the arm?"

"Displaced fracture. The doc got the pieces back together. Now they're waitin' for the swelling to go down. Then they are going to put in a pin."

"Sorry to hear that. And the rest of you?"

"I'm gonna live. Assuming the food here doesn't kill me. What about you and little blondie?"

I gave Sal a condensed version of how we found a friendly farmhouse and that Candace and I had given our statements to the RCMP. I hadn't heard if Candace had been released or if they were charging her with anything for her role in the theft of the statue—stealing from and attempting to extort money out of criminals was a bit of a legal grey area.

"If you ask me, the damn thing is cursed for sure."

"If it is the Vanderburg Jaguar, it could be worth thirty or forty million dollars."

Sal's eyes widened. "You have any idea where it is?"

I laughed. "I wish."

Sal knew the driver of the van had been killed and she told me she had a 'dose of that hyperthermia' by the time the police found her and the van. I told Sal about the Black Stilt Art Gallery and that I saw one of the men who held us captive at Landen's Museum off-loading flat crates at the gallery.

"At first, I thought the gallery might be owned by Landen and that he was dealing in stolen artwork. But when I realized that the numbers Howard had jotted down in his appointment book matched the dates of articles I found in his office about a string of other crimes and deaths, I knew there was something bigger going on. By then I also knew Landen had lied to me. He told me he gave the jaguar back to Palermo, told him it wasn't worth anything, and that someone later stole it from Palermo. He said Palermo hired Howard to find it. But so much didn't add up, including why Palermo would want Howard to find a statue he believed to be cursed, especially after Landen had told him it was worthless. That's when I decided I needed to find this Jason Gray. I was told he liked to hang out at an old cabin in Horsethief Canyon, and that's were I came across a body."

"Was it this Jason character?" asked Sal.

"I'm betting on it. Jason Gray used to work at Landen's Museum, at least until the fire—which he and Candace started to cover up the theft." I swallowed. "Looks like someone else besides me figured he took the statue and went after him. I also found Howard's wallet nearby. I think someone planted his wallet, to maybe try and make it look like Howard killed him. Anyway, pretty stupid of me to go out there alone, huh?"

A nurse arrived to check Sal, and I ran downstairs to get Sal coffee and a slice of their pumpkin spice loaf. Two police officers were hovering around her door when I returned.

Sal hoisted herself higher on the pillows as I set down her coffee and loaf. "You're a real peach, Jorja, a real peach."

"I see there are some police officers here to talk to you. I hear they've arrested Landen. This is going to take some time to figure out. We've got the RCMP from Drumheller, Olds, and Torrington involved, as well as Calgary Police Services."

"That old coot Landen is some piece of work."

By the time I got back to my parked car, I had four missed phone calls and a text message from Luis. He hadn't been phoning to say good morning. I opened the text message. *"Call me."* This was the breakup phone call I had been anticipating, and I already felt the coming rejection in my gut.

I remember something I read when I was working through my grief and anger over my parents' deaths. Fear of rejection isn't just psychological, it's biological. Our evolutionary history has programmed the fear of expulsion and rejection from our ancestral tribes right into our very cells.

I drove home and ate a bowl of cereal. Another text from Luis arrived. *"We need to talk. Can you meet me tonight?"* I thought about our last disastrous meeting, him ordering me to stay out of police business, although, as far as I knew, Howard Bergman's death wasn't being investigated by the police. It was my reference to a dirty cop that had triggered him.

I got it. He's the brilliant cop and I'm an ordinary citizen who implied something rotten was happening in his own shop. What I didn't get is how he was treating me. Stonewalling when it suited him, a way I felt was intended to keep me away. Then my awful drunken declaration that I loved him.

Did I love him? I don't know. I was starting to love him. It was happening slowly, steadily, organically, not like some bolt of lightning from Eros. I was starting to get him, and he was getting to know me in a way I had never let a man know me before. I had seen the real Luis, the tender, caring, and protective Luis that lived inside. But as quickly as that small crack into his inner psyche opened, it snapped shut just as suddenly. And if I were being truthful with myself, I wasn't all that different. It left me wondering if one could truly love someone who only showed or gave one side of themselves, keeping their real self hidden.

My finger hovered over his last text. I took a deep breath and typed. *"Yes. Where and when?"*

SIXTY-EIGHT

I arrived at Ciao's twenty minutes late. I wasn't doing it to annoy Luis, I was trying to avoid what was coming. The hostess led me to a table in the far corner where Luis was already seated. Now I wondered if Luis had specifically selected this restaurant for its name.

He stood as I got to the table and pulled the chair out for me. His jacket was already draped over the back of his chair, and he had rolled up the sleeves of his white shirt. The hostess wished us an enjoyable evening and departed. If only she knew.

We sat for several minutes, silent. As handsome as he was, there was a coldness there. He radiated cop. I could feel the pinprick of tears behind my eyes and looked away.

Luis cleared his throat. "I ordered us some wine. Would you like a glass?" He picked up the bottle, which was standing on the table.

"Yes, please." His hand trembled slightly as he poured me a glass. I felt my toes curl in my shoes. It was now or never. Might as well rip off the bandage.

"Just don't offer me another glass after this one. It…uh…seems to mess with my inhibitions. I'm really sorry about the other night."

"Don't be. I'm not," he countered quickly, leaving me confused about which part of the night he was referring to. I felt my face grow hot and took a sip of wine to avoid asking him the obvious question.

"Look, I was out of line that night. I shouldn't have jumped all over you like that. I really need to get better at leaving work behind when I head home."

So, this is what we were going to talk about, even though there was a big old elephant standing next to the table, waving its trunk.

"Well, I should know by now that certain topics are off the table."

"It's not that I don't want to discuss things with you, it's just that in certain instances I can't." His dark eyes focused on mine. I could see his pulse throbbing at the base of his throat.

"No, I get it. I really do." I took a deep breath. "I need you to know I wasn't digging for information or trying to put a spanner in the works. Sometimes I just want to vent. Or I start talking about one thing, which triggers another thought, and I suddenly find myself ruminating about it out loud. It's a bad habit of mine. I can see how that might make you feel like I'm interfering with police business or that it's my subtle way of trying to get you to look into something on my behalf. Trust me, I'm not that calculating."

I wanted to excuse myself, say I was going to the washroom. I just needed a moment alone, to try to sort out what was happening here. How to broach *the* topic. A server offered me the reprieve I desired by coming to take our order. I hadn't looked at the menu yet, so I asked for a salad, anything they had on hand. I didn't feel like eating much of anything.

"Actually, you're a brilliant investigator. I wish I had someone like you on my team. The reality is"—he held up his hand—"and I still can't talk about it, but you hit on something big that night. I was afraid that you'd derail everything we had been working on."

The conversation was going in places I never expected. Did he just call me a brilliant investigator? I looked at Luis and remembered the way his lips felt on mine, how safe and happy he made me feel when he wrapped his arms around me. I looked at the tables around us, couples, friends, sitting, talking, laughing. Connecting in ways I found difficult even after years of therapy. I was about to risk all of that now.

"What hurt me the most, Luis, was how later that night when I called you...to apologize...and yes, I was drunk, so not much of an apology...and I...I told you I love you..."

He reached over and took my hand in his.

"I'm not sorry you called that night. I know you were drunk. I know not everything that came out of your mouth that night came with full intention. But I should have acknowledged it instead of running, like I usually do. I really like you, Jorja. I've never felt like this about anyone else."

I swallowed several times as I felt my throat closing. *He liked me.* Well, he was right about one thing, I couldn't look him in the eye when I was stone-cold sober and repeat my declaration of love. And the fact that I had said those words both scared and mortified me.

"So, where do we go with this now?"

"I feel like I don't yet fully know you. Some days I don't understand you at all. But I want to get to know you better." He squeezed my hand.

"I'm not that complicated. Maybe you're not trying hard enough."

Luis laughed. "See, like now. I do love your sense of humour." He reached across the table, ran his finger down my cheek, and touched my bottom lip. "I'd like to work on that, if you'll give me the chance."

I nodded. But deep down inside, doubts were growing that we would ever mesh. Maybe I was still feeling the hurt from hearing him say he liked me, not loved me. Then again, the sentiments he and I just expressed went both ways. I didn't understand him, either.

The server returned with our meal, and Luis' phone rang. I could tell by the look on his face that something was up. Work, as usual.

Luis put his phone away, leaned back, and pulled out his wallet. "Sorry, something has come up. I need to leave. But please stay, at least have your dinner."

"I'm not really hungry, so I'll walk out with you, if that's okay." After Luis settled the bill, I followed him outside.

The trees lining the boulevard were draped with tiny lights, lending a fairy tale atmosphere to the night. Luis pulled me to him, crushing me against his chest. His mouth found mine. For a moment, there were just the two of us, two people desperate for love but afraid to show the other who was really inside.

Luis stepped back. "I gotta go." He reached down, grabbed my hand, gave it a squeeze, and walked away.

And I let him.

SIXTY-NINE

I woke the next morning to breaking news that Regina Boscovich, the owner of the Black Stilt Art Gallery, had been arrested for masterminding a cocaine-smuggling operation.

"The 49-year-old woman, fiancée of developer Franklin Dirks, was arrested as the brains behind a crime gang which smuggled cocaine from Latin America to Canada. Picture frames and art objects made of cocaine were shipped into the country along with authentic art pieces. A raid of the Black Stilt Art Gallery yielded twenty-two kilograms of the drug. Two other men have been arrested in connection with the smuggling ring, along with eccentric millionaire Milton Landen. More details will be released when they are known."

This news was followed by a video clip of Franklin Dirks arriving at his place of business. Dirks held a hand up to the camera and repeated "No comment" as he rushed into the building.

I was still sitting there, letting it all sink in, when my phone rang. It was Edith, Jeff Nickleson's ex-wife. She wanted to let me know that the police had contacted her two days earlier, wanting access to Jeff's computer and phone. They were starting to think the hit-and-run accident that killed him wasn't an accident after all. She gladly turned his devices over to the police.

She wanted me to know that a few days after she and I spoke at the pizza bar, she found the time to go through all of Jeff's files and email. There were a few she copied and would be sending to me after the call.

After getting the emails from Edith, the remaining pieces fell into place.

· · · • · • • · · ·

Mike and I arrived at Donna's place at the same time. After exchanging hugs, Donna led us into the living room where she had set out a tray of fruit, pastries, and cheese. The fireplace was lit and took the chill out of the room. The aroma of freshly brewed coffee filled the air.

"Come in, come in. Make yourselves comfortable." She waved toward the living room. "I just made coffee. I'll bring in a pot."

Mike and I sat down. "This turned into quite the case," Mike commented.

"I'm not sure we even know the half of it."

"And how are you doing?"

I had never seen Mike look this serious before. "I'm fine really, Mike. A few bumps and bruises is all."

He cleared his throat. "There's more to wellness than physical well being."

Donna brought in coffee, cutting off any further comment. We exchanged pleasantries while she poured. Finally, we were all settled.

"I'm going to let Jorja tell you what she knows. She's been dogging this case from the get-go."

"Thanks, Mike." I turned to Donna. "It's been difficult to put the pieces together, especially as several people who could have told us what was going on died, as well as Howard. Some of what I'm going to tell is still speculative, but most of it has now been confirmed."

Donna nodded.

"It all started with a pre-Columbian jade jaguar that a man named Guy Palermo picked up on one of his excursions to Colombia. He took the artifact to a friend of his to get his opinion. This friend, an archeologist, was only somewhat familiar with pre-Columbian artifacts. He, however, thought the statue might be one of the Vanderburg Jaguars, which was discovered by an archeologist named Vanderburg in the eighteenth century. The Vanderburg Jaguars were believed to be semi-religious objects, reputed to provide the owner great power. The statues were later thought to have fallen into Hitler's hands, but after the war ended, their whereabouts became unknown."

"Oh my," gushed Donna.

"Palermo was in dire financial straits and wanted to know the statue's worth. His archeologist friend gave him the name of a man who was once considered an expert in pre-Columbian art, and who is more recently a purveyor of ancient artifacts. Milton Landen. Palermo contacted Landen to see if he could authenticate the statue as one of the Vanderburg Jaguars. Palermo wanted to sell the statue for whatever it was worth, and quickly. Or at least, that's the impression he gave to his friend."

Donna frowned. "So did he think Milton Landen would buy it, if it was authentic?"

"Not necessarily, but Landen is well connected to some very rich, art...let's say connoisseurs, some of whom would pay dearly to possess a piece of history."

Mike interjected. "Some of these collectors are more interested in having something rare, even if obtained illegally, to show off to those that they want to impress, rather than for any artistic merit of the object itself."

Donna nodded. "I see. I always wondered who would buy a stolen piece of art for instance. I mean if the Mona Lisa was stolen... you couldn't very well go and advertise that you had it. I didn't mean to interrupt. Please go on."

"Feel free to interrupt anytime. This whole thing is so complex, it can be hard to follow. Anyway, we still don't know if Landen believed the statue to be real or not, but he told Palermo it was a fake. He also told Palermo that true authentication would likely take years. Landen said he could put the statue on display in his museum to generate some interest in it, then afterwards sell it to a private collector. Landen himself told me this was the plan."

"If you can believe anything that guy says," huffed Mike.

"Yes, true. He still might have been able to get a decent price for it. I suspect he planned to pawn it off on a rich but somewhat naïve collector who was more interested in being able to share an entertaining story about its supposed history with his friends, than its true authenticity. He couldn't declare it to be one of the Vanderburg Jaguars because it would generate too much attention from the historical art community, so decided to claim it came from his fathers collection."

Mike grunted. "Knowing what we now know about Landen, he would have sold it to the highest private bidder as quickly as he could."

"There was a young security guard working at the muscum at the time, and he got wind of some odd comings and goings. He got into the habit of listening in on Landen's conversations, even taking the liberty of exploring his office after hours and figuring out where Landen kept the numbers to his safe written down. He overheard Landen during several so-called 'secret phone calls,' to presumably one or more potential buyers for this statue, and heard dollar figures mentioned that were in the millions."

Donna gasped. "Really? Would someone actually pay that kind of money for an old statue?"

"Apparently, yes. Sotheby's sold a similar but slightly older object a few years ago for fifty-two million dollars."

Donna's mouth gaped open. "If I had that kind of money, I can think of a million other ways I'd want to spend it—rather than on an ancient statue."

"You and me both. Regardless of whether Landen thought he could get three million or thirty million for it, he planned on selling it for as much as possible and only paying Palermo a pittance of what he got from the sale."

"You mean by lying to Palermo about the price he would manage to get through a private sale?" Donna asked.

"Something like that. We can't be sure. What we do know is that the security guard and his girlfriend started a grass fire near the museum, forcing an emergency evacuation, and during the ensuing chaos, stole the statue along with some other objects."

"How do you get rid of something like that? Surely, they didn't plan to just take it to a pawnshop. And wouldn't a buyer want it authenticated? How would they explain how it came to be in their possession?" Donna, looked from me to Mike, shaking her head.

I laughed. "It brings up a lot of questions, doesn't it? The security guard solved a lot of those pesky problems by sending Landen a ransom note. He wanted a million dollars for the statue and for his silence. The note hinted that he knew what Landen was up to and by that, I mean his involvement in a cocaine-smuggling operation."

"Wow! He was smuggling cocaine?"

"Turns out, yes, but he wasn't the mastermind behind the whole thing. It was a woman named Regina Boscovich. You may have seen the news about her on TV. She was running the whole thing. She needed a way to get the cocaine into the country without attracting any attention. Landen was constantly buying and selling objects for his clients and the customs people got to know him. One of the men arrested along with Boscovich works for Canadian Border Services. I suspect Landen might have been paying him off."

"This Landen guy sounds like he took a lot of risks. I thought you said he was wealthy." Donna forehead wrinkled. "Why would he need the money?"

"What is slowly coming to light is that Landen was in debt. He was known as an eccentric millionaire, but his eccentricities drove him into the poor house. He had been selling the artifacts in his museum for years and replacing them with fakes. I'm not sure who approached whom, but Landen was picking up picture frames and other objects, like vases and carvings, for Boscovich and then doctoring them to look like the real thing."

"Wait," Donna said. "The picture frames and carvings hid the cocaine?"

Mike jumped in, "Actually they're made out of cocaine. Drug smugglers are getting more inventive in finding ways to conceal their illegal shipments. They were mixing cocaine into the clay of sculptures and vases decades ago. Now they're mixing it with plastic and then molding it into a variety of objects. There was a case about a year ago where cocaine traffickers created a cocaine paste and molded it into imitation designer shoes."

"What? That's insane," Donna said.

"The shoes I mentioned were actually being worn onto planes. Now there's a whole crop of traffickers using these sophisticated techniques to make anything—car parts, dinner sets, and picture frames."

"All they need is a lab on the receiving end to dissolve the resin and precipitate out the cocaine. Brilliant. Just goes to show how lucrative the drug trade is for these scumbags." I couldn't help but admire the ingenuity of humans, especially where money was concerned.

"So how did my dad get involved in all of this?"

"After the jaguar was stolen during the fire, Landen saw an opportunity to take Palermo right out of the picture. He told him the statue had been stolen. Landen suspected the security guard had taken it but had no idea he planned on ransoming the statue back to him. I think he planned to hunt down the security guard himself or get his thugs to do so. But Palermo didn't like what he was hearing, especially when he found out Landen hadn't even filed the theft with police, which he would have needed to make an insurance claim."

"I can see why he wouldn't want to make an insurance claim. Especially if some of the other items taken were fakes," Mike said.

"Palermo didn't trust what he had been told by Landen, so he hired your father to check him out and try to figure out if he was having the wool pulled over his eyes."

"That explains a lot," Donna said. "I can see why my dad was excited. Chasing something like that would have been something he could really get into. Not to mention Palermo may have offered him a good deal of money if he found the thing and it ended up being one of the Vanderburg Jaguars."

"I can see a lot of people wanting to go after it," Mike said. "If word gets out that it's missing, even the possibility of it being real would be enough to create a frenzy among all the treasure seekers out there."

"It hasn't been found?" Donna asked, turning to me.

"Not yet. The security guard was found dead in Horsethief Canyon. His girlfriend says she doesn't know where the statue is. She's now in police custody."

"You said several people died besides my father. What happened? Something must have gone wrong."

"The security guard and his girlfriend had no idea who they were really poking when they took that statue, and it set off a deadly chain reaction."

"I'm getting us more coffee," Donna announced. "I want to hear this."

SEVENTY

I told Donna and Mike how Candace had been sent by her boyfriend to pick up the ransom money, and that the jade jaguar had been apparently hidden somewhere nearby and its location would be revealed once the money had been handed over. The information Nickleson's wife provided to me further explained what happened.

"Landen didn't have a million in cash lying around to pay the ransom, and he was further worried that the security guard was onto his role in the cocaine-smuggling scheme. He went to Boscovich and told her he needed a million dollars. Boscovich hadn't built up her operation to have some security guard and Landen's greed and carelessness bring her down. One of the men working for her was her...let's say *enforcer*. She also had a cop on her payroll, to help smooth out the edges when things occasionally went wrong. A cop by the name of Raymond Bale, known to his buddies as Ace."

Donna gasped. "My dad knew. You told me he had mentioned a dirty cop to his friend Lennie."

"Good cops despise bad cops," Mike said.

"Rightly so. The security guard at the Ventura Tower where Palermo died was a former cop himself. Nickleson always suspected Bale of being on the take but couldn't prove it. This went back to his days on the police force in Winnipeg. Then a year or so after he joined Calgary Police Services, Raymond Bale—also made the leap and joined CPS. Still bothered by what happened in Winnipeg, Nickleson started watching Raymond, trying to prove he was on the take."

"Wow, so this guy had a history."

"You bet. A few years later, Nickleson left CPS but swore he would get the guy. After Landen told Boscovich that he was being blackmailed, and that Palermo had hired a private investigator, your father, to find the missing statue, she had Palermo killed. She didn't want people poking around to try and find the missing jaguar, because it would have turned the focus to Landen, possibly threatening her entire operation. Your father interviewed Nickleson about the night Palermo died. Nickleson told him his suspicions about Bale. He gave your father a video clip showing Bale in the building *before* Palermo died, and then later conveniently arriving with police to investigate his death."

"That video was on the thumb drive that was in my father's safety deposit box."

"Right. He was also the detective who went back up on the roof after Palermo's fall, and then came back down and reported to the ME that there was no sign of a scuffle or anything on the roof, further leaving the impression that it was suicide. Emails going back and forth between Nickleson and your father show that they figured Bale killed Palermo. The video shows him going up in the elevator right before Palermo's death."

"A cop buddy told me that Raymond's having a hard time explaining his presence in the building," Mike said. "Or why his fingerprints were found in the basement of Landen's museum."

"We know Howard had been following Bale the day he died. Bale, and the enforcer working for Boscovich, were ordered to make all of this go away. The only way to do that was to silence anyone and everyone associated with the statue, and its trail to Landen, which in turn could jeopardize her whole operation."

Donna topped up my coffee.

I continued, "The man who was supposed to hand over the ransom money to the security guard's girlfriend, Candace, didn't bring the money. They planned to nab her and the statue and end it all right there. But she didn't have the statue, so instead, they grabbed her, figuring she would lead them to the security guard. Candace fought back. Howard, who had followed Bale to Glenmore Reservoir, saw her struggling and came to her rescue, but the other man, whom we now believe was the enforcer working for Boscovich, out powered Howard. Now it looks as if Howard was knocked out, his wallet taken, then his body rolled into the water where he drowned."

"I knew it, I just knew it!" Donna looked over at Mike and me. "My poor dad...but that's what he was like. He would have jumped in to help, even if he had no idea who this woman was."

"Your dad was a fine man, Donna," Mike added. "A lot of people owe him their lives."

After a minute, I continued, "Nickleson and Howard were working together. Nickleson was there with Howard, but he was at the other end of the path. Bale must have spotted Nickleson and tore after him, while the enforcer wrestled with your dad. Nickleson was run down a while later on 14th Street by a grey car, which my associate, Sal, later saw being buried on Landen's property. The police have since excavated it and matched fingerprints to one of the men who abducted Sal and me, who later died when the van we were being transported in went off the road. That man had also been sent to follow and dispose of me when I turned up shortly after your father's death to pick up the trail. I had noticed a bearded man following me for days and finally he got his chance and abducted me the day I went out to Horsethief Canyon looking for Jason Gray."

"You were abducted?" Donna's hand flew to her mouth. "Oh my god, Jorja."

I rubbed the back of my neck and let out a fake laugh. "All's well that ends well."

Although no one knew for certain, Howard's attacker may have taken Howard's wallet to simply find out who he was, before rolling his body into the water. Later, Boscovich's men decided to frame Howard for the museum guard's murder by leaving Howard's wallet near his body, at the bottom of the canyon. The police now determined that Jason Gray had been killed with Howard's gun. But the timelines didn't fit, as the ME placed Howard's death and the subsequent break in at his apartment three full days before Jason Gray's death.

"Wow." Donna shook her head. "I see what you meant when you said the security guard never realized he was poking a ginormous bear. Who could have imagined that a stolen jade statue would end up exposing a huge drug ring?"

"It was a pretty slick operation," Mike said. "The drug dealers are desperate to stay one step ahead of the law. Drug smuggling is a lot more sophisticated than back in the day."

"I still can't believe they can create objects out of cocaine."

"The stuff they make is very realistic looking. Their biggest remaining threat are the drug-sniffing dogs, but if they can pay off a few people, and use the smaller international airports, they can still squeak by.”

“How can I ever thank the two of you?” Donna lay her hand over her heart. “I can’t tell you how much this means to me. And to Amanda.”

“Well, I’m sure it’s going to take a while to wrap this case up.” Mike got to his feet. “I’m predicting we’re going to see a few more arrests in the coming days. It’s too bad your father got caught in the crossfire. I’m going to miss him.” Mike turned his head away and cleared his throat.

“Me, too,” said Donna, standing up to give Mike and then me a hug.

SEVENTY-ONE

Mike's predictions were true. The following week, Regina Boscovich's empire came tumbling down. Eight arrests were made after search warrants were issued for five locations in Alberta. The searches turned up fifteen hundred kilos of cocaine, estimated to be worth close to fifty million dollars. Police also seized eighty thousand dollars in cash and several illegal weapons.

I took great pleasure in watching a TV clip of Raymond Bale being loaded into the back of a police car. Landen was led from his palatial home in handcuffs. Franklin Dirks was also being investigated. Suddenly, questions were being raised as to the source of the capital for his Saddle Ridge Raceway and the entertainment park he was developing north of the city. He continued to insist he knew nothing of his fiancée's drug-smuggling operation.

What I didn't realize is that Calgary's Special Crimes Unit, along with the force's Organized Crime Unit, had been leading a nine-month effort—with assistance from the Royal Canadian Mounted Police in Drumheller, the County of Kneehill, and several other detachments—to make the bust. Now I understood why Luis had reacted as he did, when I started talking about a potential dirty cop on the force. They already had eyes on Raymond Bale, at least according to the Police Chief's statement after Raymond was arrested.

Just about the time all this news broke, Jason Gray's former boss at 4SiteSecurity contacted police to report that a package had arrived at their office, addressed to the now deceased Jason Gray. The package contained the missing jade jaguar. It's believed that after the blackmail exchange went south, the day Candace, his girlfriend, was to have made the exchange, Jason decided the safest thing to do with the jaguar was to mail it to himself at his former employer's address. If it turned out to be the real thing, Palermo's daughter would have more than enough funds to set up the trust fund she had wanted for the plane crash and Yemen crew victims' families.

· · · · ● · ● · · · ·

I pulled the Chevy Spark up to the curb, grabbed the bag of groceries off the passenger seat and tucked my chin into my jacket as I climbed out. Winter had arrived in the weeks since Milt Landen and Regina Boscovich's arrest. Investigations were continuing into Franklin Dirk's affairs to see if his relationship with Boscovich was more than a purely personal one.

Azagora and I were back on solid footing—friends with benefits, who were 'in like' with each other. He had made a point of introducing a fellow officer to me—the woman in red I had seen him with the night a major drug deal had occurred at the Black Stilt Gallery. She was one of six undercover officers who had been working to bring down Boscovich's drug operation. On the one hand, I appreciated Azagora's attempt to smooth things over between us, on the other hand I couldn't help but thinking he did so just to prove a point.

I skirted the side of the house, eased myself down the snow-covered steps and pushed open the wooden door to the basement. I paused to let my eyes adjust to the dark. I took a step forward and jumped back as an unholy wail filled the space. A mangey, orange cat crouched on top of an old fridge, its ears flat to its head, a satanic growl emitted from between barred teeth.

"Oh." My hand flew to my chest. "Mr. Miyagi, you scared me." I tucked my chin deeper into my jacket collar and slid by, avoiding eye contact. Mr. Miyagi was one of Sal's three cats. The cats didn't actually live with Sal, but they co-existed in some sort of symbiotic relationship. Kind of like me and Azagora.

Sal opened the door to her apartment before I got there.

"Jorja. Thought I heard someone rustlin' out here."

"Just said hi to Mr. Miyagi." I nodded back over my shoulder, hoping I wouldn't spot the black cat, who she called Boss. I love cats, and the majority of them seem to like me. But Sal's cat's were special.

"I brought your groceries. They were all out of pickled herring in vinegar, so I got pickled herring in a dill sauce. Hope that's okay." I had been stopping by every three or four days to check in on Sal and run whatever errands she needed.

"That'll do Jorja, that'll do just fine. Got time for a coffee?"

"Sure, a quick one." I peered past her.

"Don't worry, the Boss is out. Just me and Eddie today."

I breathed a sigh of relief. Eddie Scissorhands, his official name, wasn't overly friendly either, but his eyesight was poor, and he moved slowly. None of Sal's cats were acquired the usual way, her cats were all strays who just somehow found her.

I entered the small space that served as her living quarters and set the grocery bag on the two feet of counter space next to a harvest gold Kenmore refrigerator. A large, wooden wire spool in the middle of the room served as the table. Two chairs, made from a wooden pallet, stood on either side.

The place was neat but crammed to the ceiling with boxes and discarded objects waiting to be made into something useful again. A well used recliner stood in the corner of the room, and an old RCA TV, in its own cabinet, stood in the opposite corner. I presumed the two doors on the far wall led to a washroom and a bedroom.

"How's the arm doing," I asked, as Sal set a cup of coffee down in front of me.

"Doc has me takin' the sling off for several hours a day. The physio guy gave me some exercises to do. Doc says I can wear the sling when my arm starts to feel sore, but otherwise it's almost good as new." Sal cackled, her laugh turning into a rumbly cough. "If you believe that, I've got a bridge in Brooklyn I'm trying to sell."

"Glad you still have your sense of humour Sal. Hey, I have something for you." I reached into my pocket and pulled out a white business envelope. "Two things actually." I slid the envelope over to her.

"What's this?" She picked up the envelope and looked at me.

"Well, there's a cheque in there from Guy Palermo's daughter—a sort of finder's fee now that the jaguar has been returned to her. And a one-page contract, from Knight Investigations, retaining you for three months to help out with the business."

Sal's eyes widened. "Don't mess with me doll. You serious?"

"I'm thinking of taking three or four weeks off. My friend Gab has been after me to take some time off—go travelling with her, once she finishes her Cordon Bleu course. I'll need someone to man the office while I'm away. No heavy lifting, just answer the phone, pick up the mail, maybe spend some time learning how to use a computer. You could take a few of those PI courses you're still missing to be able to apply for your license."

"You serious?"

I nodded. It was the least I could do for her. Sal always came through for me, and she had put her own well-being on the line for me while I hunted down the truth about what really happened to Mike's friend, Howard Bergman.

"What can I say. You're a peach Jorja, a real peach. You're not pulling my leg are you."

"You've done a lot for me over the last year Sal. With a little more work, you just might be able to get your PI licence. And I could use a licenced PI's help from time to time."

Sal turned her head, but not before I saw the small quiver in her chin.

"Go ahead, have a look at the check."

She pulled out the cheque and bent to examine it, then looked up. "What's it say doll? I don't have my glasses handy."

"It's a cheque for ten-thousand dollars. I got one too."

"No way. That's a freaking year's rent. Who gives away this much money? And why?"

"Guy Palermo's daughter said she didn't miss seeing the jade jaguar in her father's collection after he died. She didn't really think about it, but if she had, she said she would have assumed he got rid of it somehow. When I started looking into what Howard had been working on when he got killed, and then discovered that Palermo had been killed, as well as a security guard working in Palermo's building, I started to wonder if the jaguar statue could factor in. That's when I learned that it could be worth a lot of money. That in turn lead me to Milt Landen, and you know the rest."

"So the darn thing was real?"

"Well, it turns out the jaguar statue is not one of the Vanderburg jaguars, but it is indeed pre-Columbian in age, and quite unique in that it's carved out of jade. The hollow recess in the jaguar's back was made to hold a container, probably made of silver or gold, and filled with seeds and various animal fats, burnt as offerings to appease the gods. Such an object would have only been owned by someone important, a king or high priest."

"Some things never change, eh, doll?"

"Once the statue was authenticated, Palermo's daughter started getting offers for it, some from well known museums and some from private collectors. She finally sold it for 1.2 million dollars. She said without our help, she would have never come close to recovering it. She's using the proceeds to set up an orphan trust fund in her fathers name."

Sal whistled. "Well don't this just take the cake. That gal sure is showin' her true color. Her daddy would be proud."

I left Sal looking more chipper than I'd ever seen her. And I was feeling pretty chipper myself. Gab would be happy to hear that I would be joining her on her travels in a few weeks. Sal was going to make a great PI, and Azagora and I were back on track. Donna got the closure she wanted about her father, and Mike felt Howard got the justice he deserved. I climbed into the Chevy Spark and turned on the engine.

An odd thought popped into my head. Would my father be proud of me if he were still alive? I did a shoulder check and gunned the little Spark. For the first time in my life, I didn't care. I laughed out loud and merged with the rush hour traffic. I truly didn't care. I loved my crazy life. A surge of joy engulfed me. I could hardly wait to see what life brought me next.

YOUR FREE BOOK IS WAITING

She wants to prove her worth as a new PI...but first she has to survive. Find out how it all began. Knight Shift is the prequel novella to the Jorja Knight Mystery Series.

Your free copy is waiting for you at: www.alicebienia.com

ACKNOWLEDGMENTS

Writing may be a solitary endeavor but thankfully, being an author is not. Yes, there are days when I rise early to sit at my computer and type in the dim light of a desk lamp with only my thoughts and fictional characters for company, but the overall process of getting the final creation into readers hands is a much more engaging one. I'm fortunate to have the encouragement and support of so many.

As always, I'd like to thank Taija Morgan, my editor and friend, who has been on this journey with me from almost the very beginning. Her wise observations and brilliant editing have made this a better book.

I also have a small squad of alphas, betas, and other support staff in my "writer family." People who help me keep my voice true, my characters believable and my plot holes filled. You are always there for me, whether I need an opinion on a cover design, need to talk over a potential plot twist, kill a character I've fallen in love with, or just vent about my latest technology glitch. I'm grateful for your encouraging words, a much-needed laugh on a cloudy day, a set of eyes when, after so many rounds of proofreading, mine fail to recognize misspelled words or incorrectly placed commas, and help to celebrate moments of success. Thank you, Terry Bullick, Brenda Domeij, Brenda Gregoire, Kevin Heffernan, Brenda Lissel, Sue Matsalla, Anne Style, and Diane Peppinck.

Beyond connecting with readers, one treasured aspect of my writing life has been meeting and spending time with some amazing Canadian writers, some of whom I am honored to now call friends. A special thank you to my fellow Sisters in Crime – Canada West siblings – you are the most amazingly supportive and talented group of writers I've ever met.

Thank you to my husband, Kevin, who keeps the home fires burning and the cats fed while I'm off on another of my 'solitary writing adventures,' and to our children and grandchildren, Sean, Katherine, Malcolm, Leanne, Tyler, and Paige – you are the joy in my life.

ABOUT THE AUTHOR

Alice Bienia is a Canadian Crime Writer and author of the Jorja Knight mystery series.

With a Bachelor of Science degree in geology, Alice spent her early career conducting field exploration programs in remote regions of Canada, where she honed her passion for reading, storytelling, coffee, and adventure. After riding the energy industry rollercoaster for thirty years, Alice has found a way to put her inherent introversion to use and now writes full time.

When not plotting a murder, Alice amuses herself watching foreign flicks and exploring Calgary's urban parks and pathways. Visit her at www.alicebienia.com